SUDDEN TIMES

Dermot Healy

SUDDEN TIMES

McArthur & Company

Toronto

This Canadian paperback edition published in 2001
by McArthur & Company

First published in Canada by
McArthur & Company Publishing Ltd.
322 King Street West , Suite 402
Toronto, Ontario M5V 1J2

First published in Great Britain in 1999
by The Harvill Press

National Library of Canada Cataloguing in Publication Data

Healy, Dermot, 1947-
  Sudden times

ISBN 1-55278-087-2 (bound) ISBN 1-55278-183-6 (pbk.)

I. Title.

PR6058.E19S83 2001   823'.914   C99-931751-2

Designed and typeset in Optima by
Libanus Press, Marlborough

Photograph of Dermot Healy by Steve Pyke
Cover Composition, Design & F/X by *Mad Dog Design Connection Inc.*
Printed and bound in Canada by *Transcontinental Printing Inc.*
Division Imprimerie Gagné

The publisher would like to acknowledge the financial support
of the Government of Canada through the Book Publishing Industry
Development Program (BPIDP) for our publishing activities.

10 9 8 7 6 5 4 3 2 1

ACKNOWLEDGEMENTS

Parts of what became this novel first appeared in *Cyphers 31* (Summer 1989) and *Force 10* (issue 10, Autumn 1998). I would especially like to thank Leland Bardwell for her encouragement to write the piece which appeared in *Cyphers*.

SUDDEN TIMES

CONTENTS

I

On High Street

1

after London

After London it was serious.

I lay low.

I stayed with the mother a while, pottering in the garden, walking the beach with all these images in my wake. I dropped into Gerties pub the odd time, but people were wary of me at the beginning. Then I suppose they got used to me again. But in my mind's eye I kept seeing Redmond serving behind the bar. And I found it hard to talk to anyone with that constant argument in my head. Argument with the father.

Then would start the lament: *If I had done this, none of that would have happened. If I hadn't. If I hadn't. If I had.* It went on till I was sick of my own consciousness.

This guilt was stalking me.

I could not get by the first dream.

the first dream

It always happens in the first dream. If you can get by that you're away. But I was pinned to the bed by these voices. For hours on end I was interrogated by myself. *If you had. If he had not. What if. What if.* And nothing was ever resolved. Sometimes the voice was that of a barrister. Sometimes it was the voice of my father.

Sometimes it was the voice of someone I didn't know. Whoever they were they were relentless. I was a man listening to complaints and sermons, jibes and asides. This could not go on forever.

I went looking for a job. I scoured the ads in the *Champion* and walked into town. I presented myself at various places with no luck. All I got was hassle. *What were you at before? Why did you leave your last job?* That shite. More argument. Then I saw this new pub was opening. They took me on the night I called. I was set up. I moved into a room at the back. One evening – maybe two weeks later – I could tell something was wrong.

Your man, the head buck, called me aside.

I got this sickening feeling.

Ollie, he says.

Yes?

I'm afraid you are not the man we are looking for.

I went, What?

I'm sorry.

Have I done something wrong?

No.

Don't I work well for you?

It's not that, he said. I just have to be careful who I take on. You know what I mean?

He gave me an extra week's wages. So I got my gear from over-head and rather than go home, I moved into the hostel. I could not face the mother. I was shamed. Days I walked the town. It was unreal. Then I got myself a labouring job on this site near the river. Urban renewal. It was not so bad. And I liked the hostel till I met this fucker from Atlanta who claimed later he was not from Atlanta. Still and all I met Sara there and we were together for a couple of months. Then one evening I went:

What's up?

I'm breaking it off, she said.

Why?

I put a hand on her shoulder, but she shook it off. Then I knew she knew. I was bad news. I had no luck with the ladies. She left me. I was not well. I took to the bed. I walked off the site a few days later and got a job in Doyle's. Fair deuce to the man for taking me on. I told him I'd give it everything. *Doyle's for bargains!* Then I took this room with these bloomin' artists on High Street.

the attic

That was home. I had to stoop to dress because the ceiling of the room was so low. The walls of faded boards sloped in on all sides. Most of what I had hung off the back of the door. On a hanger I had what I wore to work suspended from the ceiling in see-through plastic. The clean vests and shirts sat in a biscuit box in a nook in the corner. The dirty clothes went into a bag under the bed. A pile of paintings left behind by the last tenant were stacked facing the wall at the foot of the bed.

I could have thrown them out. He was in India. He might come back. I hadn't the heart.

I'm tidy.

I had all of Marty's things round me. His atlases, *dawk-cue-ments*, travel books, his bearded heads of fishermen. I had my brother Redmond's box of cassettes. Sometimes I might play Queen or Pavarotti with the window thrown open on to the street below. The attic stood on the top of a three-storey house. You could say I was on the fourth storey but it was not really a storey, more a bird-cage under the roof. After a storm the slates, one by one, would click back into place. The beams expand with a grunt. The floorboards give. I'm not one to complain, but most mornings I woke with a start wondering what had happened. Then went to bed the next night wondering what would.

You had to watch your head. Every time. No matter where you

5

are you have to watch the head. The only place you could stand up straight was in the centre. And then there was the window. You had to duck to reach it. By day it was like any other window in the world. You crouched and looked out and saw what you saw – every jackdaw in town croaking, monks in white ascending to Harmony Hill, the roofs over High Street, shoppers, newspaper vans.

It was a light everyday melody, cheerful even. It would not do your head in.

But by night it was something else.

It's like this.

If you left the fucking window open it turned into a loud-speaker through which a town in turmoil screeched its wares.

Every sound travelled straight up from the street – drunks, women screaming, church bells, taxis, skinheads. Some frantic demon seemed to grip the folk once darkness fell. At night the whole town bedded down with me. It was a ward of the insane.

In this room I was to start my new life.

the water tank

Yes. It sat in a hardboard box in a corner of my room. Some plumber had thrown the box together out of shuttering.

I often thought of pulling the whole thing apart and doing a proper job, but I'd lost the head for carpentry. Being a chippie was a thing of the past, though in case I ever changed my mind I still kept my spirit level, saw, the two hammers, a fine chisel and one Stanley tape measure in a duffel bag under the sill.

All pipes in the house led to that confounded tank. And why wouldn't they?

What do you expect?

When I lay down in the bed I'd wait for it. Just a turn of the tap somewhere below and the beast groaned. And if one of the artists went to the toilet in the middle of the night, the tank began clanging and spilling, next it would change gear and explode, the water run downhill, the filling begin and then this drip would start.

It wasn't nice. It was cat. Every time someone went to the toilet I went with them. I heard their door open, the footsteps descend to the second floor. As they squatted I held the chain. At the first plop my heart trembled. When they rose I pulled the chain.

I wasn't sleeping.

I was losing it.

So I hung a sign in the toilet.

PLEASE DO NOT FLUSH AFTER MIDNIGHT!

That was all right. Next day I found someone had hung a sign alongside mine.

PLEASE DO NOT PUT ON LIGHTS AFTER MIDNIGHT!

That was to do with the lights on the stairs.

the bride

It was the night I moved in I saw her make her appearance. A cruel evening in November. Businesses were just closing shop, lights going off and street lights coming on. I sorted out my gear and lit up.

Then I ducked down in my new home and looked out the window – that finished it – for there on the opposite side of the street I copped the bride.

I couldn't believe it.

She was like one of the Luton ladies I used follow. She wore an illuminated wedding dress with a slight hint of pregnancy. She was faceless and still, just a white veil, nothing else. It took a while before I could make out that she was in the window of a shop. The window of a launderette and dry cleaners. I had never seen her before though I must have passed that shop many days. But

7

there she was. I looked away and lay on the bed. Went back, there she was again. All night she stayed lit beside a green tank of orange fish. She was an apparition, and the cleaners was her grotto.

Next day after thinking about it I went across with my wash. I sort of dived in before I could stop myself. There was a strong smell of male socks and motherly underwear. The washing machines were going like billy-o. I found myself perspiring. The place looked wrong and the flashback came. The woman said, Yes? *Yes?* she said again. What can I do for you? I don't know what I said. *I could have said anything.* She took my bag without a word and slung it overhead. As she wrote out my docket I turned by the way to look at the bride. She didn't exist. She wasn't there. The dress was there all right but that was all she was – a wedding dress. She had no head, no hands. The wedding veil was tawdry and under the tresses no one. Just musty warm air.

I must have made her up, I thought.

Then I saw that the windows were steaming up.

I just grabbed the docket and left.

It took me a couple of days before I worked up the courage to go back. I never enter a cleaners. Not since London. Ever. I know what the story is. And I wouldn't have gone into one that day only for to see the bride.

A ghost of happy marriages

I studied her from my room till all hours.

By day she disappeared. The light of day did not suit her. But by night the bride came into her own. As the fucking clamour increased throughout the town and squad cars piled to a stop with a screech outside the Lamp and these fuckers began cheering over nothing at the monument, the light in the launderette began to intensify. The more the tumult the more the light. The more the light the more the magic. The steam cleared from the windows and she came in from the back. She stood up in the dark to the left of the counter, drew her pleats and bridal veil up in one missing hand and with the other made some strange gesture towards the passers-by. Each side of her were racks of dry-cleaned suits, dresses, raincoats, all hung in cellophane. She was radiant, laundered and shimmering. A ghost of happy marriages smiling in a blue beam of light till the early hours.

I didn't mention her to anyone except Liz and that was in a moment of weakness.

It's something best kept to yourself.

You know what the story is.

the kitchen

It was the pits, as Liz would say.

Liz is a pal of mine. The first pal I've had since Marty and La Loo. I met her in the Rap where she was doing this mime thing on stage. Yes, Liz, looking beautiful in a slouchy way, hair boyish and fair, would disdainfully pick a single vessel out of the dirty sink, and with a sigh run it under a spout of boiling water from the kettle, scoop dried colourless beans out of a small saucepan and make a meal from there.

What she excelled at was desserts, fruit cakes and humming.

But not washing up.

The men artists were bad enough but the women worse. Why that is I don't know. Like the stairs and the rooms the kitchen reeked of various oils and plaster. If I was away for a few days I came back to find the linoleum by the gas cooker coated in grease, the hob stained with curry and Bolognese. If you turned on a ring there was a sharp smell of burning. An onion peel glowed and spat. The oven stank. And the sink was full of unwashed delph.

9

Being the oldest there, and always tidy because of something far back in my nature, way back, it fell to me to wash up. And I always did last thing at night, for there is nothing worse in this world than to wake up to a sink full of unwashed delph. I can't face into that.

I don't mind. Students are all right. But the kitchen itself was very depressing. The one window in the back door looked out on a wall a few feet away. There was just enough room in the yard for briquettes, one single flowerpot made out of a chimney flue and an overflowing dustbin. Beside it a cat's home. I made a box for the cat but not for the tank. I often looked at that wall and marvelled. It was about eighty-five foot high. Just a plain block wall at the back of a barn owned by a carpet-seller who sold Dutch furniture.

Dutch furniture mind. Fuck him.

Not a lick of paint or a taste of plaster, just a high wall shutting out the sky so that you breakfasted in darkness.

It's true.

I used to curse a lot when I was younger.

the stairs

It was like this.

I might be working late in Doyle's or be cleaning up after hours in the Rap and then I had to climb those stairs to my room. Rickety is the wrong word. The steps were very uncertain. I could not get up them in the dark no matter how I tried, so I'd put on the light and then the commotion would start on each floor. The problem was that each bedroom door had a glass partition overhead and the bulbs shone straight on to the sleepers within. The artists would start shouting. Hi, put out the fucking light! The light for fuck sake, the light! Even Liz would yell out, although she said she didn't. But I heard her.

By the time I raced the last few steps to my room I was in a lather of sweat.

At last, flipped the switch and the house below me went quiet.

But not me. I wasn't the better of it. It got so bad I was afraid to go back to the house once I went out. But if I went out I had to come in again. I bought two torches and they were nicked. Best thing was to be up there in bed before them. Then I had only the tank and the rascally town bellowing through the window to contend with. But I had to work late and those days I had no place else. And I was only being charged £25 quid a week, which wasn't bad no matter how you looked at it.

And I had Liz as a friend.

I don't complain.

The stairs were a cross I had to bear.

2

Doyle's for Bargains!

Doyle's Supermarket. *Doyle's for Bargains!* It was a great shop to think in.

I was an all-round man – giving out trolleys at £1 a head when the lad was off, sweeping up round the cashiers, stacking shelves by night. I wanted nothing too complex. I was just waiting for half-past six. Sometimes I'd say it out loud to myself – *Half-past six! Half-past-six! Half-past six!* And if I was on early nights I'd hear myself saying *Half-past two! Half-past two! Half-past two!* People often said to me that I should return to the carpentry, but after those things happened in London I was not the same. There was no looking back. You have to break out before you can learn the laws of the tribe. And you have to break inside before you can learn your true nature. There's no need being too serious.

I was serious once.

The head would not take it.

As the chippie says – I was offering it up.

Doyle's was all right. I picked up around £115 after tax at the end of a five-and-a-half-day week. There was plenty of overtime. And supermarket people are very down to earth. The cashier girls might get a bit high, but generally everything is very sensible and busy. In fact the place is a scream. I get high there myself. And then when you think that I live in High Street – well. One day people in authority turned on the butcher boy and demanded he take the ring out of his nose and put it in his ear because punters complained at the meat counter. Well I don't know. I say a ring in your nose makes you look hygienic. I didn't take them serious. I didn't want any bother. I needed a routine. Working there gave me a new lease of well-being.

The only bad thing – doing the trolleys in winter was hardship. The heat began inside the sliding doors. Where I'd camped out lay open to the elements. It had a roof against the rain, but nothing against the cold. I did myself up each day to be on the safe side, why, woollen cap scarf long johns padded shirts you name it I was wearing it.

For a time I wore gloves, long woollen gloves, but I didn't feel right in gloves somehow. No chippie does. You might saw a finger off without knowing it. In truth I think gloves are weird. Especially in evening dress. I wouldn't dream of attending the Oscars in gloves. You'd be surprised at the hang-ups you have that you don't know of.

Say nothing.

Stall the breeze.

groin bags

The day they gave me the groin bag to keep loose change in I was shamed. It was worse than the gloves but then you can't stash so many coins in your pockets.

I was stuck with the groin bag.

What the hang-up was there I don't know. It reminded me of a Sumo wrestler's belt. Or worse still those ball protectors the medievals wore. A type of jockstrap let's say. More a class of overgrown genitalia that dodos wear on their travels. For the first few days I walked round with my hands across the bag out of humiliation. You'd look down and see these things hanging off you. I don't

13

mind work. I like clean work. I always liked working. Even when I was at my worst I got a lift when someone called round and woke me out of my sleep and said will you fix the chair the table the wardrobe. Seconds was my trade – second fittings. I might not want to go, but I did.

I owe people a lot for making me do things when I didn't want to. Like the Gilmartins who gave me the part-time job behind the bar in the Rap. Like Geoffrey who took me on in Doyle's.

I may not remember the people, but I owe them. Coming to the door when I wanted to see no one. They saved my life.

Christians

You'll get that. There's a fair few knocking about.

Anyway, Doyle's was my employer. I had to put up with the groin bag. And I liked my life there. I liked the buzz first thing in the morning. Customers brought out the Christian in me. They were all cheerful sinners like myself.

Once they kept it that way.

This morning a man stops as if he knows me which he does not.

Hi Sham, he says, I come from Aitnioige. The place of the Little People. Do you know it?

No.

Well, it's out your way.

Oh.

Do you take a drink? he asks.

The odd time.

I do not.

No?

If I take a drink, I take a blackout.

Oh.

14

But I smoke, I do.

Fair enough.

Yes.

He ties his shoelace and goes on.

my own space

I don't like hearing talk of governments. Politics makes me dizzy. They're cat. If you're paranoid about government then the psyche is unsettled. You're not well. Next thing is you're standing in Saint Columba's in your pyjamas talking to some bollacks about the phallus and chewing something to bring you down. No sir. No way.

What I've discovered is – once you're moving you're thinking, it's when you're not moving that things go awry. This numbness starts in the brain and what you see would sicken you. If you're moving you can leg it through the whole alphabet. You can plan you're life. You're someone. So flying down the tiles with a mop is to me like a spell on the couch. I work out ley lines when I'm putting tins of Bachelor's peas away. I get great satisfaction from placing the last can of sardines into place. Stand back. A job well done. I'm off to the jellies. I'm among the curry jars. The trick is to to be eternally on the go.

They often say *Hi! take it easy, Ollie*, but I say *Don't be decadent! You don't have to keep up with me.*

Keep moving.

That's the one.

I get these very pleasant thoughts once I'm active.

Once there's something to do the job is Oxo.

opulence

It's just that I like the word.

The same as I like the Rory Borry Yellows. Them's the lightning before the storms.

courthouses and trials

I don't like them.

They smell like out-door toilets or maybe confession boxes, not that I've been in either for a long time. There was a toilet out the back when I was young that used fill with frogspawn.

But I once ended up in a courthouse for days.

I was looking for work when I ran into a bit of bother. Then this cunt put me through it. It was Mr Ewing this, and Mr Ewing that, and Mr Ewing *are you telling the court there are no other places in London where day-labouring can be obtained?*

There are.

Why did you not go to them?

It just happened like that.

eating

That has to be done too. At six-thirty I'd cut across the car park to the chipper. The Lamp. Maybe sometimes I'd go to the Italians, maybe the Chinese but mostly it was the chipper for me and straight to the same seat by the road. This is where myself and Marty would come for a bite before heading out on the town. I like an old-fashioned dinner. The whiting if it's on, and if it's not, the fresh cod. Beans too. A spring of scallion. Hold the sauce. The tea after not before. A read of the *Champion*. And I'll have the apple crumble, thanks Dorothy. Not at all. Never. There now. Lovely. Light a fag and look out the window of the chipper on to the Garavogue river and the swans and the crowd from the Point waiting on the bus.

Even when I was at my worst I could put away a bit of food.

The truth is I like eating, full stop.

3

the London Fire Brigade

They suddenly appeared out of nowhere one evening in May when I was having the tea.

They made the Irish in the caff look not well. They all looked like not-wells. These men were bronze and brown-eyed, very European in fact. Not all cockneys appear healthy, but on this particular evening the Irish looked a tinge grey in comparison. And the divers looked like something fresh out of the sea. When they saw me they called out my name.

Ollie, said Al.

Al, I said.

We thought you might be here.

So they sat down around me.

What's this – fresh cod? asked Al. Is that what you're having?

The cod is good, I said.

Each year they used come to me for the key of the cottage that stood on the alt. It was owned by my uncle the mountie in Canada and was empty most of the year. So they ordered fish and sat around the table talking of what had taken place between last year and this. Who got married died drowned disinherited. How things were working out for me now. And then the talk turned to London and all that had happened me there.

But why did you not ring me that time? said Al.

I meant to, I said.

You should have contacted me.

I know. I just didn't get around to it.

He shook his head.

Will you come out with us? asked Fred.

I might, I said.

Don't think about it, said Al.

It was Saturday night and I wasn't into climbing those bloomin' stairs, so I said, Right I'm with you just give me a chance to get my bearings you can drop me off at the mother's right. They had the same blue minivan with *London Fire Brigade Diving Team* stamped on the side and she was stacked full of gear – diving suits oxygen canisters webs tins of Heineken grub whiskey from the duty free. The lot. We drove up to High Street so I could change out of my gear and get the key.

Liz in a pair of men's dungarees came into my room.

Who are the sleazebags? she asked.

Friends, I said.

She opened a window to look down at the fire brigade men. She turned and studied me.

Are you going with them?

I am.

Then wear the blue shirt, she said.

OK.

It suits you better.

She tucked down my collar and I thanked her.

lust

The lads studied the lady that waved goodbye to me. They had this lust that creeps up on the tired.

They were just off the ferry from Holyhead to Dublin, sailing part of the night and driving all day, now this, the last few miles.

On into the ocean.

walking

The wind was coming off the land. We lit a fire and threw open the doors of the cottage. I gathered the mousetraps and set the electric blankets then they drove me to my house and I was about to get out when Al said, Hey, how about a drink? I said I wasn't into the drink these days.

You say that every year, said Fred.

OK, I said. Why not?

Well, we went up to Gerties. Just like that. In this life, one minute you're sitting in the Lamp thinking what to do and next thing you've landed on your feet in another dimension.

It's happening throughout the world.

You're in the Lamp sipping tea, wondering what's round the corner, looking at the river, you're planning the pictures, no, not the pictures, I don't believe in the pictures any more, the TV maybe, but possibly a lap round the town or a walk to the Point and back. If there's one thing I am that's a walker. I did a lot of walking in London. Clapham to Hammersmith. Finsbury to the Angel. Liverpool Street to anywhere. Anywhere to nowhere. I don't care if it's a schizophrenic thing to do. Fuck it. I can air my head breathe see about me. That's what I would have done if the London Fire Brigade Diving Team had not come.

I would have legged it to the Point.

Yes.

Gerties

The sun was setting beyond Ardbollan, a fellow from Denmark was sitting on a wall outside the pub, and in the dark shop a neighbour of mine was looking at the floor.

Ollie, he says.

Johnny, I say.

Are they back?

They are.

They are, he said, as he stirred his toes. Ahem.

And how are you? I asked him.

He looked at me.

I'm past it, he says.

He cleared his lungs and reached for the drink that was set on a ledge over his head. With wide eyes he drank to the third. It was as if he was looking into a harsh beam of light. Then his eyes settled and he left down the glass on the counter, shook himself and took my hand.

Stay in touch with your father, he says.

I will, I said.

He's a good man, he said and nodded.

A starling shot under the thatch. The air tightened. A girl came out the back door of the house across the way and kicked a ball out of sight. Then she went back in.

Everything began to happen in slow motion. The divers took Johnny's hand. One time he had two of their hands in his because of the divers' panic at wanting to greet him.

You're welcome back, he said, to this part of the world.

What are you having? asked Al.

Johnny raised a hand, palm out, in front of his face.

Nothing, he said, I'll stay on my own, thank you.

Just the one?

No.

Whatever you say.

Yes, thank you.

Next door in the lounge Schumacher was pulling out of a chicane and Gertie's son could not be roused. I glanced in.

Joey, I called.

He pulled a face at being brought away from the TV. Siberry was sitting alone in the dark watching the race with his cap on his knee. In another corner Pa Waters sat before a Campari and stout with his back to the proceedings. The noise was something awful. We had whiskey pints Ballygowan in the shop. All like that. That sort of thing. Straight in. And they wouldn't let me go. Another. Then another. And the dark settling outside till the lights appear on the Waterside and on the Rocks regular as clockwork. One two three, Caraways, Conways, Gurns. Out to sea the lighthouse beam spun.

Then a flash of lightning broke the water. It was the Rory Borry Yellows. A wash of light ran through Gerties.

will you bury me?

Johnny threw his arm round my shoulders.

Will you bury me? he whispered.

I will.

Good man. Good man.

He tapped the wood of the counter and whistled.

I knew you would, he said.

I will.

Say nothing.

No.

The thunder struck. The TV ran out. The lights went twice, then altogether. Joey lit candles. The talk dropped to whispers. It was like a stranger had entered. The divers settled in the middle room with the surfers and the locals gathered with them. There the talk was of the best diving places in the world – lagoons off Africa, cold waters in Dorset, the Black Sea, sea caves beyond Connemara – and then it turned to dredging up bodies out of the Thames after a dance boat went down.

They were some men.

And getting sentimental and lurid too in the shadows, nothing but

22

bodies coming up out of their consciousness from old wrecks lying in the deep: men in tight pants who had just finished the tango with women in fine rig-outs were springing, springing from the sea. Eleven days in salt water. Seven days in fresh. The eyes gone. The fingers gone. As they talked of drownings the bar went silent. Then the locals talked of drownings. Soon we were all thrashing about a hundred feet down.

Then a silence. I began to feel disturbed. In the dark a woman's face lit up as she drew on a cigarette. Johnny appeared at the doorway of the middle room, his face huge in the light of the candles.

He came and sat by me. He put his mouth to my ear.

You swear you'll bury me? he whispered.

I will, I said.

Good.

He gripped my arm and shook it. Then he put a Doyle's plastic bag of mussels collected from the shore at Lisadell into my hand. I headed off into the night. Perfect.

the Ma

The Ma was sitting by the fire with her eyes closed. She had been listening to the transistor and fallen asleep in the blackout. I sat down opposite her in my father's chair. She mumbled something and her tongue appeared in the light of the flames for an instant. She must have been dusting because she had a scarf still on her head. She was pulling faces in her sleep, while the North-West Radio in another room talked in a resounding otherworld echo of lighthouses and eel-fishing.

I sat for a quarter of an hour there in the half-light, wandering through her thoughts, without moving.

Then I heeled some turf onto the embers. She woke with a start, put a hand to her heart and drew in her breath.

Ma, I said.

What?

She grabbed the armrests. She was on the verge of a scream.

What? she said again as her eyes focused.

It's Ollie.

Her face lit up when she saw it was only me.

Ollie?

Yes.

Dear God, I didn't know who it was. I was dreaming. I was dreaming of your brother.

I'm sorry.

How long have you been sitting there?

A while, I said.

In the dark?

That's right.

Watching me?

Yes.

God blast you, she said. You're always doing that. Juking around.

old times

She offered her lips. We kissed. She took the scarf off her head and tried the light switch, but we were still in darkness.

We're back in old times, she said.

We are, I said.

What's in that ?

Mussels Johnny Waters gave me.

I simmered the shellfish in an inch of water on the gas till they opened and she filled them with bread crumbs. A squeeze of lemon and wild garlic and butter, then we sat them a minute in the pan on the flames. We ate by the fire. We felt our way through the house like sleepwalkers for a look outside at the sky. There was

24

not a light to be seen on the earth. Then a comet flared behind a cloud. There was a smell of burning. A halo of sparks flew round a transformer on an ESB pole in a further field. Lightning knifed the sea towards Donegal. The Rory Borry Yellows lit up the horizon. The summer storm was moving on. The mother led me to my room with a candle.

And the bed is stone cold, she said.

She stood by the door of the room off the kitchen, reluctant to go.

I heard from your father, she said cautiously.

Did you?

Yes, he wrote, she said, and he said to say hallo to you.

Did he?

He did, and she unearthed a letter from her housecoat pocket. Read it out, she said. I steadied the candle by the bedside table. It was a short note in pencil, dated exactly, and timed, 3.45 p.m., 6 June, with 9 DURE STREET, COVENTRY, in large capitals.

> *Dear Margaret,*
>
> *I hope you are well. Do you see Oliver? He's in my thoughts alot. Say hallo to him for me and say we must meet soon. Things are not so good here. It's nothing but unemployment and arthritis. My knee is at me. Imagine after all this time from a kick of a cow 30 years ago. I walk with a limp now. The day of the car in Coventry is gone. The Irish are walking the streets with nothing to do. The Japs have taken over. And if you work for them you have to stop a few times a day to say your prayers.*
>
> *Maybe I'll get over this summer.*
>
> *Keep well, and buy yourself something nice with the enclosed.*
>
> *Eamon*

I handed her the letter back and again she stood at the door peering at me.

Well? she said.

Well what?

Will you write to him?

I might, I said.

It's time, she said, you made up.

Leave it a while.

Still she stood there on the threshold.

Are you all right?

Yes, I said.

The Bradys see you, she said, sometimes.

I see them, I said.

Are you minding yourself?

I am.

Are you sure?

Yes.

Go on to bed, I said. The door closed. The radio sang from somewhere near midnight and I had my first good sleep in weeks. In my head, myself and the father were talking like old friends again.

fights with knives

When I woke up next morning she'd been and come back again from early Mass on the bicycle.

We had tea in the back garden in gleaming white sunshine.

That town is a dread at night, she said. I see it in the *Champion*.

It's noisy.

It's brash.

It is.

Fights, she snorted, with knives.

That's right.

26

And Lord knows what drugs.

Everything under the sun.

Such a carry on. You watch yourself now.

I will.

You know what happened before.

I do.

With a sigh she got up to inspect a pink rose. A lone bee hovered and the cat caught him in her mouth. Twooo! spat the mother. We walked to the well under the firs and cleared it of leaves and needles. I caught the reflection of our two heads in the water. We were ethereal. We walked the Long Square at the back of the house. The cattle in the next field were buck-lepping. The sea rose in a plume beyond the alt.

4

the body politic

I took the Ma's bike and cycled to Day's shop to buy whatever came
to mind, oh porridge fig rolls bootlaces candles rashers. Things. Just
things.

When I came in the shop was dark and my head struck a wreath
that was hanging overhead. Do I need signs? That brought me
back. There was a crowd of our neighbours there in after late Mass.
Christian names were called. Whole families lay over the counter.
Some sat outside in their cars reading the sports pages in the Sunday
newspapers. Lads in baseball hats were propped up against the
wall watching the next arrivals. They give impish waves to tractors
steaming by.

An emergency lorry from the ESB rose a ladder to a pole looking
to see where the fault lay. This was watched by the young Gallagher
girls who sat like boxers on the window sill of the shop in the
sun. They wore jeans, trainers and puffed-out waterproof jackets. A
woman who had left her husband whispered into the phone in the
telephone box.

A fine smell of dung wafted in from the lower meadows. In the
football field a few cars were drawn in along the goals to watch a
game of soccer.

How are *things*, Ollie? asked Mr Day as he struggled to make up
bills with a pen because the till was still off the air.

Things are grand, I said.

He was wearing a red flashy tie and a bright sports jacket. Through the partially open door behind him I saw a newly timbered coffin on struts.

I'm glad to hear it.

And how are *things* with you?

Spot on. Except I've forgotten how to count. Unconcerned, he laboured on with his pen as a queue formed. Mrs Young stared a long time at her watch, sighed and spun the winder. Mr Day straightened up and looked me in the eye.

Whisper, he said.

Yes?

The one thing that gets me is those words *the body politic.*

The body politic, I repeated.

It's on the radio till I'm sick of it.

Is that so?

Yes, he said going back to his notes, *the body politic.* Who they are when they're at home I'd like to know.

The people, proffered Michael-Joseph.

That's another thing I can't grasp, said Mr Day scornfully, *the people.* Who are they?

Ah cripes, said Mickey-Joe.

dancing

The queue was chattering away as Mr Day totted. Then said Mrs Young to no one in particular:

Dancing! she spat.

Oh I know.

Till all hours.

Yes.

Of all things – *dancing*!

Then Day's daughter arrived with a calculator. She had an urchin's face and nearly too-intelligent eyes. Her father handed the calculations over to her and the queue moved on.

Mrs Young took her provisions and shook her head at whatever the dancing had done to her.

Cunla

I tipped my cap to the wee priest in his old Volkswagen. Then the travellers trotted up in a horse and cart, followed by a posse of mangy curs who immediately knocked over the dustbin and swallowed ice-cream wrappers whole. I called out a timid greeting to a girl in blue who used busk with a ukelele in town. The blind man rounded the corner in a Russian hat and oversized light-blue jeans. The mother's bike flew.

I thought my own shadow ahead of me on the road was someone coming, but there was no one, not this time anyway. *Only myself, said Cunla.*

O Cunla, dear, don't come any closer
O Cunla, dear, don't come any closer

Only myself, same as usual.

I passed old damp sitting rooms where visiting babies slept in high prams. An elderly couple were on their hunkers planting flowers in the graveyard. I stopped the bike and walked through the graves to see that all was well with the lads. I peeled off a few tufts of grass and stood there a while studying the sea-stones.

Not so bad, says Marty, though I had not asked him how he was. Not so bad, Ollie, Marty said, as if I had asked him how he was, which I hadn't.

Then on past the Long Squares. The Pound. The alt. A Mr Pheasant with a sharp red comb was nipping the bottom of Mrs Pheasant on the shore road. Every time she bent to eat he prodded her on. *Go on out of that!* A young hare shot across the beach, stopping with erect ears every few yards to contemplate what lay ahead, and then he sat on a rock alongside a questioning heron to view the sea.

Cormorants.

Spiders, righting the damage the storms had done, were spinning on every available tree. The hawk shivered in the sea breeze on a gate at Gypsy Green. Under the low bushes the plucked brighter grass. I got off to walk the hill. Into the house.

the quarter finals

There was a door into the back kitchen had come off its hinge and I fixed that. There was a window slipping in her room and I fixed that. The rain chased across the fields and the blackness lifted. A spot of weeding. At three all the lights in the house came back on and we watched the quarter finals match between Kildare and Dublin where the Kildare midfielder got clocked.

Look at that, said the mother, and he done nothing.

I started laughing.

For dinner I picked a pot of Maugherow Roosters in the garden and peeled the spuds into the sink, uprooted a cabbage head that sprouted out of a bed of seaweed, and the fire brigade called round at eight. The mother came to Gerties for the waltzing. The cockneys settled in the middle room, my neighbours gathered in the shop and the one-man-band from above Skreen played a keyboard in the back room all down through the piece. There was a mark on the ceiling that his head used hop off. For the ceiling in Gerties is low too. The divers had been down off the rocks at dawn, sixty foot or so, all eight of them since early morning among the lobsters and the crabs, the lights on their heads bouncing off the stones.

A different world, they said. Pure. Purest water in the world.

You can see better down there than you can here, said Al.

I can imagine it, I said.

Some elderly couples, who danced with each other every Sunday night, took very large strides across the timbered floor. My mother danced with Dom Feeney to a song of Kris Kristofferson with her head down watching her toes, then she took her seat again among the widows. The crowd stood with their backs to the bar to watch the floor. I joined the mother for a jive.

the meaning of sin

I copped a low-slung man swing out of the toilet whistling an introduction to some idea that was going through his head. He stopped up to consider what he wanted to say, his forehead creased, then he bit the nails of his right hand. I'm glad you asked me that, he said to himself, yes. Then he went back to the shop.

I followed him for no good reason.

And that's how I found the German psychiatrist sitting by the stove. We often talked mental problems together when he'd come to his summer home on holidays. Ollay! he said. A pint beside him as he tapped tobacco into a cigarette paper, then he dabbed it with his lips, lit her, and kissed my cheek.

And before you start asking me, he said, I don't feel guilty.

I wasn't going to mention it.

You always do.

No I don't.

Yah, you do.

It's always you that starts it.

No, he said.

It's my shout, I said. I bought us two gins. He wiped his face with a handkerchief soaked in perfume.

32

Well, I have no problem feeling guilty, I said.

Ah the Irish.

What do you mean – *Ah the Irish*?

Because you have little to feel to feel guilty about.

I have, I said, a certain sufficiency.

Please?

I have enough guilt to be getting by, I said.

Of course.

Of course is the wrong word.

Please?

You should have said – *I understand.*

Of course, he said nodding.

That's right, I said. Keep her going.

Please?

Nothing.

What do you mean – *nothing*?

It was a joke.

A joke?

Yes.

I have something for you, he said, something special.

Yes?

Do you know, he asked, the meaning of the word sin?

I have an idea.

You are thinking of religion.

I suppose I am.

I mean the meaning of the word.

OK, I said, fire ahead.

It means, in most languages, he said, to be. To exist.

Go 'long.

It is true, and he nodded emphatically. Yah. I found it in a dictionary in Berlin and thought of you.

That threw me.

To be, I said.

33

Yah.

I'll have to look it up.

One of my neighbours interrupted us and the psychiatrist disappeared. The mother went ahead home with the Feeneys and I joined the divers and the surfers.

bad versions

This often happens. The divers and the surfers had begun to sing bad versions of Irish songs and were telling stories in Irish accents. I had heard this shit before. It got too crazy for me after a while, too much going on for me to keep abreast of. I was losing my place. I grew distracted. Something like cowardice.

The want to be away.

As if I was losing at the horses and couldn't recoup, no matter how hard I tried. Now the last race was over so I said good night, slipped the latch and stepped out into the dark. Lasses were chatting in the arched porch. Mammy, a child called to her mother, come back here. The storm from the northwest was hurrying in from the Atlantic, and as it came thundering across the sea, it drove before it a barrage of bright sparkling lights.

I stood behind the battery wall.

To be, I thought.

5

Joe Green

What happened was I stood into the ditch to let a car go by, then the driver threw open the passenger door. It was him – Joe Green. I sat in.

the problem

Are you listening?

I am.

Right. The problem is I make enough money and yet I have nothing. Do you understand?

I do.

Well, it beats me. And what use is the TV? Feck all. The thing you like they take off. I miss the fucking wrestling on a Saturday. I loved the wrestling. Do you understand?

Yes, Joe.

What are you saying!

I'm saying I understand.

How could you understand?

What?

What are you saying?

Nothing.

I'm sorry for you, he said.

Is that so.
You know why?
Why?
Because you can't face it.

bad things

You never miss the shelter of the bush till it's cut, said Joe quietly.
Isn't that true. And I knew he was referring to Redmond and Marty.
It is.
But you have to have the true nature. *You have to have the true nature* – that's the key. Will you believe this! I had a quiet calf and she wouldn't go to the hay. *Pass out there! Pass out there!* I said to the calf and she paid me no heed. And she died.
That's a pity.
The first of January that calf died. I was supposed to keep him for a year and a day. And a day.
He shook his head.
That's a strange thing – *a year and a day*, he said, isn't it?
It is.
A year and a day, he said with wonder. Then the calf died.
He slowed the car down till we were nearly at a standstill. I love animals, I do, he said looking at me.
I know that, I repeated.
The trouble with Joe Green is that he just won't just let go of his beasts. His cattle are pets and he goes with the moon.

tendencies

And he has them too. He told me once that he had such a huge member that when he got an erection the blood would drain from

36

his face. So that's Joe. The Golf comes to a stop a hundred yards from my house.

Come back, he says, to the mobile for a drink.

I can't, I say.

He turns on the overhead light.

It gets awful lonely, he said.

We sit there without moving. He gives off a wide dank angry smell. He looks at the rain and seems for a few moments to be unaware of my presence. Then he turns, sees me sitting there and we coast to my door. He looks ahead as I get out.

Good night, Joe, I call.

Never mind, he says.

He heads off into the dark, the right-hand indicator blinking furiously as he motors down the sea road and it is still going all the way out to the alt, ticking along the ridge like a distress signal at sea, until first the headlights are doused, then at last the indicator. Joe Green is home.

Sean McGuilty

I stood at our gable out of the wind and had a smoke. A figure passed in the rain.

Who's that? I shouted.

Sean McGuilty, said the German psychiatrist.

Tell me this, I asked him, did your father ever surrender?

No. And you tell me this, Ollie. Vot is it like to speak in the language of the conqueror?

I had no answer to that.

I heard Wagner from the German's cottage. Then jazz. A tractor taking the new road. *To be is to sin.* Only one dream that night. It was spacious and there were certain familiars there, people long gone out of my life, the figures in the high cupola at the airport, a figure in the back of a lorry. Then Redmond appeared behind the bar of Gerties. He held a glass up to the light. Very high. I was delighted to see him and started to explain in a hurry all that had happened.

Never mind that, he says.

I just came up to see you for a minute, I said joyfully.

Work away, he says.

I'm sorry, I said, that I could not get here earlier.

Never mind.

It's great to see you.

Sure.

I tried to explain that I'd been planning to get to see him. Never mind that, he said. Then he stepped away. I would have gone with him, but my father was in the way. This emptiness. They were there, but the following morning I couldn't piece it together, it was all a haze, and again came that sense of something missing.

I have taken more risks in my dreams then I have in reality. A hundred times more.

I'd dropped something.

I'd forgotten the thing that tells me who I am.

6

the General

I was on the road next morning in teeming rain seeing things that weren't there. Along the new road I was followed by a cat who was simple. Scat cat, I said. Not now, boss. He watched me through clouded pupils narrowing to slits, and reluctantly he moved off with one long querulous meow.

Smoke reared from the General's chimney and his door was open. I saw him at his kitchen table in his shirt sleeves.

My my.

The thought of him within preparing for the day ahead struck me like a revelation. The first cup of scalded tea, his aired trousers, the fire lit from the embers of the night before. *My my.*

I walked through that parish of bachelors with a light step. I've always been in my element walking abroad at first light. Especially of a Monday because I start at nine and that leaves me the whole early morning to myself. No pressure, just take her nice and cushy. *Nice and cushy. That's the one.*

I greeted the Italian who was standing out of the rain under a tree in his back garden. Saw Elvis counting his beasts on the crest of a hill. We waved.

good morning hare

I stand in the transport box of a neighbour who stopped on the new road for me and we take off over bumps birdlife scatters thunder past the cemetery John Pete lifts his cap and blesses himself with the peak I salute a hare darts across the road Good morning hare.

He drops me at the creamery.

tell them we're still here

A few other tractors were already there, their engines turning over, so we took our turn and waited for the creamery to open. Soon Eddie Flynn came down the road in bright dungarees. He flings the galvanize doors wide and the trailers back in. We stand in the high-ceilinged shed listening to the birds flitting from beam to beam on the tin roof. They sang, chewed seeds and shed white droppings with a small splash onto cement bags then swooped out over the heads of the farmers who were gathered over milk churns in the forecourt. Bales of wire coal fencing posts fertilizer bags coarse grain animal feed were stacked against the bare walls.

Eddie Flynn stood at his high counter ticking off purchases into a tall blue-backed ledger.

I'll give you a hand, I said to John Pete.

He made a clocking noise. His eyes were a runny blue and he had large hands. We lifted bags of calf nuts and fertilizer, some briquettes and a bag of Polish coal onto the transport box. I sat up behind him, we lit fags and watched cats drink from a spill in the pump that was sucking milk from a churn. Then Marty's father, Mr Kilgallon, pulled into the yard on his tractor. He saw me.

Ollie.

Mr Kilgallon.

He looked at me a long time, shook his head and went on in. The school bus appeared and I waved it down.

Tell them all in the city that I was asking for them, says John Pete.

I will.

Tell them we're still here.

I will. I will.

no mountain

The bus fills with lads in blue and distracted girls in brown gymslips on their way to the Mercy. The ladies are still in the dream world, or somewhere in between that world and this.

So there we are on a Monday morning.

The General has reached wherever he's going the mother is up John Pete is nearly home Joe Green is walking his beasts and soon I'm like the girls, staring off into the future. *What are you saying? To sin is to exist. Tell them we're still here.* It's like I've been making this journey for years and the mountain is away again. For much of the year Ben Bulben is hardly ever there. It ascends into the clouds and goes off the earth. It's taken down for the winter. It's up there in the dark rain and the driving hail. Clouds are moving so dense at its foot that you would think that there was no mountain.

None in the wide.

No mountain, no Yeats.

Go for it, says the driver to the radio, *my old son.*

We stop at every other corner taking on more ladies. The door slaps shut and we're away. Go for it, he says. His hair is a rich deep white like an elderly woman's. A split runs straight across the centre of his skull. Looking at his head I think of my own and try to get rid of the thought.

That was close.

the pothole

We booted by the church at Drumcliff and raced over a pothole. A girl held her breast. With Willie Nelson singing of heartbreak, I get off at the Line. The girls watch me absent-mindedly. Rain falling in sheets on the Garavogue river. Ten to nine by the post office clock.

That'd be her.

What a to-do, as the elderly gentleman said.

II

The Rap

7

the Rap

When I finished in Doyle's that evening I cut across to the Wild Raparee. Of course the Raparee is not the Raparee at all these days. It's the Inishfree, but we still call it the Rap. Everyone knows that.

It's where the art students, young doctors and some of the solicitors hang out. I used come here when it was a kind of soccer bar. Then the pub changed hands, the fans moved out and the artists moved in. Down came the stapled photos of Giles and Best and up went gilt-framed prints of works by Picasso, Henry and Jack Yeats from the £1 shop.

Mrs Marise Gilmartin, the proprietor, saw to that.

It's in the Rap I met the bloomin' artists I share the house with. The house on High Street.

It's all right there except for the stairs.

my love life

The pub is all right too except the Boss and his wife are going through bad times. I think that's why they gave me the job, because of what had happened in my love life. People take great leeway. They tried groping into my past when I first started. I was vulnerable and said things in confidence that I should not have.

I'll start again. I had been living in the hostel since myself and this lady Sara broke up, sharing rooms with travellers from all over the world, and that was fine.

One night we were in Australia, another night in the forests of Maine. I found it hard to sleep what with trying to put the pieces back together again.

The intimacy you once had with someone is hard to forget at the beginning. It returns stronger than ever before.

I would say I was not right in the head.

That's right.

High all the time on sorrow, and low because of what you think is being said about you. I heard babies crying everywhere. Then the father started ranting. Fathers are difficult. He went on. And on. I said OK. Somebody came and put another in my place. The lady was gone. I was away with the fairies. I was stopping in the hostel with a chap from Atlanta. He popped some speed in my tea. That's the second time that happened me. And it came right at the wrong time. Like it did before. There was nothing for it but to give off a smile, and nod, nod again, then give one of those laughs that bounce along the top of the throat, and then the shame at being a hypocrite, being stoned and rabbiting on.

Hold it there now, hold it there.

But I couldn't.

It all came back. The worst thing is I turned sort of religious. That can happen. It can happen the best of us. I walked to the window in the hostel and looked out at the monastery that had not been inhabited in over two centuries. In my head I heard beautiful psalms. This need of mine for God is a travesty. The traveller wanted to speak of Aristotle and I wanted to speak of St Paul. You'll get that. You push too much onto someone.

I started to tell your man from Atlanta about the lady. I saw his aura shift towards dark, and his strangeness came back like a flood across the room. The spiral started. Next thing I was weeping. The bloke split.

I lay there wondering who was at the window.

Atlanta

I have never been to Atlanta. He was born there. So when I heard him come in later that night, I said, Tell me about Atlanta, though I really wanted to ask him about the speed he put in my tea.

What? he said.

Atlanta, I said, where you come from.

I don't come from Atlanta, he said.

But you told me you did.

I guess not. It must have been someone else.

What are you saying?

I'm saying I'm not from Atlanta. You have the wrong guy.

Then who is from Atlanta?

I don't know.

But it's you.

No, he said. Never.

I turned to look at him, but I couldn't see him. He had not put the light on. He got into bed in the dark and we each lay there in silence.

I couldn't trust myself to say anything even though I wanted to explain. I was afraid I might find myself back babbling. I framed the question a few times – *Why did you put speed in my tea? Why did you put speed in my tea? Why did you put speed in my tea, hah?* – but I said nothing. Because this must be another man entirely and yet his voice sounded exactly like the first fellow.

But who had they put in his place – I couldn't tell.

Then my body separated at the groin into two halves.

47

the top of me

The top part of me was death. The bottom of me was life. My head was deathly cold. The upper part of my trunk had come free. And my groin was warm. If I could fit the two together I'd save myself. And if I didn't do it sudden I was dead.

I fought and woke to find myself in the dormitory of the empty hostel. Whoever the new fellow was he was gone. I'd never know if it had been the man from Atlanta denying me. The woman came to change the beds and I said I was ill. Four days I lay there without a bite, drinking water from the tap, while in the other beds travellers came and went in various languages, made love, boiled soup and did their nails. I got up at last to get my tools off the site.

Where were you? asked the head buck.

I wasn't well.

You don't look it either.

Does he know too? I wondered. *Does everyone know?*

I'm quitting.

Fair enough, he said. Are you going to take on the big world by yourself?

I might.

Good luck so. I think you'll do well.

You think so?

I do.

Why?

A Sligo man never loses any sweat.

I watched closely the way he looked at me but I couldn't tell.

the fashion show

I went into the Rap for to plan ahead. I mind it was a lonely day, the place empty and smelling of disinfectant and that awful polish

48

they spray onto tables and counters that catches in the throat. My mouth was dry and I was feeling weak. Mrs Gilmartin was watching the fashion show on Sky News.

It was hell. I bought a vodka and orange. Then I was afraid to drink it – just in case. She propped her chin on her upturned palms and watched me. Every time I looked up, her eyes were on me. *Jesus.* It got hard to think what with the scrutiny. I watched the fashion show with great care. I counted the girls on the boardwalk. Then she came over and sat down.

We both stared at the TV.

I believe, she says, that you've broken up with Sara.

How did you hear? I demanded.

Oh I can't remember.

You mean the whole town knows?

No, it was told to me in confidence.

Blah!

Honestly.

They have little to talk about.

Well now, she said, it's not the end of the world.

Do you say so?

Someone else will happen along.

I doubt it

That's what I said.

Oh come on, she said. You're only young. If I had the chance I would long ago have left your man.

Do you mean that?

No.

Well, you should not say it. It's not something that should be joked about.

My God, but you're serious.

I took a drink quickly.

Who told you about me and Sara? I said.

Does it matter?

Yes.

What difference does it make who told me?

Because I want to know what they're saying. Some one is bad-mouthing me.

Jesus, she said.

That's right, I nodded.

You'd want to take it easy, Ollie.

Who was it for Christ sake? I yelled.

Sara, she said.

What?

She told me herself. Are you satisfied now?

I am, I said sheepishly.

She stood.

Do you mind looking after the shop for a minute, she said, I want to hop down to the bakers.

I sat there on my own. I remembered another conversation that ended like that – and now I was sorry I had ever asked. It was as if I had just stepped into a draught. An eternity passed. I thought it was some joke to leave me there alone in the pub. I thought they were watching to see if I'd steal something. I felt like I should be doing something but there was nothing to do. On the TV the last of the models curtsied, then all arrived back on for the finale, accompanied by a young male designer in leather. And that was the end of the fashion show.

Then I thought – *this is all a front.*

Life is pretending to be normal.

But I'll adapt.

trials?

Don't start that.
　Leave it out.
　Trials?
　No, thank you.

the clientele

This is what happened.

Joe Martin came in and stood at the bar just as the music ended. Thinking he was alone he studied himself cheerfully in the bar mirror, straightened his tie and made a face. He ran his tongue round his upper teeth and pursed his lips.

Japers, he said, seeing me behind him.

Joe.

What's the story? asked Joe.

She's gone to the bakery.

A' course.

All of a sudden like?

Aye.

He rattled the coins in his pocket, selected one and dropped it into the Sea Rescue Lifeboat collection box.

Well, I'm not going to wait here much longer, he said.

Hold on, I said. I went behind the bar and pulled him a pint.

I prodded the till suspiciously, but she shot open. Now. I got two hot whiskeys for the Waterses. The crowd for the Strandhill bus came in and I served them. An hour later Mrs Gilmartin returned to find the pub half full.

Well, well, she said. I knew the shop was in safe hands.

Aha-ha, I said.

Could you do the bar this evening – you'd be doing me a great favour?

I will, I said, if Sara is never mentioned.

Hand on my heart, she said.

And that's how the Gilmartins offered me a part-time job. Gilmartin is something above in the Court House and she runs the pub full-time. Their one son Gabriel went to Art College. Hence the artists among the clientele. That's the story.

So I'm here four nights a week. Yes sir. If I had not stepped through the door of the pub that day I would not be where I am now. If your man had not put the speed in my tea I'd still be labouring on the site. And if I can hold on a bit longer I might find purchase.

Sara

What was the first thing Gilmartin said when he greeted me that evening? He said I hear you're on the loose again. I looked around for an escape, but there was none. The world is your oyster, son. From here on out, he added. And he winked. And what did I do?

8

mirror images

The boss is in position on the other side of the bar at seven. He eats his dinner at the counter opposite me.

I do this four evenings a week, £15 a shift, a few drinks, no questions asked, and I get the tea. So this evening again I sit facing him. We commence eating. I try to head my gestures off into a different direction, but it's no good, I'm trapped in this ritual ever since I returned that wink a couple of years ago. He shakes the salt cellar, taps it off the bar, shakes it again and hands it to me.

I shake the salt, tap the bar and set the cellar down. The pepper goes through the same procedure, then the Chef sauce.

His mouth opens. I can see into his lungs.

Quiet, this evening, he says.

I nod.

We forage on.

I hear they have a cure for impotence, he says.

Have they? I ask guardedly.

They have indeed. I saw it in the *Sun*. Your lad will stand round the clock.

Now.

With an extra inch added on for good intentions.

Very good.

Do ya think so? He laughs knowingly. Lifts a forkful of food. I do the same. Have you seen any ladies lately?

No.

No?

No.

He pauses.

Are you gone celibate or what?

Never mind.

I try to turn the conversation off in another direction when it strikes me, not for the first time, that we're eating in unison. If I lift a spud to my mouth he does the same. I cut my chop, he does his. So I slow down and try to vary my moves but darn it if he doesn't do the same.

Are you copying me? I ask and leave my utensils down.

What are you talking about, professor? he says and leaves down his.

You're eating the same as me.

What do you expect? he asks astounded. Weren't we given the same shagging dinner?

that's not what I mean

– I said.

I lift my knife and fork. And of course so does he.

Did you ever, I say, start humming a tune and the man beside you takes up the exact same tune?

I've seen it happen.

Well, that's what I mean.

You have me.

Find your own tune, I say.

He studies me with merry contempt.

Would you like, he says, to order something different from me? Tell herself, tell sweet Marise. Let her cook two different dinners.

You have it all wrong, I said.

Suddenly I pinned a sprout and shot it into my mouth. He studied this move.

Got you, I said, chewing.

He shook his head.

Can I go on? he asks.

Whatever you like.

He slowly resumes his meal. We work at two different rhythms, but slowly we fall into line again, mimicking each other except this time I don't know whether it's me imitating him, or he me. Whenever Gilmartin is around I feel I'm the victim of mirror images. Why I should have chosen him, or he me, is one of those facts of life. Oh, it was a very difficult meal, one of the worst, me aware of his every move, every morsel he sends into his mouth. Throughout dessert he watches Ollie warily. We finish together, exactly. And on cue she reaches in for the plates.

Lovely stuff, he says.

the man in the quiz show

That's who I am, as far as they are concerned.

She does not speak to him. He does not speak to her. It's not healthy working for two people that don't speak to each other.

Of course they both speak to me, sometimes at the same time. I get up and walk along the bar looking back at him till I'm out of his orbit. He lifts the newspaper. He calls out questions from the crossword. She asks, What did he say? I tell her though I know she's heard him.

She answers him through me. She says the name of a horse. He says the name of someone who's been hospitalized.

I hand the news of the day to and fro between the two.

It's something else, it's not easy. You lose your way among lost souls.

where were we?

I shoot blue down the toilets, scour the sinks and mop the floor then read the new graffiti on the back of the doors.

Often enough the nudes in the gents are quite delicate and erotic. The artists of course. Funny enough, there's few drawings in the ladies.

More words than pictures there.

Run a mop down the corridor. Done.

Where were we?

parachuting

Ah. By the time I've finished the jacks the students arrive and the parachuting starts.

Marise Gilmartin likes the students. She gives out free grub when they celebrate parties and exams in the pub. There's draws for big hampers at Xmas, ads for student magazines. She sponsors walks. There is a certain cheerfulness abroad tonight not only because it's grant day but because Marise over the weekend sponsored a parachute drop.

So how did it go?

I couldn't do it, said May.

Aw.

I couldn't do it. She shook her head furiously. I looked out and I thought, *I can't.*

Hah, said Gilmartin, and he tapped a fag with his little finger. What did I tell you?

I looked down at the fields and the little roads, said May, then the inspector said go.

The instructor, said Fintan.

Whatever you call him.

Go on, said Marise.

But I couldn't.

No.

So they circled again and there was these ones here behind me, Fintan and Sheila and Do, and they were to go after me, but I couldn't.

And that made it worse, said Fintan.

Right, said Do.

So the plane came round a second time and my head felt light, no, not this time, then they came round a third and I wanted to do it, I swear, didn't I?

You did, said Do.

Just to step right out.

That's it, said Fintan.

I saw myself doing it, said May, but I couldn't, so he put Fintan first and Fintan went.

I did.

Then Sheila.

I didn't look, I just went, she said.

And round again one more time and Do was in front of me and I'm saying to myself the next time, the next time I will, but Do went and I was alone and I didn't and it was terrible.

Ah well.

To have gone all that way for nothing, for nothing, said May sadly.

There'll be another time, said Marise.

Never, said May, shaking her head, never.

And she sat down.

the instructor

I was polishing a glass by the till.

Does anything ever go wrong? I asked Fintan.

What sort of thing? asks Gilmartin.

Well, explained Do, the man most at risk is the inspector.

The instructor, said Fintan, correcting her.

Whoever he is, said Do, he's the man in danger.

Do you tell me so? asked Gilmartin, and he swung round on his stool. How the fuck is that?

Tell him to listen to Do, will you? said Marise.

Listen to Do, I said.

I am listening.

Well, stay quiet, said Marise.

What I want to know is how the bloody instructor can be at risk when these folk are only novices?

Because he's up there with you, announced Do. And you've all jumped out and he thinks I might as well go as well. He thinks to himself I'll be quicker going down with this lot than going back by plane.

What's wrong with that?

Well, you see, he has no parachute on.

Fuck me, said Gilmartin and his eyes bulged. What the fuck did he jump for?

He forgot.

He forgot?

He forgot he had no parachute on.

Fuck me, said Gilmartin and he whistled.

9

could you hug someone?

In the Rap that night they talked parachuting flying coasting planes jets the speed of light paradiving the force of gravity Dunnes Stores black holes ley lines mental telepathy sonic booms suicide, then the Lotto winner Annie Levi and her husband came in.

They'd picked up two hundred and fifty grand maybe a month previously and had not been seen since. The town was rife with rumours. They had gone back to his native Italy, they were in New York. They'd sold up. They were going to court to fight each other over the cash. Now here they were, dressed as usual, being congratulated on all sides. Each trip I made to their table I came back with a fair tip.

Gilmartin knew this. He was watching through the mirror all that was going on behind his back.

I see you chatting the rich, he said.

Don't be a silly fellow, I said.

Do you notice, he sneered, how they are smiling a little too often?

Wouldn't you?

And touching each other.

It's normal.

Do you see that?

See what?

They're at it.

Well, don't look.

I can't help looking. Jesus, they've just done it again.

Done what.

Touching! You'd swear they had only just met.

You're jealous.

Come here.

What?

Come here to me.

I'm here.

Could you hug someone? he hissed.

What brought this on?

Never mind. I asked you *Could you hug someone?*

You're joking.

I'm serious.

Man or woman?

Makes no difference.

A' course I could.

I could never hug anyone. *Anyone*, he repeated, and he went back to the mirror.

Jimmy Quinlivan

Watch out, said Marise, there's Jimmy.

Jimmy Quinlivan was a dapper, middle-aged customer who chatted incessantly. He was going through his second childhood. In a cap and wide red tie, white runners and brightly brilliantined grey hair he moved among the students, having a glass of Guinness with the Claremorris lesbians, a whiskey with the sculptors from Westport. Jimmy likes slumming among the students. It gives him a kick.

He's something in the kitchen in the hospital and rides round town on a Honda in a long black coat.

He looks in most nights.

If the shop is quiet he heads off elsewhere. Other nights, like now, he goes from group to group talking like someone stoned. Sometimes the students bring him home to their parties. He'd even slept on the couch in High Street and wandered the house till all hours fretting over some slight.

Jimmy, I said, what can I get you?

A Powers, he said. Have you any change for Scotch dollars?

Ah balls, Jimmy.

He suddenly saw the Lottery couple. He studied them from afar, took his whiskey and, before I could stop him, he lit across the room and landed as if by chance at the table next to them.

He smiled, they smiled.

Keep an eye on him, said Marise, he's high.

I came over.

Are you all right, Jimmy?

Why wouldn't I be? I'm just chatting Annie here. I knew your mother, he said.

You did? asked Annie.

Why wouldn't I? he said and leaned in and tipped his glass off theirs.

Two hundred and fifty thou', he shook his head. That's a fair lump of lolly. He gave an erratic laugh and was consumed by a long drawn-out cough.

They looked at me.

Jimmy, I said.

It's my birthday tomorrow, he said.

Happy birthday, I said.

Yes, said Jimmy, I'm all of sixty-two.

The couple began emptying their glasses.

I said, I'm sixty-two.

I heard you, said Annie.

Hold on there and let me get you a drink.

No thank you, she said.

Sure, aren't we all the one?

Excuse me, said her husband.

Excuse me, my arse. A few weeks ago you were slinging hash just like myself.

That'll do, I told Jimmy.

Are you speaking to me?

Yes, I am.

He's speaking to me, he said to Annie, and me minding my own business.

Fine, I said.

Sure we're only having a bit of fun, said Jimmy. Isn't that right?

That's right, said Annie.

that's right

That's right, said a student in marketing who'd just come out of the toilet pocketing the remains of a joint. He sat down at the wrong table, with the solicitors, helped himself to a cigarette and looked round for a light.

Do you mind? he asked.

No.

He met the eye of the man that held the flaming match.

Do I know you?

Just to see.

Yous have changed.

Over the years, laughed the solicitor.

Larry took the light and looked round at the others.

I don't know. Yous are not the people I was with, he said.

No, said the solicitor.

I thought so. What did you do with them?

We hijacked them.

Good for you, said Larry. Still and all they were nice people.

If you say so.

Seriously though.

Yes?

Where are they?

Who?

My crowd.

Larry, I said, your crowd are over there.

Did they move or what?

No you did.

Jazus. How did that happen?

He got up and shook hands with everyone.

That was very nice, he said. Yous are very nice people.

He took my elbow.

Are you all right now? I asked as I steered him towards his table.

Never better.

He studied Do.

Is that you, Do? he asked.

That's me, she said.

Good. He sits and calls me with a fluttering hand. He brings his mouth to my ear. Who were those suits I was with?

The law, I said.

Hit me, he says.

All airs and graces, shouts Jimmy.

Hit me, says Larry.

You'll not look down on me, roars Jimmy, and he's on his feet. He spat on the floor and toed it into the carpet.

Hit me with your rhythm stick, shouts Larry.

I should have jumped, says May.

do you wanna wake up with a crowd aroun' ya?

The Italian who won the Lotto rises. He prods a finger into Jimmy's face, says nothing and sits again. Annie puts her hands on her husband's shoulder, leans over and looks long and hard at Jimmy.

Mister, she says, do you wanna wake up with a crowd aroun' ya?

What's that?

You heard me.

Did you hear what she said to me? shouts Jimmy.

C'mon, I say.

She threatened me! She threatened Jimmy Quinlivan, an auld man.

Jimmy, I say.

But I did nothing wrong.

C'mon.

He drains his drink and says, But it's my birthday tomorrow.

Happy birthday, I say.

He walks ahead of me. At the door he stops and considers shouting back one more time.

Don't, Jimmy.

You can't do this to me.

You're annoying the customers.

They're not customers. They're tramps.

Come back tomorrow.

Never! I'll never set foot in this kip again.

Suit yourself.

He takes a gander over my shoulder.

Go on, Jimmy.

You can't do this, he says, I'm a republican.

Go on home.

And I'm a chef as well.

Good night, Jimmy.

You'll be hearing from me, he says.

It's all go, Jimmy.

I know about you, boy, he whispered. The boys across the water did for you.

The door closes behind him.

10

he's growing old

We pull the blinds. I start on the jacks and work backwards to the tables ending up by the door. Marise clears the till. The boss stacks the glasses and bottles and mops the floor. He heads into the back quarters and returns in his carpet slippers with the Alsatian leaping behind him.

Go down, Judo!

The dog runs to me. I avoid making eye contact with the animal. Gilmartin sits in his place changing stations. The dog snuggles by his feet. I throw a last few darts at the dartboard then douse the main lights and sit by the window that looks into the yard. Marise brings us ham and tomato sandwiches. The boss scoffs his with tendons straining. The dog has crisps. He picks them carefully out of the bag one at a time. Marise brings me my first pint of the night. I light a Major. She sits at the far end of the room sipping a gin and water. No ice. No lemon. Just plain Gordons.

She opens the evening newspaper to the racing pages. She ponders a while.

Would you enquire of the lady how her gambling is going these days?

I look her way.

Tell him it's going fine.

I look back at him.

I'm glad to hear it, he says. It's nice to know that the joint will be here when I get home.

Anything else? I ask.

If she happens upon a good thing, tell her I'd be obliged if she'd let you know.

He puts a hand in under his armpit and smelt his fingers then he bounced backwards and forwards on his seat.

What's wrong with ya? I ask.

I'm stiff.

He's growing old, says Marise.

Tell her that has to happen too.

I hear ya.

Yes, he says, contentedly, that has to happen too.

This wonderful sense of randomness sets in. The light on the till glows. The bar grows comfortable and strange. *I should have jumped. Flip me, but you're an innocent type of a man. What are you saying? Do ya wanna wake up with a crowd around' ya?* The ice machine clatters. Nothing much happens. Then it starts again. Is Scots Bob out yet? Has he done his time, and if he has, will they come looking?

the Cavan bus

The best time to be in a bar is when it's closed, says Gilmartin.

You're right, I said. I have a touch of vertigo tonight.

Well, don't look over the edge.

I won't.

We sit in our separate silences while transvestites talk on Channel 4 of out-of-body experiences. I take a second pint and grow benign, meaning it goes straight to me head.

He switches to a black-and-white thirties comedy on TNT.

Did you know, I said, that Sligo is on the same ley line as Paris and Rome and Egypt and the pyramids?

Is that what's wrong? he says.

Is he trying to be funny? she says.

What's the difference between being cross and being paranoid? I ask the boss.

There's a slim line between the two, he replies.

I dare say.

I wouldn't dwell on it, he says.

I get a fit of laughter.

Marise comes across to my table with another drink. She turns her wedding ring round.

Jimmy was high, she says.

He was, I say.

Gilmartin snorts. He's straight in off the Cavan bus, he says.

Don't be making fun of poor Jimmy, says Marise. He's all right.

He flicks off the TV and comes over and sits at our table. With a loud sigh Judo gets up and follows him. We sit in silence a while, doodling mentally, travelling away from where we are, making cross sections of what has happened, and what will.

The poor banished children of Eve, he says.

Ah balls.

The three of us there like old faithfuls. He lifts his pint in the half-light and I lift mine, hold it back just in time. The mirror image has started again. As he drinks, I catch a glimpse of my own reflection.

a woman's heels

As I pass the £1 shop a figure steps out from under the awnings.

She watches me pass. A woman's heels clicking smartly behind me.

She steps by me, holding her skirt down.

The top of one black boot bounces as she walks.

The woman from Veritas.

The truth folk are following me about the town.

the cast

The light was on in the kitchen though it was well gone one, and Liz was there.

Do you mind if I take a cast of your face? she asks me.

I don't mind.

You see, I have to have a project in by tomorrow.

What do you want me to do?

I want you to lie on the floor.

Oh. I lay down. Like this?

That's perfect.

She knelt down with the basin beside her and began to pat the plaster gently into place round my cheeks and chin.

It's like being at a ladies' beauty parlour, I say.

Don't talk any more.

OK.

Are you comfortable?

Hm!

It's nice and wet, isn't it?

Hm!

We have to watch, she said, that we don't catch your eyelashes.

She patted two eye patches into place. The room went black. Her hands hurried.

And you'll have to breathe through your nose.

Hm!

Don't move.

Her hands cupped my face.

OK?

She undid my shirt.

We don't want to get it dirty, do we? she said. Are we panicking in there?

Ah!

Don't talk.

It's all right, she said, it'll only take a few minutes.

She put the flat of her hand on my chest.

It's grand, she said, it's coming along nicely.

Ah!

Sh! You'll crack the mould

I hear the kettle boiling. Her steps, water pouring, a chair righted, my own breathing.

Now, she says, I'll tell you what I'll do. I'll put on some nice music.

I listened to Brahms as the plaster hardened. She ran her fingers round my neck.

Not too long now, she said.

An itch began on my right cheek. It beat like a trapped fly.

Is the plaster very cold?

She tapped it. The sound echoed through my head.

We're nearly there, she said.

She combs my hair back.

Right, she said.

She lifted the cast off and took the linen from my eyes. I lay there shirtless.

You were very good, she said.

Thank you, I said, sitting up.

Look, she said.

She showed me the cast.

That's you in there.

There I was, from inside out. Smiling.

the bed

Because she's with me I can climb the stairs in peace. I wish Lizzie good night at her door. I undress according to my system, but get the order wrong as regards the boots after the shirt because the shirt is already off. Anyway according to the system it's best to have the shirt just before the socks. I sit a while on the edge of the bed looking at my feet. I think I hear someone moving.

No.

I dart a look out the window just in case. No one.

I look back at the bed and I'm afraid of that bed. I know that I have a long night's thinking ahead of me. So I put on Queen low and climb beneath the sheets. Then it starts. *The Irish are too fucking Irish, don't you agree?* says Scots Bob. *Are you all right, mate? You look a bit pale.* I switch the tape off. Someone passes below on the street. Their conversation reaches my room and in my mind it turns into another conversation altogether. This happens a few times, so that I'm thinking other people's thoughts and making them my own without meaning to till I've gone far beyond the expectations I had when I lay down. Then the talk goes into the interior. The window of the cleaners steams up. The lorry pulls in and I know what I will find in the back.

I don't want to look. I go searching for a sound outside myself. *Time to go! Time to go! Rain! Rain! Rain!*

When I wake a few minutes later it sounds as if I'd left the radio on.

I've been singing Ry Cooder in my sleep. There's a lot of static in the consciousness. Where was I? If I start to think I get the tenses mixed. It's neither here nor there.

Just a clicking noise from the tank above.

I wait for it, but it doesn't happen. So I tiptoe into Liz's room. She is sleeping lovely.

I'm nearly away again when this crowd come out of a nightclub up the street. Men's shoes, women's shoes, an argument that's not yet finished.

The mother starts calling.

Come here, Natasha! she screeches.

No!

Come here, Natasha, she yells again, this very moment.

There is a sudden dash across the street. Heels strike the pavement.

If I catch you, I'll strangle you! Come here!

No!

Natasha!

I'll slow dance with Daddy if I want to! shouts Natasha.

NATASHA!

Natasha takes off. Mother takes off after her. Their footsteps race into the distance.

11

the morning shift

Step onto the street and close the door quietly. Eureka! The breezy town of Sligo below me is still sleeping. Cartons from the chipper fly crazily round the foot of the monument. The night staff let me in at seven. Not a soul but the butchers and the vegetable men. Vapour from the freezers drifts like incense behind the meat counter as the prawns are arranged in trays.

Lorries arrive from the east coast with tons of potatoes and cabbages that are tipped onto pallets. George, in his straw hat with the blue ribbon, and his white coat with the blue collar, is trimming chops and slicing ham. The pizza fillings are spread. The fish van from Donegal stalls in the car park. Bread from the midlands is wheeled by.

I'm stacking shelves at seven-thirty, sweeping down between the aisles and packing frozen foods. Then I unlock the trolleys by half-past eight. Plug in Postman Pat.

The tills start ringing. The crowds trundle in.

We're off.

small talk

That's what keeps me alive.

that crowd

I don't mention any more to anyone about the crowd that are after me.

When I did, their eyes would go all hazy. You could tell they thought I was out of my tree.

I'm at the cereals

This is supposed to have happened, but since I did not witness it I can't be sure. A bloke stopped up in one of the aisles and put the mobile phone to his ear.

I'm at the cereals, he said.

Fuck me.

out on the roof

It's where we go for the break. I bought some luncheon meat at ten and stepped onto the flat roof with Frieda. Below us shoppers moved aimlessly like survivors heading home from the wars. Frieda lit up and told me she was O-negative and her man was O-positive.

Is that bad news?

Flip me, she said. If you're pregnant it is.

I see.

And I'm pregnant.

So what do you do?

Nothing now, till the child is born. Then if I get pregnant again I have to get an injection. But if I had known at the beginning it would still make no difference. You don't turn over to your man in the bed and say *Hauld on Jimmy, put that thing away, put that thing back a minute, and tell me are you positive or negative?*

No, you can't.

Flip me.

We sat talking of sex pregnancy wages and sunshine while beneath us the shoppers milled by. As Frieda talks of Majorca my mind wanders. I have always had a soft spot for pregnant ladies. She has a soothing voice that opens a gap onto solace. I go over the rooftops. The twenty minutes are gone. I'm off. I pause for blue cheese from Kerry on a water biscuit.

A bottle crashes behind the wine counter.

Over the intercom comes my name.

Will Mr Ewing go to the car park, please?

Mrs Brady

I make my way back whistling. Gerry nods towards Mrs Brady who is standing by the trolleys.

Morning, Mrs Brady, I say cheerfully.

I push her provisions out to the car.

Things are something terrible, she says. You can't trust anybody.

No.

It's come to a sorry pass.

It has.

There's hormones in the beef and tranquillizers in the bacon. There's men with breasts and women with mickeys. All from eating meat.

Now.

I steer a path between a crowd of people while she keeps step alongside.

Can you believe it – they're feeding the pigs Valium. If you boil a bit of bacon you have to lie down afterwards. Dear oh dear.

Yes, I nod.

The thought of food makes me ill.

75

The pigs are getting depressed in those sheds. If they get depressed they lose weight. So they tranquillize them. Where will it end?

I don't know, Mrs Brady, I say. I begin filling the boot.

That's why I started buying lamb. Then along came Chernobyl. Now you can't even have lamb stew or you'll light up at night! I swear. And when they've left you with nothing safe to eat, next thing they come along and tell you you can't live in your own house.

I haven't heard of that one, Mrs Brady.

Listen to me. She took my elbow. It could all happen that you're in your own house and the next thing is there's radiation bubbling under the floorboards.

What?

It comes out right at you through the foundations. Watch the yogurts. Did you hear of that?

No.

I saw it in the *Champion*. Did you not see it in the *Champion*?

I might have.

No wonder we're not right.

I brought the lid of the boot down. She sits into the car very decorously and snaps her bag open on her lap. She winds down the window and gives me 50p for myself and £1 for the trolley.

panties

Thank you, Mrs Brady.

She switches the radio on, dons her dark glasses and feels round in her bag for her key.

Just then the both of us hear the lady talking to the announcer on Radio 2.

Say that word *panties* again, Gerry, please.

Panties, says Gerry and the word shoots across the car park.

Oh Gerry, I love how you say that *word.*

My God, says Mrs Brady, and she gave a giant rev.

Say it again, says the lady.

Panties, repeats Gerry.

Mrs Brady took off.

anybody

Patsy Boyle lights a cigarette and stands by the trolleys looking out at a summer shower sweeping over the car park. A crowd gather around us with lowered umbrellas.

He edges close to me.

It happens, he says.

It does.

We stare out at the rain. It smells like bottled Guinness. It pelts the roofs of cars like hail.

Who's that fellow coming? he asks.

I don't know.

I thought I knew him to see. Patsy considered the man as he shuffled towards us, head down, in the rain. It's very peculiar. *Very peculiar.* I suppose he could be anybody.

That's exactly who he is, Patsy.

Just anybody.

That's the one.

The man we'd been watching passed between us.

I could have sworn, says Patsy, and he shook his head.

a handy concept

The hands of the clock move on. The shower eases off. The crowd hoist their umbrellas and run across the car park.

Did you ever think you were here before? asks Patsy.

Sometimes.

It's a handy concept. Whatever goes wrong is not your fault. It was the fellow in the other life is to blame. Yes. Well I suppose, he says, I better venture.

He turns up his collar under his ears and darts away.

who was that man?

Who was that man? asks a woman who is sitting on the bench with her head wrapped in a scarf, like an Arab.

That was Patsy Boyle, I say.

Was that him? she says as she stows her bags between her legs.

The same.

I thought so. He was with Telecom once, wasn't he?

He was.

So was my fellow, Jimmy. *My husband*, she explains, giving the word husband a rarefied twang, then she nods. He should be here for me, but he's not.

Two New Age travellers sit down by her and begin to eat a Mars bar each, taking small, polite, measured bites.

She brings the bags closer to her.

You see, she says, he had to go off to the station to collect Georgina. I'd made a list for the big shop, and with all the to-ing and fro-ing I lost the list. He usually keeps the list and walks round with me ticking things off. He's good at certain items, you see. But when I looked I didn't have it. I looked everywhere, she continued. Now I don't know what I've bought.

She looks into her bags.

I could have bought anything.

She lies back and sighs.

Anything under the sun.

She closes her eyes a second.

As a matter of fact, I'll bet you he still has the list in his pocket. It wouldn't surprise me.

She takes a look at the travellers and moistens her lips, taps the scarf on her head and looks in one of the bags.

So at least I got steaks.

She pats her lap.

What time is it?

It's twenty to one.

Where is he?

She throws her eyes to heaven.

And you know the Sligo train is very uncertain.

She looks round her.

And I'm left sitting here, mind ya.

the nerves

She points to where Patsy had been.

And that's when I saw Patsy Brady. That's Patsy Brady, I said to myself.

She pauses and her voice drops.

I think they let him go, didn't they? she whispers and puts a hand to her mouth as if she has said something dreadful.

I couldn't tell you.

The nerves, she intimated with staring eyes.

Oh.

The poor fellow.

Then she nods.

A nice man, she says, nodding again.

She looks into her bags.

What have I bought at all?

She unearths a marigold biscuit, she turns towards the car

park, peers about her, then cracks the biscuit in half and slowly, with forefinger and thumb, she eases it into her mouth. Then she suddenly shrieks.

There's Jimmy! she says and she jumps to her feet. Jimmy! she yells and she gathers her parcels.

I'll love you and leave ya.

Good luck, I shout.

Jimmy, she waves. Here! *Jimmy!*

these are my days

These are my days. This is my life.

III

Blessed Be This Day

12

studying a hair

On Wine Street I stand in the chemist's with the *Daily Mirror* tucked into my pocket waiting till a shower passed. Then Jimmy Quinlivan in his motorcycle helmet lands.

Am I barred? he asks.

What?

After the other night, he says loudly, am I barred?

No, I say.

Are you sure?

Yes, I'm sure.

I don't want to be embarrassed.

You're not barred.

You might be only telling me that.

I'm not.

I don't want Gilmartin giving me a hard time.

You'll be fine.

He picks something out of his mouth, a hair maybe, studies whatever it is and shakes it free of his fingers. Then he stands in beside me. I do not want him there. I'm thinking of bad things.

very touchy

We seem to be in there a long time. After a while he speaks.

What are you doing standing here? he asks.

I'm standing in out of the rain, Jimmy.

It's stopped.

I know.

So?

So what?

He peers up the street.

You waiting on someone?

No. I'm keeping an eye out.

For what?

Just in case.

Japers. He feels his nose very carefully. How long have you been here?

Since yesterday.

I was only asking. He takes something else out of his mouth and throws it away. You're very touchy, he says.

There's this crowd, you see, I said. I'm keeping an eye out for them.

Very touchy indeed, he says.

Then I was in the bookies.

So you were in the bookies?

Yes.

How did you do?

Not so good.

He purses his lips.

I used to do the nags, he said raising his eyes, once upon a time.

Did you indeed?

I did. But I gave them up as a bad job.

Good for you, Jimmy.

And I've never looked back.

Great.

Gilmartin, he says, should not be let near that bar.

No.

He's driving people away.

Is he?

He is, the bollacks. But you say I'm OK.

You're OK.

I'm OK in the Rap?

Yes, Jimmy.

the old hippy

He steps onto the pavement and feels both his cheeks with his fingertips. He pats his dapper trousers. Then he looks at the sky and looks at me.

Are you going to stop there much longer?

I might.

Will you come across for one?

No.

Fair enough.

Thanks all the same.

Would you, he asks, by any chance, be a class of an old hippy?

I might.

I thought so.

He turns to go.

Oh, Jimmy.

Yes?

Happy birthday.

Thank you.

Be seeing you.

Good luck so, he says and he takes off his helmet and saunters wide-footed up Wine Street.

good luck, Jimmy

I went back to London.

A swathe of streets.

I catch a glimpse of a vague place I once was daily. The vagueness hurts. It has no name. I try the streets and the smells that lead there, but they taper off. It's funny. I thought it was all stored someplace nice. I have a past that's troubling me. I walk through Clapham station again across a platform with people going south. Then I lose it.

There's another thing –

It goes.

I search for a familiar place, a place I'd be most days. I have to try very hard. No one's there but ghosts, fast-receding ghosts. Voices recede, nothing really except for the briefest knowledge that I was once there, wherever that is. And then I realize that where I am now, in this chemist's doorway, will in the distant future be forgotten. Like where I was yesterday. And the day before.

The ground is disappearing under my feet. And I get a longing, a sickening nostalgia.

I try to put myself there as I once was.

In the Portakabin waiting on Marty.

the cable

I've been out late. I'm after leaving the Greek caff off Hammersmith. I'm wringing. I'm after hauling cable at low tide along a dark beach in a sort of wasteland. She was a long thick black electricity cable for a power station over there to the left.

The engineer had a trick.

I have a plan, he said, bracing himself against the east wind.

He got the idea that the tide would take the cable out. Instead of digging a drain and going round by the land he'd put her into

86

the sea. Then when the tide took her she'd drift far out and lie underwater out of harm's way. So we winched the cable along the sand for a couple of hours and sat in the lorry watching. We had to wait for the tide to turn. There must have been an airport near for every so often these aeroplanes flew low overhead. They looked warm and bright inside. Outside it was bitter cold. The sea slopped. The engineer must have got the time for high tide wrong because it was dark when the waters started charging back. In his plaid shirt and leather jacket, he comes up the line, walking heavily in the manner of a labourer.

Right, he says. You're all on overtime.

Some men stood out in the sea hauling on ropes. She does not budge. Others stand knee-deep in the water trying to lever her forwards with poles into the tide.

She won't go.

The ganger shouted Heave! Heave! The men pulled, we levered like fuck and the cable lurched between the rollers. Heave! The winch screamed. The cable inched forwards. The ganger and the engineer with water swirling round their boots are disappearing behind us in the last light.

One more time.

But the sea is moving too fast. Someone loses their footing in the currents. We give up.

She won't go. Drenched, we climb into the back. The lorry skids home along the motorway. The escalator emerges from the underground. I skip off at the top step, but instead of going into the wide space of the many-peopled station I head for the Greek caff. My good friend is not there. There is a smell of shepherd's pie. The place is lovely and warm. I could sleep there if I was let. But Marty does not show.

Not long after that, I found speed in my tea in the fancy place and bones in the back of a lorry.

just bones

That's what Marty was. Just bones.

the brother

Redmond was two years younger than me.

I think of him breakfasting by a jukebox going across a car park with his bag of tools entering the venereal disease department of Paddington Hospital eating mushrooms in Hyde Park. I have it now, a whole street to myself and he's on it. Walking by the cinema that's become a warehouse standing a moment by the Seaman's Mission the Jesuit Home of Renewal the Lego Box Charlie's Nook the Top Shelf.

I could go on.

I'll have to stop this. *You'll get that. We're only passing through.* And you might add, if you like, that there is no life after this one. And so on regardless. Go the whole hog. Go to town! No bother, sham, just pile it on! The regrets come with a vengeance. The want of revenge comes with a vengeance. The finite. The fucking finite within the fucking infinite.

The lament going full throttle.

I've got to stop this. I'm away. I'd be obliged if you'd lay off, will you? Thank you. Thanks awfully. Wait a moment. Has the whole bile surfaced? We mustn't away while there's more wretchedness to be uncovered. On the pillow the ancient face from the grave I woke up beside. The flames. The smell of petrol. Flesh burning. Is there anything else? Run that by me one more time. Got you.

I'm obliged. No, not at all.

It's me should be thanking you. I'm in your debt.

that was close

It was.

keeping watch

I don't want ever to go back to London, there's men after me there.
  And the worst thing is – they know where I come from.
  They could even get me here.
  So that's why I'm standing in this doorway. I'm keeping watch.
I've been keeping watch since I came home.

the six o'clock news

That's what my subconscious is. All in a few minutes the sordid
other life overtook me. You'd think the good things would surface.
No way. Just a list of slights, murders, abuse and terror. Followed
by the weather. I feel like running. The first time you do wrong
is bad enough. The actual event will bring its own shame. But
it's when you run it through your brain, again and again, down
the years, that it grows enormous.
  The afterlife of sin is more horrendous than the sin itself.

to sin is to be.

I shouldn't be let out. But even if I was locked away in a cell
I'd find a reason for remorse. It's built in. There's always wrong-
doing in the years ahead, too, no matter where you are. That'd be
her. That'd be the story. Good job no one is listening in.

A presence loomed behind me and a hand came down on my shoulder. I got a fierce turn.

It was Broderick, the chemist.

What? I shouted

Are you all right?

I am, I say.

Well, you're blocking the entrance.

Sorry.

He closed the door again. I found myself clutching the *Daily Mirror* like a club. I immediately sped off. I looked down O'Connell Street and saw there were too many witnesses on the right-hand side so I took the left and braced myself for Harmony Hill. Took a side street and wondered whether a cardboard box lying against the door of the scout den was a tombstone. My heart pounded.

Then I noticed how the tone of voice, even in my head, had changed. As I considered what appeared to be irrational the tone turned scholarly. The tenses kept shifting. A new voice occupies my mind as I wander home on High Street. But as the security of the house loomed things looked up. I got a mental lift to find myself back among familiar objects again. The minute I'm inside I'll be safe. I will be. I will. I arrived at last to my green door and beyond it the cursed stairs and across the street the bride in her grotto.

I tried the pockets in the correct order without the least sign of panic.

Arriving at the final pocket I found no key.

So I knocked and slouched a little, the voice gone back into the vernacular, the usual man returning home after a day at work. Liz! Knocked again and studied my feet. No one. Slip away now quick! Back down High Street. No sign of that crowd, thanks be to God. Sunday will come and with a bit of luck Monday. Better not to think ahead. Keep walking. You are where you are, but generally you're elsewhere. And even doing a bit better over there where you're not.

That's right.

a knife slice

I remember walking across the wide floor of the room outside the courtroom and I stood there waiting for my solicitor. Then I saw Silver John.

He smiled across at me over the heads of the men he was with. He did not stop talking as he looked at me.

Then he just made this movement of his hand.

A knife slice across the throat.

Just the once. I felt it.

the mental stutter

This mental stutter starts. It's where the words go awry. So I stepped smartly into the Hub bar, wondering if this was another one of many wrong decisions I'd made. The cartoons were blaring on the TV. I ambled to the bar, laid down the *Daily Mirror* and Pat Keohane wiped the counter down and turned Tom and Jerry low.

Givadaint, I heard myself say.

What? he asked wide-eyed.

So I open my hands and cup an imaginary glass.

A pint?

I nod.

Of what? he asks.

I indicate the tap.

Guinness?

I nod again.

As he pours the pint he stares steadfastly ahead at the cartoons. I watch him. When I look away I can find his eyes on me. Now it's my turn to watch the cartoons. If I look back, he's facing the other way again.

Then I inadvertently speak before I am ready.

Tatat!

He looks at me wildly. I give him a false smile and light up. What I want to say rings through my head with blinding clarity.

Ilostthekeyiddahise, I say.

He studies the aluminium draining board and gives it a lick with his cloth.

Did you indeed? he says.

Did.

I laugh. He laughs.

Then as he turns away I see him in the mirror making a face to himself. He furrows his brows and widens his eyes and raises them heavenward.

hoses

I go that way sometimes, he nodded sympathetically.

Yado?

I do indeed.

Nuw.

In my case I wake up high from sleeping on my back.

Istaso so?

It is.

He placed the pint before me on a beer mat and rang up the till with a sharp rap of staccato.

In my case, I say, itslossingonhoses.

Hoses?

Hosessorry.

Jesus.

Snags, I explain. Bluednags

Oh. He gives me my change.

Lostdalot, I said.

Lostdalot?

Aye. Everydingdong!

He reads the front page of my *Mirror*, then folds the paper and brings it away with him. Over the top of it he considers me from afar.

Morocco

You should get away for a while, you know, he says.

I nod.

Did you ever think of taking a holiday? he asks.

I shake my head.

I'm just back from Morroco, he says.

Gad?

Spot on.

He retires at a further remove from me.

And, he adds, the crowd on the plane saw a UFO at Manchester airport.

Didnot?

Did.

No!

The whole planeload saw it. It was unreal.

Jeepers.

He laid down the newspaper and showed me the tan on his arms.

It was fine in Morocco except for one thing, he says, there were no cartoons on the telly and the gins were on the dear side.

He watches the TV.

Do you mind? he asks.

Notatall.

He lifts the gizmo, turns up the sound and we travel into a magical forest. A toad lands on the moon and raises an umbrella. A mouse drives a hearse to a mouse funeral in Montana. Best leg it. Quick now!

the price of a can

I find myself in Connolly Street, elated. I buy a hamburger read what they'd underlined in red in the Bible propped open in the Veritas shop stood a moment looking at the monument got my breath back. The guards go slowly by in a squad car. A man vomits in the alcove where the Bank of Ireland pass machine is.

He puts his hands against the wall and leans far forwards to miss his black slip-ons and white socks.

I go back to the Veritas shop. *And blessed be Thy advice, and blessed be Thou, which has kept me this day from coming to shed blood, and from avenging myself with mine own hand.* I stand there considering revenge and feel strangely elated again. On High Street a crowd goes by singing a pop song I don't know. I don't like the look of what's going on outside the Pepper so I cut round to Harmony Hill. It's peaceful there. Not a soul. I go through the marketplace. The light is still on in the gypsy caravan. Its satellite dish shimmers in moonlight. The generator hums. As I pass, the door of the caravan opens and the old fellow emerges to take the night air.

The square fills with the rattle of horses' hooves and gunfire. The Indians are herding buffalo within.

Night, I say.

G'night boss. Have you the price of a can?

No.

He hitches his trousers, ascends the step, the caravan lurches, the door closes. *Only myself, said Cunla.* I go through the archway onto upper High Street and emerge facing the bride. The light from her wedding dress floods out onto the pavement.

oh, that Ollie

The house is deadly dark. I stand watching it for a while to see if there is any sign of trouble. Maybe they came and changed the locks. There's nothing for it so I knock loudly. The sound carries down the street and before the echo dies I knock again, twice. Liz's window opens on the third storey.

Who's that?

Ollie, I say.

What do you want?

I want to get in.

Oh, that Ollie!

She disappears and a few seconds later a clump of keys clatters onto the roof of a Fiat parked outside.

And don't put on the light, she shouts.

I leave her keys on the kitchen table and think what is it I wanted to do, but I can't remember so I ascend the blasted stairs cracking a match on each floor feeling my way through the dark with the boys looking out at me from the darkness with the flame in their eyes and find the switch in my room at least three foot to the left of where it should be. I get into bed. Alone at last with the body, close the eyes and the interior lights up for a second and Pavarotti is singing in the Portakabin and everything is back to where it was before all that happened then it goes grey goes awry what was it grey that I forgot grey what was it fucking thing next thing very slowly round the top of the friary wall there's shells coming only a small puff as they strike the walls I'm trying to wake Liz, Liz I say, it's started, but I can't get her to wake, I run to the basement

window the grass is lit like it's the middle of the day the invasion
has begun the first bombs have struck down the street the gunner's
changing direction the first shells come towards us, Liz, I shout, Liz
for God's sake don't.

Next thing I'm in the empty room my chest running in sweat
wondering what war had started in my dream.

who's talking to you?

Later still that night I heard them going past in the dark. I was
back thinking of my brother. I was thinking of Liz of trolleys loaves
thinking of tins of tomatoes seaweed cabbage waves Knocklane
the graveyard ghosts lightning openings Rory Borry Yellows storms
boats being underwater Aithnioige Clapham the Lag Redmond my
brother myself Marty then there was this cheering and cursing
outside.

A group had gathered right under my window. I did not want
their voices. I wanted the silence. And as always happens their
voices accumulated. Their roars got worse. I thought I would go
mad in the bed so I opened the window and leant out.

Would you ever fuck off! I shouted.

The girl looked up, the rest went quiet.

One fellow stepped into the centre of the road.

What's wrong with you, you bollacks?

It's four in the morning, I said.

Who's talking to you?

I'm talking to you!

And who are you, you cunt?

What did you say?

I said, who's talking to you, you cunt?

I backed off got into my jeans and came down the steps of the
stairs two at a time. I opened the front door.

Were you talking to me? I said to him.

He leant over and grabbed the aerial of the Fiat Liz had thrown her keys onto.

He bent it slowly looking at me.

I started to laugh.

Go on, son! I said.

Let's go, said the girl.

See, he said, I don't give a fuck for your money, and he snapped the aerial.

Doesn't matter to me, I said. That's not my car. I don't have a car. I never had a car, Mr Feeney, I said.

He looked perplexed.

How do you know my name?

I know your mother.

Are you fucking serious?

I'm serious.

How do you know my mother?

I work with her.

Let's go, said the girl. I know who he is.

What?

I said I know who he is.

I don't give a fuck who he is.

LET'S GET OUT OF HERE! she screeched. That's Ollie Ewing!

Who the fuck is Ollie Ewing?

He's all right, said one of the lads, I know him. He does the trolleys.

I don't know him, Feeney said, offended.

How could you? I said. You don't know people like me. Who am I to you, you shitehawk?

He turned to the others.

What's he on about? he asked.

Let's go, she repeated and she took his arm.

And I need my sleep, I said. I can't sleep. And you sound like

97

you're in the room with me. I don't want you in the room with me.

He's nuts, he said.

That's right, I agreed. I have been trying to see the funny side of things for far too long.

We're going, boss, said one.

Looking back at me, my scourge moved off. The cat came out of the friary gate and curled itself round my bare feet.

Come in, said Liz.

She was standing in the doorway behind me.

You'll get your death, she said.

I'm all right here, I snapped.

You have the street awake, she whispered.

Oh.

Now I looked up and saw that some of my neighbours were standing by their lit windows looking down. And above them again the full moon on a thread. The crowd went on up the middle of the road singing. I headed off up those stairs behind Liz. Into sleeplessness again to find that the lack of sleep has a smell all to itself. It smells arid, like burning, then dank like the smell in an unlived-in room. I ironed a pair of trousers and sat on the edge of the bed.

I thought of whitewash and ash and went from lust to grief. Do other people go on like this? Well, if they do I'm sorry for them every last son of a bitch and their pretences and jingoism and their up in the morning and into bed last thing at night with them starlings and swans and geese every last one of them barking, the Sligo flag, the Berlin Wall, the Archipelagos, the Curlews, the Saint Paddy's Day Parade, the site in Hammersmith, the flat in Clapham, all of them. I'm back in a room I can't quite recognize. It's a room I'll be in someday. I know that. Now if I knew the right thing to do to get out of here I'd do it, but I've made the wrong decision. I'm stuck with this, but not forever like. Come and get me, you bastards, I say, last thing.

Then I remember what I had forgotten earlier.

To pray. *Blessed be this day. And Blessed be Thy advice.*

and lying there

And lying there I heard her say my name *That's Ollie Ewing!* It struck me one day I'll have to go through it all again if I'm going to go on living.

I tried getting off the Ryan air shuttle at Luton.

But my father was in the way. I could not go down the steps.

I was terrified of what would come after.

not so bad

Not so bad, says Marty, last thing. Not so bad, Ollie, Marty said, as if I had asked him how he was, which I hadn't.

13

Bolognese for breakfast

I woke on the wrong side of what goes on normally. I was ashamed of myself and all my doings. Daylight was streaming across the friary roof. The bride was gone.

Downstairs Liz has her non-fattening butter and low-fat milk in front of her on the table.

You're up early, I says.

I couldn't sleep after all the commotion.

I'm sorry. I didn't sleep myself.

I know.

You do?

Yes, she said. You were babbling for hours.

She is drinking from her own cup and eating the last of a wheat-germ loaf from Tír-na-nÓg. Jim Bolger the sculptor arrives down, splashes his face with water from the sink and sits down in front of his solitary fare – Dairigold butter and egg his own miniature white loaf a cup that says DADDY a large incongruous silver knife. Not a word is spoken as I heat up the last of the Bolognese, get one of my own tea bags and dunk it in a mug of boiling water. I drink it straight cause I've got no milk. We sup like fools.

I couldn't eat my dinner for breakfast, says Bolger.

That so?

It's repellent, says Liz.

They both watch as I dip a slice of bread in the sauce.

I like my food, I say. Once you pass twenty you get less choosy. The problem is until then you're spoiled. Then it begins to wear off.

Oh yeah, she says.

That's the way it is.

When I turn twenty, she said thoughtfully, I'd like my own space. A big barn with plenty of light.

I see it, says Bolger.

No clutter.

Right.

A bunk bed at the top of a ladder in a little recess. Do you know what I mean?

I do, I say.

Oh dear, she laughs. What I want is a big barn, huge, and she cups her face in her hands.

OK, I say.

I'm not saying you can't live there too, Ollie, she says raising her face again. You can share the space with me if you want to.

Thank you, Liz.

Excuse me, she said, I need to go to the toilet.

Work away.

what about me?

She fluttered in and sat back.

Where was I?

In the barn.

With you, she said.

That's right.

And what about me? asked Jim.

We can all live there if you like, said Liz. But I'd have to think about that.

She spooned thick yogurt onto her tongue.

The truth is I don't want to end up by myself. I have a dread of finding myself alone when I grow old. An old lady taking her dog to do his poo poo. I couldn't stand that. You understand?

I understand.

Oh, by the way, she says.

Yes?

Never mind.

She rose and stacked her dishes neatly in the sink. Her things went back into her section of the fridge. Jim's went into his. Mine, mine. Everything went back to its proper place in the cupboard. I wiped the table she swept the floor Jim fed the puss and then we all washed our teeth. I counted the money that was left in my pocket.

We stepped out the door together.

I stopped a moment to view the bride that was not there.

Postman Pat

We went on down the hill. Liz was wearing a farmer's fair-day cap low over her forehead. A single earing in her left ear glistened. Her lips were honey red. She was carrying canvases that were too big for her. Jim Bolger was wearing baggy corduroys stuffed into Dutch Army boots, a Palestinian scarf and a blue cardigan that reached his knees. He had a black dustbin bag over his shoulder in which he had all his needs. His walk was poncy and his body cast an errant shadow on the footpath ahead as if he in fact were someone else.

I'd seen the same man once poring over a book in Hammersmith Library opposite the copshop.

Yes.

I myself was in my green shopcoat. I love it.

This is what we looked like this particular morning as we stood by the Garavogue river feeding the swans with bread. The swans cruised out into midstream the pair headed to college and

I went along the corridor of the supermarket switched on Postman Pat's mail van and the rocking motorbike. The arcade filled. At eight-thirty I unlocked the first of the trolleys and stood looking over the car park at the glaze of heat rising from the bakery.

Smarties

Glad to be alive, I stepped out onto the flat roof of Doyle's for tea at eleven. The girls sucked fags and bitched. From our perch we looked over the shoppers at the rooks screeching round the cathedral firs. A posse of Hari Krishnas shimmied in orange through the car park. A Ford backed into a Mazda. The world appeared a small place.

You hear what happened today, Ollie? asks Julie.

No, I say.

Well this Dolly-Anne with a full trolley comes to the counter for rashers.

Don't tell him, says Mary, I'll only wet myself.

Go on, I say.

Rashers, half-a-pound, she says all la-de-da, and I don't want ones that sweat like milk on the pan.

All right, I say.

Give me Smarties, shouts her son.

The mother pays him no heed.

And five slices of ham, she adds.

Smarties, he shouts.

Make it six, your best, roasted.

Smarties, he yells.

Shut up you! she screeches. Then she turns to me. Do you call that your best ham?

Yes.

Well, it doesn't look right to me.

It's our best, I say.

OK, she says, if I have to.

The young fellow swings out of her arm.

And I'll have a pizza with anchovies, she adds.

Smarties, he roars.

I like anchovies, she says, as if the child wasn't there.

If you don't get me Smarties, he says loud enough for his voice to carry the length of the counter, I'll tell everyone that you had Daddy's mickey in your mouth this morning.

Oh God, says Mary, giggling.

Well, the place went silent.

The shame of it, says Mary.

So your one abandoned the trolley and everything in it and flew out the door with him in the air behind her.

Jesus, I said.

That took the wind out of the bitch.

I wouldn't like to be him when she got him home, I say.

Me neither.

Stop it, said Mary, it hurts.

In her mouth, laughs Julie.

Jesus!

The cow, Julie added and she put her fag out with the toe of her shoe. Below us the sound of the beating cymbals and drums went off into the distance. We climbed down the fire escape in bits.

the moon

Just before closing time the man who goes with the moon comes in.

How are you, Joe?

I'm rushing, says Joe Green.

I push a trolley behind him. He buys three pieces of boiling bacon, three cabbages, one turnip and a pound of butter. A six-pack of Smithwicks. A box of candles for the storms.

Never let it be said, he says.

He takes an oilcloth from his shirt pocket. He tips me £1, he tips the cashier £1, then he bids me good night and heads off to the Irish House. I chain his trolley to the others and turn the key in the lock. Over the rooftops behind me the full moon is hanging in the blue sky.

Morocco

A voice follows me everywhere telling me what to buy, then someone switches it off and it's replaced by another voice that says the store is closing. *The store is closing! London calling! The store is closing!*

Where's Geoffrey? I asked Maisie.

He's in the office.

I knock guiltily. He waves me in. The manager is in a light-blue suit. He's brightly shaved. He's on the phone ticking off things in a ledger with a coloured pen. His green cap on the table is festooned with salmon flies. A rod stands in the corner. Still talking and ticking away he points me to a chair.

He cups the phone.

Do you know what problems I have to deal with mostly, Mr Ewing?

Staff? I offered cautiously.

He shook his head.

Buying in?

Try again.

Sales?

No, he says. Complaints. It's an industry in itself.

And he lifts the phone to his ear again. An exchange ensues in which he is mostly silent. I drift off. Everything becomes very plain and simple. *Tell them all I was asking for them.* Then when he turned to me I had forgotten about his existence.

Well, Mr Ewing?

Yes?

You wanted to speak to me?

That's right.

Well?

Oh. I bobbed in the chair. I'd like to take my holidays.

What?

I nodded.

Now?

As soon as possible.

Are you on the list?

I'm down for September.

But it's only July.

I know.

He lifts down the staff book and flicks through it.

Is there anything wrong?

No.

You left this very late.

I'm sorry, Geoffrey.

Can you do a couple of nights before you go?

I can.

Can you do tonight?

Yes.

Then there's no problem, he says, and he scores a line through the month. I'm short tonight. If you can do tonight you can leave tomorrow.

Thank you, Geoffrey. It's good of you.

No problem.

I stand to leave.

Are you going far?

I hesitate.

I might take a week in Morocco.

Oh.

the Kellogg's freak

Already the night staff have gathered to pack and unpack the shelves and I join them.

Some nights nothing happens. For weeks everything remains more or less where it is. The ciders and honeys and cornflakes come to rest. The mango chutneys settle. The Worcester, Yorkshire and Chef sauces sit content. And just when we know where everything is, Geoffrey has a whim, he grows fretful, and the whole thing starts all over.

This evening that's what happens. He walks the aisles behind me brooding on variety. Whole commodities move house and turn up elsewhere. Creamed rice is upgraded, it moves from among the peas and beans to a shelf next door to the wines. In a few days, much diminished, it will return back to where it was. Or maybe head on somewhere else. All the tins of Roma tomatoes are on the move. They find themselves next the cheeses, then the cheese takes off, along with the yogurts, to a new refrigerator by the meats.

Curry pastes are on the go.

Toilet rolls take up a new position by the floor polish.

Geoffrey goes up on his toes and views the displays from various perspectives, makes an adjustment here and there, lifts a can and studies it, replaces it, stands back and feels his bottom lip with the fingers of his right hand. He goes by colour. He looks through the eyes of the potential customer. He strides to and fro becoming a shopper from the Point, a wine bibber from Tubber, a Kellogg's freak down off the mountain, an obsessive meat eater from anywhere, till at last he steps out into the summer evening with his rod.

The rock music comes on. We attack the heights. Then someone sets off the alarm. Feeling sentimental, I stack jelly near where the biscuits have been, shift deodorants to the other side of the toiletries, and pack the previous day's bread into boxes for the old folk's home and the asylum. A lorry backs into the shed and one of the men sings in a tenor voice. A tenor voice is a blessing.

half-two!

Half-two! Half-two! The night passes. At last we step out into the car park with plastic bags of meat and chicken that have reached their sell-by date.

The night staff stream in various directions home.

I walk the town like a UFO.

the buffs

The streets were empty. The night sky olive. I found myself alone at the bottom of High Street. I stopped to read what new message they had underlined for me in the Bible in Veritas.

Señor, a voice says from overhead.

I stepped back.

Is that you, Ray? I called up.

That's me. He was leaning out on the sill in his shirt sleeves.

So what's new?

I'm going to be Santa Claus again this year.

Are you?

I am indeed. Are you in a hurry?

No.

Then stop there.

A few minutes later he stepped out onto the street and pulled the gate of the shop behind him.

I couldn't sleep from thinking of the match.

What match?

What match? he repeated. What match? You're out of touch, señor. We're playing Shamrock Rovers tomorrow.

We stood on the dark street watching crows pick rubbish by the monument. Ray looks sickly in the street light. His eyes are dark and huge, and his chin is unshaven. His large belly is tied laxly by a thick belt. His jeans ride low over his buttocks. He's wearing spotless black shoes. I light up.

It's fifteen years since I smoked a cigarette, to the very day, he says.

You remember the exact day?

I do.

You're tough. I can't remember what I was doing yesterday.

Well, this is it. You're mind is contaminated. Think of Job. You know your Job?

I do.

Well, everything was against him and look what he done. Right?

Right.

Job was the boy.

He was.

So which way are we going?

We took off towards the Cathedral.

We strolled cross the gravel path then tipped away into the dark moonless grounds.

I was on the radio yesterday, says Ray.

You'd have a nice radio voice.

Do you say so? Well, I told the buck that there were no good people in politics. The people that put you in want their pound of flesh, I said, so what the politician does is pay his dues and

109

stash a bit away. The town of Sligo should be a paradise, I said to him, but it's not.

It's not, I said.

Aye. But the buck laughed. He didn't want to know. He thought he was talking to an idiot. But I said, Listen, listen to what Marx has to say, so I quoted him Marx. I gave him a dollop of that, and I followed up by knocking Darwin and evolution and then I mentioned Jesus. Jesus too had his struggles with the dealers and the conmen, I said. He put them out of the temple.

He did.

That was a rare man, señor.

He was.

He is!

That's right.

We cut across through the car park.

If Sligo Rovers win tonight you know what I'm going to do?

What's that?

I'm going to refrain from sweet things for a week. If you don't do your penance you'll be visited. You have to watch out if you're doing wrong. But you have to be twice as careful if things are going well. That's when you're in trouble.

We passed over the bridge and stopped to look at the sky.

What star are you? he asked me.

Pisces.

Don't rush things, he says. That'd be your main bother.

And you?

He looked at me with haughtiness.

I'm Aries, he says, the ram.

You look like a ram.

A saintly ram, he said. You see I'm on the cusp. The brother is Cancer. He's highly strung. Up all night long.

Like ourselves.

That's right. But since he found God he's easy enough to live with.

We headed along the Garavogue. With a sort of sadness, I saw one of my trolleys had been dumped and upended in the river.

The late mother was born on the full moon in February, continued Ray. It was a terrible house to grow up in.

Now.

We studied the new apartments.

See what the buffs built, he says. You get the buff in from the country and he'll build fucking anything. He'd pave over the fucking river if you let him.

We went up the alley and came out again at the monument.

That's better, says Ray. I'm the better of that.

See you, Ray.

Good night, señor, he says. And watch the auld personality problems, he added, closing the gate behind him. Then he climbed to the one-room flat he has over Veritas.

the dance

Liz was asleep on the sofa in the living room with a sheet thrown over her. I touched her shoulder.

Where were you? she asked.

Out and about.

You know I can't sleep if you're not home.

I'm sorry.

She sat up.

I was waiting on you, she said.

I was working late.

I thought you were on days.

I was, but then I had to work nights, I said.

But it's half-past four in the morning.

She pulled the sheet around her shoulders.

And you won't, she said, be able to get up in the morning.

I don't have to. I'm going on holidays.

What? she said, offended.

I'm going on holidays.

You didn't tell me that.

I only decided this evening.

She got up and waltzed across the floor. I watched her thinking of what she must not be thinking. She dropped the sheet and stepped through her upright arms. Took graceful aim with her nostrils. Hummed. With her hands made wheels. Waded with slow steps across the linoleum. Advanced, turned. Brought herself serenely serenely slowly slowly to a stop. With a humble obeisance. A closing of the eyes. A nod.

Where? she asked, where are you going?

Morocco, I said.

the Sligo Champion

Ollie, she said.

Aye.

Ollie, she said. Please stop looking into my room at night.

OK, I said.

I can feel you there when you do it.

Can you?

It's very unnerving. She studied me. Will you take me with you?

I will.

Then I'll bake a fruit cake for the train, she said. I spread the *Sligo Champion* across the kitchen table while Liz put the kettle on.

The dreams I had, she said. I was rowing out to Inishmurray Island in a tea chest.

Jesus, I said.

And I ran into your room, but you weren't there.

She put her head under the kitchen tap and began to wash her

112

hair over the dishes, tittering away, then she towelled her scalp vigorously and sat opposite me, a cup in her hand and her head done up in a turban.

You looked in again at me last night, didn't you?

I did.

I thought so.

Only for a second.

Tut-tut, she said. I can always tell when you are in the room.

She stood and commenced a series of cat sounds as she looked into the cupboard, she leaned forwards with an ironic moan, lifted a jar of coffee and purred, sat, away in her own world, started a series of coos, half-bird, half-cat, and looked me in the eye.

Tomorrow?

The day after.

She sprung to her feet.

I better pack, she said.

I read the paper from cover to cover and climbed the stairs in the dark. The door to her room was open, She was lying fully dressed on the bed with one arm thrown over her head. A duffel bag sat gorged on the floor. I pulled her door quietly to, then went to bed to bed to bed and beyond.

the Long Squares

The mother was bathing her corns on a chair outside in the sunshine. The radio on the sill was playing dance music.

I'm glad to see you, says she. If I don't see you I begin to think you don't exist.

A car goes by, twinkling on the Ox Mountains. A calf flies by like a car on the new road. I go inside and feed her dog with scraps from Doyle's.

There was a robbery in Grange this morning, she shouted.

No, I says.

Yes. The bucks are out. Do you know what I was thinking before you came along, she continued. I was thinking to myself *Why are there so many love songs?*

We spend a lot of time, I suppose, in procreation.

So we do. But that is no excuse. If they didn't have so many childer there would not be such a pull in the boat. Do you hear me?

I do.

And if you weren't in the humour for love it would be hard to listen to the radio.

I put my head out the door.

Gilmartin said he could never hug anyone.

The Gilmartins were not known for affection.

I went in again. She was silent a while.

What are you doing in there? she called.

I'm ironing.

Ironing, is it?

A shirt or two.

Are you going someplace?

I'm going on my holidays.

Bless us. With who? she called.

Liz.

That lady that lives below ya?

Yes.

She came indoors in her bare feet and towelled them. The sun went behind a cloud. A shadow suddenly passed the kitchen window. I made tea and served it up with fresh scones I'd brought. She got into her carpet slippers and we moved to the garden. Along the hedge the mallows were in bloom. The hay shifters were charging up the hill spilling grass. The square balers and the round balers were shooting down the Long Squares.

In twenty weeks it'll be Christmas, she says.

114

And I know who Santa Claus is, I said.

So they told you at last, says my mother. Now that you know it, you should write it down.

I will.

She unearthed a comb from her pocket and did her hair.

And how is all in the friggin' town?

Not so bad.

Plenty of courting?

Plenty of ladies.

You can turn off that too, she says.

She faced me.

Your father is on my mind.

Is he?

I wonder is there something wrong?

I took the mother's bag and headed off. It had an old Aer Lingus sticker still attached to the handle from her travels in years gone by. I thought that sticker might bring me luck. The shifters passed, dropping clumps of grass along the middle of the road. Tractors with gangs of young fellows in the trailers tore to and fro like aeroplanes.

The air on the hill was filled with the salty smell of sea manure.

14

let that be Barney

After I finished in the Rap I took various routes home just in case that crowd were out then I let myself into the house in High Street. I was feeling great about going away.

Liz had her duffel bag and case ready in the hallway.

I went to her room and looked in. She was fast asleep. I went to the kitchen to eat a tin of anchovies and found another one open on the table. Liz had been feasting. Soon so would I. She differs from me only in her handwriting. On the table stood the fruit cake sitting face down on a baking sheet. I read the crossword in the paper and lost my place. Why is it I can remember only the bad things?

The bad things they said of me.

Hah! Why, Ollie?

I went back to the crossword. Then some word made me step down off a train in France. One word and I'm away. For a long period I walked the docks listening to the sailors. There were fine boats in port. After a long trip through fields of wheat, I bed down for the night in Montmartre. Under my window a man seated in the square makes bird sounds.

Then I said *Let that be* to Barney McKeown. *Let that be, Barney.* But he wouldn't. He was a lad I'd been to school with. He'd come back to reprimand me over something I'd long forgotten. Something to do with something left behind.

the lorry

I'll try to explain. I approached the lorry in which were the charred remains. My feet were burning in whatever the acid was. The cops were everywhere. I told them all I knew, but I could tell they were not believing me, no, they didn't believe Ollie, Ollie knew that, so I crossed the park in a swish of summer light. The whole country lay before me. I knew who I had to find. So I confronted a man that I should not confront. I ask him about my friend. He says one thing, then he says another. Within seconds he has broken his word.

This is not what you said a moment ago, I say.

He is trying to get on with the business at hand. Again I say this is wrong. *This is not what you said a moment ago.* And now I approach him.

The others behind me go quiet. I'm overdoing it.

You're out of your depth, he says.

Never mind that, I say.

He smiles at me.

Someone take this fucker away, he says, before I kill him!

I go closer, wondering at my own audacity and knowing too with a sudden start what blows feel like.

Brady's

Next I walked into Brady's in Cloonagh. The whitewash was gleaming. I pushed the door in. Mr Brady was sitting at the table in front of his tablets. He suffers with his blood. He was about to take the tablets when I walked in, shattering his privacy. He let the pill box fall. The pills scattered over the floor. He looked at me in consternation.

Then I found that the people I was with, maybe they were the

Fire Brigade, maybe not, had gone ahead of me down the long ladder at the pier. It must have been forty foot down. They stood looking up at me as I climbed over the top. The first rungs were very high. I had to swing myself out over the edge to get my first foothold. Then I started down. I could see the folk in the distance below, standing in a rocking boat.

It was a long climb. Sometimes I was hanging on for dear life. The distance between the rungs became greater and greater, or sometimes they were so close that I lost my footing.

I was filled with dread and the sense that this was a dangerous climb that I need not have undertaken. Then sometime before I reached the bottom I fell to the floor at the céilidh. I should not have gone out to dance at all because I was drunk. I was shamed. The moon rose. The pup galloped. I went into Liz's room and her head had turned into that of an old face in a grave. She had aged. She had shining luminous grey hair. I was near tears.

Come back Liz, I said, *come back.*

We arrive to the grave with our shovels. Mr Brady bends down to gather his pills. I find myself back at the Simplex Crossword in the small kitchen at the bottom of the house.

I'm terrified.

working back

The night ticks away beyond the window. Mir the spaceship is passing somewhere overhead. The Fire Brigade are on the Irish sea. Where was I? I begin working back through all the regrets. *The grave.* Yes. *Liz.* Yes. *Mr Brady.* Yes. *The rungs at the pier.*

Yes.

I dance and fall and meet again the man I was foolish enough to confront. The smile is still there. He pities me does Silver John.

That's not what you said a moment ago, I say and I'm terrified.

Then suddenly there before me stands Barney McKeown in the happy act of reprimanding me.

Let that be, Barney.

the train from France

He ushers in the train from France.

Here we are again, thankfully, with the man in Montmartre making bird sounds on the seat below.

IV

Old Grudges

15

the Sligo train

Where are we?

Cooloney.

Oh God, is that all?

Liz searches in her pockets and puts her glasses on the table.

I'd like, she says, to be able to transport myself ahead to wherever I'm going without having to bother with the tedious bits in between.

She gets up and takes her bag down from overhead. She puts her novel on the folded newspaper, her glasses on the novel and watches my reflection in the window.

There's something wrong with you.

Not a thing, I say.

How can you sit there in that seat? she asks.

What?

It's facing the wrong way.

Oh, I see.

I don't know how anyone can sit facing back the way we've come.

It doesn't bother me.

I could never do that. She made a sour face. I have to be facing the way I'm going.

We rocked along towards Boyle.

We drove straight into a herd of cattle once, she says. There was blood everywhere. They came from nowhere.

That's where they always come from.

Who?

That crowd.

From nowhere?

Yes.

She starts the crossword and mouths the clue to herself. *C something something something.* I don't know why I bother, she says. She tosses the paper aside. I can never read on a train. And I can't read in a car. Can you?

Yes.

She looks into the far distance.

Never mind my mind. My mind is beyond redemption. Like yours.

Then she took down the fruit cake, and cut two slices.

Nice, I say.

ears

Near Drumod she says: I have a phobia about my ears.

That's strange, I say.

Yes, my ears, she says, nodding. And I only mentioned it in passing. It's not something I'm inclined to talk of.

I suppose not.

It's personal.

OK.

She lifts the plastic cup and shakes it, hoists it high and drinks. She looks out the train window.

And that's why I'm afraid to sleep.

Because of your ears?

Stop laughing at me.

I can't help it.

124

Well it's not funny.

I'm sorry.

You're not sorry. If I was you and you were me I'd be laughing too.

You are laughing.

That's because I can't help it.

Oh.

I'm having an identity crisis.

I see.

It's private. Tell no one.

I won't.

You swear?

I do.

Good. You see – her eyes open alarmingly wide – I get afraid that something might crawl into my ears.

While you're asleep.

Yes.

You mean bed bugs?

I mean slugs. *Slugs*, she repeats with relish.

By God.

Oh yes.

they're always hanging about in there

I had a feather got into my ear once, I says. It came out of a pillow and reached my brain.

It did not, she gasps.

It did.

Was it painful?

Very.

Jesus. She looked at me anew. How did you get it out?

I woke screaming and the lady I was with pulled it out.

125

She shook her head, sat back and joined her hands. Was it a long feather? she whispered.

It wasn't short.

If that happened to me I'd die. But I suppose the good thing is a feather is inanimate. A living thing will head on in and then its *good night!* Her eyes turned glassy and she looked away. And who, pray, was the lady that was so nippy with the feather?

An old girlfriend.

There is no such thing, says Liz adamantly. They're always hanging about in there somewhere, and she tapped her skull.

faces

She lifts her bag onto her lap to get a magazine and a middle-aged woman from Drumod promptly sits down beside her.

Excuse me, she says, are yous well?

We're grand, I say. We were talking about ears. Liz here has a phobia about ears.

We all have our fads, the lady says. I'm like that about looking into people's faces.

No.

Oh yes. Girls are always eyeing other women. I can't speak about fellows, but I'd say they spend a while looking at the girls as well. Well I can't. Not me. I'd look anywhere but at a woman. I can never look into a woman's face. For instance right now – am I looking at you?

You might be, says Liz

Well, I'm not.

That's weird, says Liz.

And I have a way of looking at men as well. She peers in my direction. Now am I looking at you?

I think so, I say

126

I'm not, not really. What happens is I pick a spot and I speak to it. You see men have more spots than women. Oh the women might be more beautiful but somehow I can't look at them. Can you look at a woman? she asks me.

Sometimes.

The whole face?

Maybe.

Look at a woman – no thank you! She shook her head in distaste. It gives me the willies. And she shivered. She narrowed her eyes and peered sideways at Liz. And you, she says, can you look at faces?

I suppose I can, says Liz. Did you know you can tell a woman's figure from her ears.

No! And the woman laughed heartily. From her lugs? Never.

There's something very naked about an ear, says Liz blissfully. Now that I come to think about it, you're right.

Yes. It's a very very sensitive organ.

Sensitive organ is nice, I say.

the AI man

Then Liz whispers, Watch out!

Ah?

Behind you – if he joins us I'm off.

Who?

Don't look.

I won't look.

Tell him the seat is taken if he asks, and Liz looks purposefully out the window.

The man, swinging his plastic bag, stops momentarily. Myself and the lady pretend idiocy. Sligo soccer fans press by him. He passes on.

127

Christ, says Liz. That was close.

Do you know him? asked the woman.

Not at all.

Then the man she'd been trying to avoid turns, comes back and throws his bag overhead.

How are yous doing? he says.

Not so bad, I answer him.

Liz looks skywards. He sits by me, unearths a sandwich from a bag and chews politely onto a napkin that holds a tomato.

Are ye from Sligo?

We are, I say, pointing to Liz and myself.

It's a county I know best from the air. Lovely place Strandhill. Not the friendliest of places, Sligo, they say.

I'm Drumod, says the woman.

I'm Longford myself. But I'm getting off at Mullingar, I have a woman there, we're doing a line this two years.

You're the lucky fellow, says the woman.

She's Cavan. And he roared laughing. Her father throws me the odd glance. You'd swear I was the AI man coming.

AI? asks Liz.

It stands for artificial insemination, the woman tells Liz.

Dear God! Is that what you do?

It's what I used to do.

She stares at him.

They were not appreciated in the old days either, he continued. The AI man you see was not appreciated because of the job. The women didn't like to think what you were after handling.

Lovely, says Liz.

If you were fool enough to tell a woman back then what you were at she'd leave you standing in the middle of the hall. She would. And yet if you were a vet she'd never leave your side.

You're right, says Drumod and she nods severely.

But do you want to know the truth? he asks in a whisper.

Certainly, says the women.

He calls her in with his finger and draws her head towards his.

There was no more hygienic job than what the AI man did, he says very slowly, then he slumps back into his seat.

Now, agreed the woman.

We were clean as a whistle. If we weren't, you wouldn't be in the job.

the Cavan woman

Are you working? he asks me.

I'm in a supermarket.

Good luck to you.

Are you not working? asked the Drumod lady.

I am not, not since the day they closed down the abattoir. And damned if I hadn't started flying lessons above in Strandhill a few months before I got the chop. That put a stop to my aerobatics.

That's sad, says Liz.

It is. But the Cavan woman stood by me. My only regret is that I never got her up in the air.

I like the sound of her, says Liz.

Why wouldn't you. The Cavan woman is very loyal.

I flew once, said the Drumod lady, with his nibs to Glasgow but my ears were destroyed.

Oh, says Liz.

You'll get that, explained the Longford man. What you're talking about there is pressure on the inner.

Oh dear, says Liz.

You see you have three parts to the ear. You have the drum, then the inner and the outer. Then the pressure builds.

Stop.

And when you get to the inner you're up against the brain.

129

Excuse me, please, said Liz.

The woman from Drumod stood to let Liz out and she headed off to the bar.

the canal started

I trundled from side to side and joined Liz. She was cradling a plastic cup of gin and tonic.

Jesus, she said. I knew it the minute I laid eyes on him.

I ordered another two and we stood on the somersaulting floor between the toilets. She sneezed.

Bless you, I said.

We watched the towns and countryside fly past. The canal started. Horses in fields appeared.

She took my hand.

Never mind me, she says.

16

a small world

We stopped in front of a travel agency on Grafton Street and looked at the cheap flights to all parts of the world. We had to give up on Morocco. One minute we were for Tunisia, next Mexico. We looked at Greece. We looked at Turkey.

Then we sauntered through Stephen's Green and sat down on a bench to look at the ducks.

What will we do now?

I don't know.

We stepped through the park towards Baggot Street and on towards the canal. A man I knew from Sligo saluted us. It's a small world, I said. From that moment on I knew we would not be journeying far. The bags felt lighter. We sat on a seat and looked into the canal where bottles and leaves and bags had come to a stop at the lock.

Do you think in words?

Wait till I see, said Liz.

Hurry up.

I can't hurry.

You have to hurry or you'll get the wrong answer.

You're making me dizzy.

I waited a while.

Well?

I don't know. I think I think in pictures.

Very good, I said.

ducks

Then we stopped talking because first a lone woman in a raincoat arrived and sat chewing chicken sandwiches very daintily. She was a pleasure to watch. Then a man in a suit lay out under a tree and bit into a bar of chocolate. A lad arrived with chips. A girl with salami. Soon we were surrounded by bank girls and insurance agents and people from offices sprawled on the grass. They drank orange drinks and yogurts and ate biscuits and salad sandwiches and coleslaw. Soon there were hundreds chatting away.

Like a pair of buffs we went quiet and studied them.

When the man who went deaf was asked what did he miss most – Music? Talking to someone? Intimacy? – No, he said, what he missed most was overhearing, overhearing on buses, in streets, cafés, All the time I had my hearing I was unconsciously over-hearing the din in the background, he said, and that's what I miss most. Confidences between strangers, sentences that don't finish and bring back memories, absurdities, single words, directions, things you could never understand, *non sequiturs*, whispers, chat, names, the giving of and the words of affection, secrets, abomina-tions, hearsay, suggestions, gossip, the canal water, the traffic, the trees, the hum of the city.

All that, and ducks.

Then we went across to the Mespil Hotel and booked in at a special rate. The manager there being from Sligo he charged you less per room if you hailed from home. We ordered cod in sauce to the room and a bottle of white wine in a bucket of ice. It was lovely. Night fell and across the road the prostitutes gathered in the dark by the canal. For a long time Liz watched their comings and goings from the window.

My mother is obsessed with prostitutes, she explained. Once we had to go up and down the canal in my older sister's car so that the mother could see all that was happening.

And was she satisfied at that?

No, she never is.

the glass cupola

We woke next morning to the sound of ducks. I lay wondering what to do. Then I thought of the father. I saw him and me that day sitting in a dreadful silence at Luton airport waiting to come home. Above our heads, figures strolled in the glass cupola of the high watchtower.

What time is it? he asks me.

Four.

Another hour to go.

Yep.

Do you think is Redmond on board yet?

I don't know.

I watched one of the men lift a pair of binoculars in the watchtower. He peered out towards the runway. He disappeared.

This is hopeless, the father says.

Leave it.

I just want to make sure of one thing.

What's that?

When this is over, you and me are finished. OK?

If that's what you want.

That's what I want.

that's what I want

That's what he said.

the broken cup

Myself and Liz walked down Dure Street in Coventry the following afternoon. I knocked on the door of my father's lodgings. The woman let us in. We climbed the stairs.

I tried the handle of his door and swung it open.

He was sitting in his vest by the table reading a newspaper. He looked at us in astonishment and let the cup he had in his hand fall. It was like the time I walked into Brady's in Cloonagh and Mr Brady dropped his pills. The cup clattered in pieces across the floor and my father rose with a finger in the air as if to correct me.

Dad, I said.

He sat again and shook his head in disbelief.

This is Liz.

He stood and nervously pushed the chair back. Welcome, he said. They shook hands. He looked round him in dismay.

If only he had told me, I could have done something about the place, he said.

Never mind, said Liz.

He gave her his chair and he sat on a small bed. He felt the white stubble on his chin. He wrung his hands.

We're booked in round the corner, I said.

Ah Jazus, he said.

He rose to sweep up the bits of the broken cup.

Dear God, Ollie, he said. I was thinking of you just the very minute before you walked in the door.

He shook his head in consternation. Awkwardly, as if he might any moment fall, he swept the bits of delph into a neat pile and lifted them onto a small shovel, then he stood in the middle of the room with the shovel in his hand wondering where to put them.

I'm moidered, he said.

I got a plastic bag and he shovelled them in.

Then he stood with the bag in the middle of the room.

Let me get on a shirt, he said.

He went off into the kitchen. It was then I saw the limp for the first time. We sat in the small room, two stories up. It faced on to the snarling traffic below. At the bottom of the unmade bed sat a portable TV on a chair and beside it was a pile of crosswords and a pair of moccasin shoes. My mother's picture was on a chest of drawers. Redmond's picture was on the wall. I was nowhere to be seen. I looked at what he was reading. It was an old copy of the *Sligo Champion*, open at the sports page.

You gave him a terrible shock, said Liz.

He came back a few moments later freshly shaved in a white shirt buttoned to the neck.

He pulled the sheet up on the bed. Then he started tying his white runners.

I'm only out of bed, he said, you caught me on the hop.

I should have knocked, I said

I was on nights. I get the odd night. Security at Watt's. Watt's warehouse.

Ah.

Did you hear what happened? He straightened up and looked at me. That other crowd let me go.

I heard.

They did. They let me go a while back. He lowered his head again and finished the last knot with a flourish. After all those years. He looked towards the window. And I'm not the only one. No, he said, I'm not the only one.

That was terrible, Mr Ewing, said Liz.

It was not right.

He went back and sat on the bed

When did you arrive?

This morning.

You're an awful man, he said. You caught me on a bad day. I haven't a thing in the house.

Never mind, said Liz.

And look at the cut of me.

We can leave and come back I said.

Not at all, he said, you're not leaving without me.

He sprang into action, took an old blue raincoat off a hanger in the wardrobe and put it on. As he did so he whistled. Went back to the kitchen and did his hair. Then presented himself at the door in a blue baseball cap.

After you, he said. He stood aside. We trooped down the stairs and he came after us.

the tour

See that mosque over there?

Yes.

That used to be the Bam-ba, he laughed. An Irish dance house. So what do you want to do?

Take a walk, I suppose.

Take a walk, he repeated. Take a walk?

He seemed confounded. Suddenly he strode off, then, just as suddenly, stopped and turned sharply into a supermarket. He headed straight for the vegetables.

Look, he said, what they have here these days. Look at them lads.

Aubergines, said Liz.

You know them?

I do.

And these.

Chinese cabbages, I said.

He looked at me with a glint of furious sadness.

There you go, he said.

I felt like apologizing to him. He went through the supermarket swing doors ahead of us. Although he was smaller, he felt taller than me on the High Street, as he nodded to ladies he knew. A man with a fox on a lead stood waiting at the traffic lights and the father leaned down and patted the animal.

How are you, George? he said.

I'm a bit short today, Eamon, said the owner. Maybe tomorrow.

What are you talking about? said my father.

Oh, I'm dreadfully sorry, he said seeing us.

My father blanched, glared at him, then pressed on as if he hadn't heard. He led us proudly through all that was familiar to him. Halls of residence, Radiators Ltd, Day Centres for Asian Elders, Toupee specialists, Rehoboth Baptist Church, 1857 – *I know that my Redeemer Liveth.*

We strolled round the sky-blue hospitality suites and executive boxes of Coventry City football ground.

We walked through a playground that was guarded by a life-size golden tiger. Blue and red double-deckers shot by. He brought us to Coventry cathedral. The roofless nave that was bombed out in the Blitz was full of cooing pigeons. Stone bulldogs on their rumps sat on the walls. A bell rang. He pointed out the bookies and the restaurants.

Do you want to go in here?

Why not.

We walked through the Daimlers and Humbers and Hillmans at the car museum. Inside a re-enactment of the Blitz was taking place. A small model of Coventry was laid out. The light went off, planes began droning, a siren sounded, there was an explosion and a little puff of smoke rose.

It's very good really, said the guide, isn't it?

Like a sea captain Da lurched into the Town Crier.

It had one long round bar divided by glass partitions into four lots. In ours a jukebox was belling.

He called out to cronies he knew over the noise. They shuffled towards us like men in a float on a Saint Paddy's Day parade. Genially they saluted to the viewing stand, then passed by. Liz slipped off to the ladies.

A fine lady, he said.

She is.

I hope you are treating her well.

I hope so.

Don't end up like me, he said bitterly. People are all right.

Same as that.

He ordered a drink and out of habit slipped some of the change into a slot machine. I stood behind him to watch the fruits spin. There it was again. I lost my place and began to panic. I saw us at Luton airport, the two of us, sitting in silence. The top of my spine hardened into a knot. I stepped back trying to get my breath. As he turned to face me I saw his mouth move but I could not take in the words. He went a dangerous colour. I tipped my forehead, said Just a mo, and as he watched me in bewilderment I stepped onto the street. I found it hard to get my breath. I put a hand against the post of a zebra crossing.

When the voices went, along came the signs.

The fox, the jukebox, the slot machine.

I don't like these signs. I've seen them before. They were everywhere, on the boat across, the train, in slight changes of consciousness. The moment we decided on England it started, the broken cup that spilled pills, the quirks of light on the street, sudden shifts in perspective. The signs on the journey had accumulated as the voices receded. I could no longer overhear.

I was in a world of signs. I don't know how long I stood there but eventually I went to an Indian shop and bought some cigarettes.

the fiver

I stood well back from view in the alcove of a cinema and lit up. Jesus. And then my father rounded the corner and saw me.

What are you doing there? he asked.

Having a draw.

Well I don't know, he said.

I ran out of fags, I said.

Is it me?

What do you mean?

Is it me? Is it seeing me?

No, I said.

I don't know, he repeated. Is it money?

No.

It's seeing me, isn't it?

Never mind.

How can I?

We stood there a while by a poster of an extraterrestrial. I offered him a Players Blue. As he took a light, he darted a shy look at me. We stayed there till I was ready. I followed him back to the bar. Liz had fallen into conversation with an ex-boxer from Belfast. His chin was silvered and wore old scars. He clapped me on the back.

I'm glad to meet you, he said, you've a good auld man.

Don't listen to him, said my father. He talks rameish.

You're one good fellow, said the boxer.

You say that to all the girls.

My father beamed. He grew raucous.

This is my gasun, he said to the barman.

The boxer spilled a bag of watches onto the bar and told me to take my pick for Liz. I chose a small wrist-watch with a leather strap and she slipped it onto her wrist, held it to her ear, tuned it. A crowd from Mayo joined us. The father went up on to his good leg and called a round. Liz sang "Ain't Misbehavin'". Then, despite my protests, he phoned work to say he would not be in. Next thing we were on the street. He was carrying a bottle of port.

We walked him home through crowds spilling onto the street from a disco. Girls in minidresses stood with cigarettes slanted at half-mast by their thighs. Laughter turned to screeching. A fellow took off his shirt in the middle of the street and called on the man he wanted to slaughter. His girlfriend began pulling him away. Liz linked my father's arm. They strode ahead like old friends. We said good night at his door but nothing would do him but that he walk us home, so back again we went through the selfsame streets and the dancers arguing in small groups as police watched them. The father strolled through them as if they were not there, a woman on his arm, his eyes straight ahead, a man who knew how to avoid trouble, unlike me.

At our hotel we stood on the steps.

Do you know what? The last time I stood inside here was after a christening, he said.

The bar might be open, I said.

There's a man from Leitrim behind that bar, he said. I know him. The Leitrim man is as decent as any.

He stepped into the foyer and patted the buttons of his raincoat. The night porter came out from behind his desk and looked down at the paper bag in my father's hand.

Are you residents? he asked.

Myself and the lady are, I said.

And you?

Since November of 1968, said my father. I think I have earned my keep. Can we get a drink?

The barman is gone home, he said.

140

Louis. Is Louis still with you?

Louis who?

Louis Ging.

I'm sorry, I don't know the name.

Oh dearie. Beads collected on his brow. But you're still here. So?

I'm sorry.

Ah, now.

Residents can have a drink in their room.

Ah, surely you could spare us a drop down here? said my father.

The bar is closed, he said.

Leave it, I said.

Oh that would be it, said my father. He seemed on the verge of tears.

Look, I said, we'll see you tomorrow.

Aye.

He hesitated on the threshold and eyed the porter. We said good night. The father left. We ordered two gin and tonics to be delivered to our room then climbed to Number 405. A few minutes later there was a tap on the door. There stood my father, grinning, with a tray of drinks in his hands.

Good evening, sir, he said. Where would you like me to put these?

How did you manage that?

A fiver works wonders, he said proudly.

she's tough

We perched on the two small beds and he sat in the only armchair.

He hoisted his port, we our gin, and touched glasses.

Good luck, Mr Ewing, Liz said.

Eamon, he said and went all coy.

And where are you from?

Westport, says Liz.

Ah, he said knowingly. I had an aunt there was condemned on the altar for marrying a Protestant.

No.

Yes.

You'll get that.

You will.

Oh dearie, dearie me, he said, but you're great gas.

He looked at me.

Ollie.

Yes?

Nothing. I was only saying your name. I was trying it out for sound. You see I hardly ever see him, he explained to Liz. He patted her knee and looked round the room. This place is grand.

It's forty-five pounds a night for the room.

Very good.

It's not so bad, I said.

You're landed.

We are.

Now.

He tried the TV. A late-night chat show came on. He flicked through the stations and counted them, then turned the TV off. He inspected the bathroom and the extractor fan boomed. A nosy yoke that, he said. He tried the sash of the window, looked out on the city, came back and sat down.

You must have a few bob, he said and winked.

The mother told me you might be coming over this summer.

I might. He lowered his head. How is she?

She's fine.

The poor wee thing, he said. She's tough.

She is.

You see, he explained to Liz, patting her knee again, I wanted her to stop here but she wouldn't have it. She was beside herself

142

with grief in this town. He looked at me. No, she wouldn't have it.

We were going to go to Morocco, said Liz gaily.

By Jingo, is that so?

He kept his eye on mine.

Well, I'm glad you landed in this neck of the woods. It's time we had a few days together. He looked away. And after this, what will you do?

Go to London, says Liz.

London, he said. His shoulders gave an involuntarily shiver. But you'll not be going all of a sudden?

We're in no hurry.

Good. He nodded and swished his glass. Things are not so hot down there either.

So I heard, I said.

Maggie Thatcher saw to that. I should have gone home when I had the chance.

You could still go, said Liz.

No. It's too late now.

the orchestra

Tell us this, he said. He set down his glass and put the bottoms of his two fists on his thighs. How is Joe Green?

The divers have him annoyed.

Aha. He laughed. And Johnny? Johnny Gurn?

He's there.

The General?

The General is fine.

Tell them I miss them.

His voice cracked on the word *miss* and his eyes watered. He took off his baseball cap and ran a hand through his hair and felt the top button of his shirt.

143

And all in Gerties?

The orchestra is still playing, Eamon.

Good, he said. They're tough. They're tough. Lord above but I'm going on. I'll have to stop talking. I'll have to quit that. So what are we doing tomorrow?

Me not know, I said.

Now that we saw the museum, we could go to the zoo, said Liz sleepily.

The zoo by God. I couldn't even tell you if there is one.

No matter.

We'll find one. But maybe you don't want an old fellow dragging out of ye.

We'll take her as she comes, I said.

That's fine by me.

Liz crept beneath the sheet of one of the single beds.

Are you leaving us?

I'm moving on, she said.

The lady is tired, he said.

Don't mind me, she said. As you were talking I started to dream.

She curled in the bed and sighed. She put the back of her hand on her forehead like someone about to swoon. A few seconds later she gave a sweet snore. The father put a finger to his lips and poured the two of us a port. He wrung out the lemon from the gins into his glass and lay back.

A fine lady, he whispered.

Yes, I whispered.

We drank in silence.

What time is it? he asked me.

It must be gone two.

Two by God?

About that.

This place is grand, he said.

He closed his eyes. After a while his chin dropped. The freckled

144

hands joined loosely at the groin looked cold. I took his glass from the groove between his fingers and threw a spare blanket over him. He darted awake and scrutinized me with wild eyes but didn't move. I got into the other single bed and turned off the bedside lamp and immediately in the mind's eye saw the bride light up across the street.

17

I was thinking

When I woke in the morning I felt this pressure against my back and turned to find a pair of feet with cracked nails and dark brown heels sticking out of the sheets onto the pillow. The father was lying beside me, top to bottom. I looked down into his face. His eyes were open.

Good morning, he said.

I lay back.

Good morning yourself.

I got a crick in the back of my neck, he explained, so I climbed into the bed behind you.

I never even felt you get in.

You were dead to the world.

We lay staring at the ceiling.

I was thinking, he said.

Go ahead.

I was thinking that we might visit the barber's.

Good enough, I said.

The barber's, then a feed.

Right.

And then, ahem, the hair of the dog, he added cheerfully.

I heard these voices, said Liz from across the room. Then I said to myself, Them's the Ewings. Still talking.

We're going to the barber's, I said.

Then the zoo, added the father.

Nice one, she said.

She stepped out fully dressed and threw open the windows. Then, whistling, went to the bathroom.

"On Top of Old Smokey"

When the door closed he got out of bed. His legs were shocking thin and white like mine and the veins on the back of the calves bulged.

He sat in the armchair in his vest and wrapped his arms round his chest. He wrinkled his toes.

Tell me this – am I intruding?

Not at all. It's you we came to see.

Are you sure – because if you like I can make myself scarce.

No, not at all, I said.

He reached for his trousers and put them on sitting down.

We had a good old laugh, he said.

We did.

And we're not finished yet.

No.

Liz came back and plugged in a small kettle on the dressing table. She washed one of the glasses and set out two cups and dropped tea bags into them.

Do you mind if I have a shower? the father asked cheerfully.

Go ahead.

He gathered his clothes very carefully, the hat onto the head, the shirt over the arm, the tie in the shirt pocket, the socks stuffed neatly into the shoes. The jacket on a hanger. The lock clicked behind him. Liz pulled her hair tight back from her head. She sat down to look at her face. She grew serious.

He's a nice man, your father.

Aye.

She filled a glass of milkless tea for herself and a milky cup for me and then she stood looking out the window. From the bathroom we could hear my father chanting some old hymn in Latin, repeating over and over *O Salutaris* and *Credo in Unum Deo*. Then he went on to "On Top of Old Smokey". Next thing we were off in search of a fiddler from Gurteen.

Birmingham

With a posse of retired, low-slung Sligo and Mayo men ahead of us we marched through Birmingham Station. Over the tannoy came an announcement that the train was leaving for Holyhead, the port for Ireland.

Keep moving, said Lee Jones of Westport, we don't want to get caught up in that.

It would only make you lonely, said someone else.

The father led the way with a little rucksack on his back. THE PALISADES WELCOMES YOU TO BIRMINGHAM, said a sign. And another read:

BRITISH TRANSPORT POLICE

Volunteers wanted

£10 an hour

For Identification Parade at New St
Station. Description: Light-skinned
Afro-Caribbean Male, 26–36 yrs,
5' 9" to 5' 11", short black hair,
average build, full beard, and
moustache closely cropped.
Casual dress.

12 VOLUNTEERS SOUGHT

Not us, unfortunately, said Lee Jones of Westport.

We passed through the Bull Ring.

Let's stop for a look round the market, said Eddie.

If we stop we'll never get anywhere, said my father.

Aw.

He fled through the crowds without a backward look. We were in the middle of life. Ambulances shot by overhead in what sounded like second gear, their alarms ringing. A motorcyclist coming down braked before a box of tomatoes that had fallen from a lorry. His front wheel clipped the pavement and he slithered to a stop in front of us.

He took off his helmet.

Did you see that? he said.

There was a frightened innocent look in his eye.

You were lucky, very lucky, said my father. He tugged at his baseball cap. C'mon.

searching

When we landed to the door of the fiddler's boarding house we found he had left his former lodgings and moved on. The woman there gave us his new address, and so the search began. First we tried the pubs. The Dubliner, which said it was Birmingham's Number One Irish pub, was empty. The Irish Centre in the High Street was closed. Streets went everywhere. The traffic sounded like the sea. The concrete walls were blistering. We walked through a huge shopping mall and came out on another road of huge blood-red buildings. The stink of fish followed us.

Where are we for now, Eamon? asked Matt Foy of Sooey.

This way, said my father.

We went to a certain seat in a small artificial park of sorry green, but the fiddler wasn't there. It was the sort of thing my father would do, go searching for a man he couldn't find. And as we went across the grass I suddenly remembered I'd been on a class of a search like this before in another life. The memory made me uneasy, but I said nothing. He was enjoying himself my father was. An urchin gave an impish wave to Liz then turned and looked a long time at his watch as he spun the winder. Then he headed off stamping on leaves.

A head-the-ball, said Sooey Tay.

Then we got a bus to Sparkhill, then Sparkbrook, and finally Springfield, and alighted by a church that said START A NEW DAY WITH JESUS. Good luck, said my father. The streets were thronged with Sikhs and Muslims. Our crowd went quiet and walked with averted eyes. In a shop Liz bought an eternity ring while the men busied themselves outside discussing what way to go. We passed Pakistani shops that sold *methi, abbi* and *pecak*. In Springfield we met a white man, a buck from Belfast.

Do you know Parr Street, boss?

Never heard of it. Are ye on the raz lads?

We are.

Well, have a nice day.

Liz headed into an Indian fabric and textile shop to pick through the material. We waited on the footpath outside.

Let's go back, Eamon, said Aidan Carr. We'll never bucking find him.

No way, said my father.

A smell of dead flesh crossed the street. Small Indians in caps eyed us quizzically. We asked directions of a man who shook his head sadly as if we were a sorry bunch. We asked him again. He shook his head and watched us with amazement as we strolled off.

Are you sure you have the right place? I asked.

I am, said my father sternly.

We took off again. We went into the Community Hall at Hall Green but there was no white folk there. We asked direction of another man who came with us for the walk. He was named

Sagreed. He entered into conversation with shopowners along the way who looked from him to us and back again. He laughed. They pointed this way, that way. We waited, wondering. This way please, said Sagreed. At 6 Ivor Street he stopped and signalled that this was the place.

But this is Ivor Street.

Never mind, said Sagreed.

But we're looking for Parr Street.

Please? and he rose his hand.

What does he want me to do? said Sooey Tay.

He wants you to knock.

So Sooey knocked on the door. But there was no one home.

Again please, said Sagreed.

This is fucking out-of-order, said Sooey.

Ah, just humour the buck, said my father.

We knocked again and the woman next door drew her blind. Then Sagreed knocked on her door. We'll be fucking murdered, said Sooey. She held it ajar about an inch and Sagreed and her entered into a wild discourse. When she closed the door in his face he cursed and shouted some form of obscenity.

Easy son, said Sooey.

That woman is barmy, he shouted.

Parr Street, said my father.

Yes, nodded Sagreed and he pursed his lips.

Sagreed, said Liz

Yes?

Parr Street is where we are looking for, said Liz.

Ah, Parr, said Sagreed and he nodded vehemently. Parr Street, Parr Street, Parr Street.

He clicked his fingers.

Off again, said Sooey.

Here we go, said Lee Jones.

Sagreed led us past the Kasmir Book Centre, back again by Hall

Green Shilon's Unisex Mendhi Bridal Fashions Mustaq's Sweets Khoobsurat Gaudi Siddique textiles. He stopped and stood aside while Liz searched around in Sai Datha Sarees. He spoke to the proprietor of Hala, Balti Chef of the Year.

But no sign of the man from Gurteen.

Only this long bazaar of vegetables and fruit and silks and children's dresses. We looked into Gibb's Mew. No. This way, said Sagreed. This could end in fucking trouble, said Lee Jones. We went up a deserted street. Liz took my arm. The men halted.

Let's go back, said Aidan Carr.

No please, you follow, said Sagreed.

This is far enough for me, said Sooey.

You follow, please, said Sagreed, and he turned and we went after him reluctantly.

Then suddenly there was Parr Street. Sagreed threw a victorious arm in the air. You could hear the sound of timber being axed in some back garden and the father knocked on the door of the Gurteen man's lodgings. An old man in wide blue jeans answered it.

But the fiddler wasn't there.

He knocks around the Bull Ring of a Friday, he said.

Now we'll have to go back where we started from, said Aidan Carr, sadly.

Are ye off on a session? the man asked.

We are.

Hold on, he said, till I get my coat.

That, explained my father, is Doctor John of Grange. We could have done without him.

Bye bye now, said Sagreed.

We headed back to the Bull Ring with Doctor John in tow and fought through the traffic. Hughie stopped a straight-backed woman on a low bike with a dress to her ankles. Her white hair was done up in a bun. No, she hadn't seen him.

This is the Year of the Ram, she said and pedalled off into the traffic.

Under Doctor John's guidance we visited a stonemason's yard where the Gurteen fiddler used labour and sat watching the mason in a small shed chisel onto the stone the name FANNY ELEANOR WYNNE – JUST AS I AM, WITHOUT ONE PLEA. On a monument beyond that the inscription read – I AM THE TRUE VINE. He had no news of Joe.

Did you try to get him on the blower?

We did.

We supped tea in a caff called Fair Do's where the cups shook from lorries passing. The lady from Laois had not seen him either.

We questioned a road gang.

The ganger stepped over a pipe that ran clean through the cutting. Then he stood on the ear of his shovel and contemplated the cracked tarmacadam below him. He stirred a stone with his foot and shook his head. There was no sign of Joe Coyle.

Are you coming with us?

I am not, he said sternly. I am not going drinking.

Right then.

He turned back down into the cutting.

I am not, he repeated, going with you.

Suit yourself.

I will, thank you.

We stood there watching him work.

Can we not forget about who we are looking for? I said to the father.

No, he said. Never.

the Bull Ring

We entered the Bull Ring and the men from Maugherow inspected the red spuds in the mall. We passed wreaths. Sprays. Bouquets. Screwdrivers. Clay pots. Mouth organs. Wool.

We thought we saw him at the Vests.

But no.

Nor at the Socks.

We passed a litter of pups. Budgies. Engine parts.

He could be anywhere, said Sooey Tay.

He could be, said Aidan Carr.

We saw porcelain dolls from around the world. We saw Leather For Less. We saw The Underworld where briefs and bras and knickers and lace basques were displayed on the sheer bodies of serving-maids. A girl came down the ramp and took off her shoe at the Mini Heel Bar. She stood at the counter patiently dangling her bare foot. We went on.

Past Just Sweets. Just Sew. Just So.

Animal Magic. Stressed ladies? No need for stress! No need! Strawboaters Zorro hats the simple wellington line-dancers' hats. A shelf of scissors. Jellied eels. Live crabs. Doctor John of Grange inspected Flash Harry's hot-water bottles. On to the Nut Centre. Would you like a set of two ducks? The Great British Banger Sausage. Stan and Ollie bookends at Short and Curley's. Carry on to the duck eggs.

Is that him beyant?

Is it?

White Elephants. Thermal socks. Jogging suits. No fiddler, but suspender belts and Genuine Swiss watches. Blue Stiltons, matching curtains, boxer shorts, and lastly, Sam's perfumes.

Out by Edgbaston Street and into the flea market.

The Bull Ring proclaims God's love in the heart of the city!

Where you can consult the Romany Gypsy about Love and

Money and Business.

Swedes put hair on your chest, shouts George.

Twenty-five pee the bananas, says Eddie. All fresh and nice, he says, twenty-five the bananas, and mushrooms, oh lovely mushrooms fifty pee a pint. Moroccan orange juices large grapefruits cooking apples seedless oranges at Dora's. Ha la! Halo! Anyone else there today? Hi there! Twenty-five the bananas!

Fuchsia curtains. Ladies Casuals. Watch straps. Joss sticks. Mushrooms!

Look at the lovely mush! Look! Feel free! I thank you, madam! Fifty pee, thank you!

You want a tasty bit of cod?

Nice? Did I say nice?

Look! Hallo! Hera! One pound a mush! Ala hera!

Famous tangerines! Lovely the apples!

Lovely the pears!

Pigeons.

Gentlemen what can I get you? Come along gentlemen, what can I interest you in?

Nothing, no thank you, we're just looking.

And why would the gentlemen not look? Feel free! We headed off, the cheers of the stallholders, like Indians on the warpath, fading into the distance, down below us the green roofed, galvanized stalls.

Bananas!

And we ended up in an old pub, throwing rings.

Matt Foy phoned round for Joe.

Then the talk turned to aliens.

aliens

Do you believe that you can be possessed by aliens? my father asked Liz.

I do, certainly.

I knew it. You see I'm not the man I once was, he said, and he broke into a fit of laughter.

It's no laugh, said Doctor John. The alien is a different matter entirely.

He is, I said.

He is not, said my father.

And what about New Mexico? Hah? Who were those lads when they were about?

I don't know, I said.

If I was looking at you, said John, and you were looking at me, just as I am now, just looking and maybe we were talking, maybe, and you were in my eye and I was in yours, so that you could see yourself in my eye and I could see myself in your eye, and if one of us looked away which of us would be there? Hah? Who would be left?

He stared at me. Wild flecks snowed through his brown pupils.

Hah?

Stop that, Doc, said my father. Stop the madness.

I'm only saying, said the Doc.

Enough of that crack.

You have to keep your ring clean, an old tunneller from Drumard told me.

Is that the trick?

It is. Yes. Take a wet cloth to your hole every day.

Blimey.

Give neither counsel nor salt, said his mate from Faughts Bridge, unless you're asked for it.

Ah, balls, said Drumard.

No sign of Joe, said Matt Foy.

He'll be with Brid White, I'll warrant you.

Whoa! Whoa now! said Hughie.

What's wrong? asked my father.

I want to make a statement.

Yis?

I want to explain my discomfiture.

What do you mean?

I'm hungry, said Hughie.

Out of the haversack on his back my father extracted pork pies and a jar of English mustard. The Doc sat down by Liz.

Are you better now? he asked her.

Better of what?

I don't know.

The first round landed. Sligo's "Noble Six" was sung. Liz sang "Eleanor Rigby". The father spat on his hands, took off his cap and dragged a wave off his temple. His new hair-do shone. He took my hand.

See, he said, wringing it.

It was the first time he really looked me in the eye.

some old grudge

But they soon tired of that place because of some old grudge against the landlord. It was back again through the Bull Ring. A belch, a cough, a sign of misery from Doctor John.

I thought he was a nice fellow, he said.

Who?

Your son.

So he is.

And then you wouldn't let me talk to him.

That's because you were at that loony talk.

What loony talk?

Never mind.

Do you hear what he's saying?

Whist now.

I'm only saying, said the Doc.

The search for Joe Coyle the fiddler brought us on to another shop where we had a few rounds of Twenty-Five. They cracked their fists off the table to announce a winning card. And this was answered in another corner of the bar where some West Indians were hopping dominoes. A Dutch man with wild eyes sat down with us to speak of evil.

It's numbers, he said.

I know what you mean, said the Doc.

C'mon to hell, said Drumard.

We left.

A druggie, said Matt Foy, that's all we need.

At teatime we sat into two vans coming off a site and journeyed quietly on swaying boards to an Irish hotel on the outskirts of the city. It had road signs for Athy and Buninadden directing you to the toilet.

A detective joined the gang. He knew them all by their first names. Sooey Tay leaned over to me.

What speed are we travelling at? asked the pilot over the intercom the last time I came across, he says. He didn't know we heard. And that was the last time I flew by air.

We taxied to and fro searching for music. There was talk of going to see some mud-wrestling. In one pub, instead of a musician a comedian came on. Our crowd had no time for that. We left and demanded our money back at the door. We didn't get it. And we never found music.

Below one of the flyovers, Sooey Tay got sick with one hand held in the air to keep us back.

It's telling on him, said Hughie.

Can we go to the zoo now? asked Liz.

a pity about your father

We went back with all talk of the old grudge forgotten to the pub with the rings. They talked of deaths.

That's a good one, said the Doc. *What speed are we travelling at?* Then he looked at me. Don't you think so?

I do, I said.

And then he got sick, said the Doc and he looked sorrowfully at Sooey Tay. Come here, he said.

He put his mouth to my ear.

It's a pity about your father, he said.

Losing the job?

Losing everything, he hissed and rose his eyes to heaven.

What are you whispering about there? asked my father.

Nothing, said Doctor John.

Much later that night the fiddler showed up, but everyone had forgotten about him by then, same as they had forgotten about the grudge. Seemingly he stood about at the edge of the party then left.

Matt Foy went to the bar and said to the landlord: Did you see Joe Coyle the fiddler?

He just left.

What do you mean?

He came in, said the landlord, and he went out. Right?

Fucking wrong. If he came in why didn't you tell him we were here?

He saw you.

I didn't see him.

That's not my fault, fellow.

Do you hear this? said Matt Foy. Do you hear this fucker?

Sit down, said Drumard.

That's right, said the Doc.

Every time we come in here, complained Matt, it's the same fucking story.

He sat and glared at the landlord.

Why did we come here in the first place?

The old grudge, whatever it was, had resurfaced. We called it a day. The Birmingham men walked us to the train station through the deserted Bull Ring. The Coventry men sat squeezed tight against each other on a seat on the platform.

It's a pity Joe Coyle didn't show, said the father.

But he did, said Liz.

He looked at her strangely.

He did? He shook his head. And you're going tomorrow?

That's right.

Do you have to? he asked.

I'd like to see London, said Liz.

What train are you getting?

The 12.10, I said.

Ah, he muttered. It was a wasted day.

No, she said, I enjoyed myself.

You did? And then he turned and looked at me.

And so did I, I said.

poor Joe

Poor Joe, the father said last thing behind me in the bed.

Cut that out! my father shouted in his sleep.

What are you saying? I said.

Fuck off now! he shouted.

I put on the light.

What's wrong with you? I asked him.

Fuck off! he said.

Stop it, I said as I watched him sneer. Don't go like that!

Like what?

I'm going back to sleep, I said.

Go where you like!

He hurled himself out of bed and sat hostile in the single armchair, and watched me with deep gloom. These angry tics I knew from another time began. And there was this stench. So I said to myself that I wouldn't talk to him.

He'll be out soon, he said.

I didn't answer.

If he's not out already.

He waited a while.

Something has to be done there, he said quietly.

I turned the other way.

Do you hear me? he said. His time is up. He will soon be stepping through the gates.

Who? asked Liz suddenly.

I thought you were asleep, I said.

Well I wasn't. What fellow?

No one.

Has he not told you? said my father. The fucker that killed his brother – that's who.

You shouldn't bring it up.

What?

You should not have said that.

What are you on about?

I said you should not have said that!

He'll be soon walking out of that jail and we should be there to greet him.

Leave it, Daddy.

Leave it?

Yes, leave it.

Is that why you wear a leather jacket? he jumped to his feet. Is that why you fuck yourself up? Hah! He started to dress. I'll meet him by myself.

Do.

I will.

Leave it now, I said.

This is crazy, said Liz.

It is.

He stood there in his trousers and vest and worked his hands. I'll go through you, he said to me.

So do, I said.

Ollie! shouted Liz.

He stopped a moment there, looking forlorn.

I mean I'll go by you, he said sadly.

Do.

Stop, said Liz, stop it!

I thought, said my father, that my own son –

Stop, I said.

Yes, stop it now, Mr Ewing, said Liz.

His time is up, repeated my father, buttoning his shirt.

I don't want to hear another word, said Liz, and she cut the light.

I could hear him sit back down in the armchair in the darkness. There was the flash of a match. I didn't want to shake or say anything. The anger and the fear made me breathless. Ollie was afraid. Then I felt him move across the room. He sat on the edge

162

of my bed and took off his shoes quietly. A few minutes later he got in.

I'm out of order, he said.

It did my head in once, I said, and I don't want it to happen again.

I know.

I thought he wouldn't like that phrase – *it did my head in.* It would, I thought, have struck him as wrong. The way he said *I know* I wasn't sure. A few minutes before I thought he would hit me. I knew he wanted to. He stirred at my feet.

It did my head in too, he said.

the return of Doctor John

When I woke next morning he was gone. Liz, with her head propped up against a pillow, was lying against the wall at the side of her bed. She had a sheet to her chin.

What do we do now?

Pack.

And go to London?

Yes.

I don't mind if you want to stay here.

No.

And what about your father?

I don't know yet.

I went in and washed the teeth. I peered into my eyes and saw Doctor John of Grange looking out at me. *What speed are we travelling at? It's a pity about your father!* The same wild flecks snowed across the irises. It was wicked. I pulled away and sat on the jacks. Then the words flowed through again, all disjointed as before, reams of them, leading nowhere. I had heard all this before. It was time to be going.

163

We paid and called a cab.

I was about to say, Hey, stop at Dure Street a moment, boss! but instead I said nothing, neither did Liz, and we went on to the station and there on the platform was my father in his baseball cap, white runners and blue raincoat, waiting to say goodbye to us with a bunch of flowers he did not know the name of.

V

The Party

18

walls

I flew over with Ryanair from Dublin to Luton on February 9th for £40.

And was put to knocking down walls, though I was a chippie.

Stuff was poured on my hair. They were making a bollacks of me on the site. I nearly got caught up in the crack the first day I was there. You could say the job was well protected. It was like a wood. But as they say – they have eradicated the side effects of the drugs over the years. But when the ground jigs under your feet, you'd wonder.

But I was young and healthy enough then. I'd brought with me from Sligo my leather pouch and nails, a tape measure and a hammer. There was a stag party behind me on the plane, all sleeping. The things I saw in the air were a river gleaming like a seam of silver in the sunshine somewhere in Wales, then little pools of mercury, and at last a city and this little cloud, all on its own, hanging like a dust-mote. The plane began jibbering, we fell sideways and the wing on my side cocked up like the leg of a dog. We'd struck an air-pocket. Dearie me, someone said. I closed my eyes. We landed among a bunch of butty planes. A red radar spun like a windmill. Spectators sat on wooden benches watching the skies. Figures strolled round the glass cupola on top of the high watchtower. And on one shed there was a weather vane with a plane, not a bird, on top.

It was a bright clear day.

I declared the hammer at customs. And was put to knocking down walls.

yuppies

Yuppies did me no harm. When they talk disparagingly of the yuppies you can tell it's an escape route for the mind. The yuppies were sound enough. They had no resentments, not that you'd notice.

Here I go again with my suitcase in my hands, said an Irish fellow, who was drunk, to a yuppie.

The yuppie up and hit him hard, straightened himself up and went on wherever. The yuppie is a hippie with a job. There were plenty of yuppies at Luton airport when I arrived. When I declared the hammer, a hand came down on my shoulder.

Sorry about this, I heard a voice say.

I turned to explain my case but who was it but La Loo in a security uniform. I couldn't believe it.

Come along, mate, he says.

Fuck me, La Loo.

The bould Ollie, he says. How are things?

Grand.

He hoisted his shoulders and gave a laugh.

This way, sir, he says.

He led me through customs with his walkie-talkie chatting away.

Is this what you're at? I asked.

Oh, only part-time. I'm doing toxicology at Luton University, he said. Don't tell them at home that you saw me working.

I won't.

You see, said La Loo, I want to make it on my own. By the way, Marty's waiting for you outside.

168

Good man, Marty. He made it.

I think he's in some sort of bother.

What sort?

I don't know.

Out through the special gates and on into arrivals, where a crowd were hanging round. My best friend, Marty Kilgallon, was standing among them waiting on me. They all had name cards in the air except him. He knew who he was looking for. The Pakistani taxi driver done up in a turban didn't.

You Mr Jennings? he asked me.

No, said La Loo, he's not.

Where is he then? the taxi driver asked in consternation.

I said I didn't know.

Not so bad, Ollie, Marty said, as if I had asked him how he was which I hadn't. My two friends took me across the crowded floor. Then an old man in a jumpsuit and glasses hanging down over his pot belly grabbed La Loo's arm.

I should not be in Luton, he said. I should be in Gatwick.

Go to Information, says La Loo.

I've been there already, he said.

Then you'll have to go by rail.

It's not good enough, complained the man. It's not good enough. You get nothing but frustration.

He waded off. Everyone in Luton was wearing safety helmets some blue some yellow some white and all very new. The comical hard hats hovered over their skulls. Ryanair air hostesses were marching around. The place was at high-doh. There were beagles in cages, rap music over the intercom and Avis girls with red cravats calling out to each other. We sped off across the crowded floor.

Come on for a coffee, said La Loo.

No, said Marty, we better head.

What's your hurry?

Business.

Good luck then.

Good luck.

La Loo saluted at the door. Myself and Marty headed to the car park. I thought he looked frightened. Things were not so good, he said. He told me this protection crowd were after him.

The best thing, he said, is not to stick to the one job. They have all the sites sewn up. The only thing is to keep moving ahead of them.

We headed towards his lorry. H122 ZFY. He walked me round her proudly. He pulled up an edge of the tarpaulin that covered the tipper and stood back. Inside was a scattering of fridges and computers, still in their packing.

Not so bad, he said. I shouldn't be carrying them around like this. Then he put a finger to his lips and winked and pulled the tarpaulin down.

We headed past Vauxhall Motors and on into London town along the super highway. The motor was a beaut: diesel, twin-tyred, a high American-style bonnet, a bit heavy round the gear box but she booted fine. He put a cassette on and sang along with the tenor as we jaunted from lane to lane.

Do you hear that voice? he said.

I do.

Hear that, he said, he's just about to leave her. And she doesn't like it.

She does not, I said.

She doesn't like it at all, he said.

No sir, I agreed.

Up Sligo!

He took me to this deserted site somewhere near Hammersmith and got down from the cab.

TRESPASSERS WILL BE PROSECUTED, a sign read, KEEP OUT. Then another sign in bright red: WARNING. THESE PREMISES ARE PROTECTED BY EXECUTIVE SECURITY PATROLS. The wooden shuttering on the fence to the front was painted a deep crimson. On the next wall big red balloons were painted on a mauve background. Then life-size people hurrying with umbrellas. To the sides, wire fencing reached to about ten feet. He got a key and threw open the high wide gates, drove in and locked them behind us. On a sign inside it said NO HAT NO BOOTS NO JOB! and further on ALL VISITORS PLEASE REPORT TO THE SITE MANAGER. SITE SAFETY STARTS HERE.

I didn't know what was going on. I thought we were looking for trouble.

Marty, I said, maybe we should go.

Take it handy, he laughed.

We drove through piles of sand and building blocks and great steel girders. FIRE ACTION! FIRE ACTION! said blue posters hammered into the ground. Hundreds of bricks sat in cellophane. Red arrows pointed up, blue arrows pointed down. SAFETY HELMETS MUST BE WORN AT ALL TIMES ON THIS SITE! A crane stood silent in the centre like a great fishing rod. From the top, the Mayo colours flew. FIRE ACTION! All round us the ground was gutted and yellow sewer pipes ran to and fro. PROTECTIVE FOOTWEAR MUST BE WORN IN THIS AREA! Rods for rein-forcing concrete sat on palettes. Others shot out of cement casings like cacti.

It's a Japanese job, he says. Going to be some sort of insurance outfit. They ran out of shekels.

I didn't know where we were going. The muck was a foot deep. Some of the foundations were set in place and pools of water had collected in the concrete. It looked like an abandoned place all right where money had run out in a hurry. Then away at the back of the site Marty pulled up. This is home, he said.

I was sorta disappointed but I said nothing. He had half a garage for the lorry and a bed for himself in a Portakabin that said on the side: WE APOLOGIZE FOR ANY INCONVENIENCE CAUSED WHILST CARRYING OUT THIS ESSENTIAL WORK ON BEHALF OF MC KENNA'S. Tacked to the back was another sign that repeated what was said at the entrance: NO HAT NO BOOTS NO JOB!

They took their safety serious in London.

The mobile was raised on wooden struts and looked like a pillbox against the wall of the office block next door.

Who are you? I asked him.

I'm the crowd on the gate – Executive Security Patrol, he said. I keep an eye on things and they let me stop here till building starts.

I thought we were going to rough it, but when I stepped up the ladder and into the mobile it was a wonder. UP SLIGO, it said on the door. He had electricity and running water, courtesy of the builders. There was a deep crimson carpet he'd taken from a skip. A camp bed and a sofa with angry springs that turned into a single. A gas cooker from the bring-and-buy and a brand new aluminium sink with the price tag still stuck to it. A small gas fridge into which I put the couple o' pound of sausages and rashers I'd brought from home. He had a stack of opera cassettes. He had a shelf of books on space, a pile of travel brochures from Thomas Cook, travel books on South America, editions of Yeats's poetry, and a pile of pictorial atlases of the world. Small porcelain heads of bearded fishermen hung from the timber frames. And there was an old grey photo of Rosses Point above his bed.

He lit the gas and we feasted on shepherd's pie and listened to Pavarotti sing Puccini's *Nessun Dorma*. He put her high.

As we ate he told the story of the opera.

Then we sat out on blocks on the site and had a smoke. The night sky was cramped and blue-grey. Away in the sky the Mayo flag fluttered. To the left was a small side street dominated by a coal-black church. One of the stained-glass windows was lit from behind and a few apostles in flowing robes were gathered in the light.

These protection rackets have me fucked, said Marty warily. You can't believe the shit that's going down. A whiff of paraffin floated through the air. A fox came out into the open and stared at us for just a moment with a backwards look then went on. Through the open door of the cabin, Pavarotti went on to sing *Questa O Quella* by Verdi. Marty told the story of that one too. The music thundered through the site as if it were the setting for the opera. The tape ended. Cats screeched. In the distance the traffic to and from the airport flew by.

Hould your whist, Marty said, and don't be talking.

He hit a switch. Lights from overhead on the crane blazed down on the site.

That item over there, he said, is the toilet in case you're wondering.

I was home and dry.

don't they know it's Sunday?

Next morning I made him a fry while he pulled weights and showered in a health-and-fitness place across the road. This black tom he had as a pet landed a mouse on the doorstep. A thrush on the roof stood waiting on crumbs then bathed in the foundations. When it rained the bulb blinked. There was a single toll from a bell. A few worshippers hurried by. Soon distant singing began.

They were coming out of the church and chatting when he reversed on to the street. We drove to north London, through streets filled with African churchgoers in wide hats and collarless suits. They flocked in little groups like rare birds. Students from France and Italy raced along the footpaths. Fellows washed cars in the forecourts of blocks of flats. A Paddy in a suit was sitting on a step reading the *Sunday Independent*. We pulled in and I jumped down.

Ring the bell, said Marty, and speak into the intercom.

Jenkins here, a crackly voice said.

Hallo.

Who is that?

Ollie Ewing, I said.

You wha?

Ah . . .

You the delivery?

Yes.

About time too.

The gates swung open and Marty backed into the council yard. We began unloading the fridges and computers onto a few pallets in a Portakabin. The security man appeared.

Rainy day, said Marty

It's good, ain't it? said Mr Jenkins to himself.

I lowered an Apple onto the deck. As I straightened up I found his face next to mine.

Do you know what time it is?

I shrugged. He followed me out to the wagon, passing Marty who was on his way in.

Hi matey, he said as I climbed onto the lorry.

Yes, Mr Jenkins?

You hear me speak to you?

It's around ten, I said, I think.

As I pulled the next fridge down off the back he tapped me on the shoulder.

Who is the boss here?

You, Mr Jenkins.

Stop fucking mucking around.

I pointed at Marty who was coming out of the shed.

Is he the boss?

Yes, I said.

Another tough guy, he said.

174

He turned about.

Hi you!

Marty said nothing.

You were supposed to be here at eight!

Is that right?

It bloody well is!

Now, said Marty.

Marty went round him and just kept moving and so did I. I dropped the edge of a fridge onto his outstretched arms, jumped down and took the front and headed inside. Your man continued whinging. Then the packing came undone and the door of the fridge fell open.

Could you take the door, please, Mr Jenkins? I said.

Fucking hell!

I wanted to answer him, but couldn't and Marty wouldn't. We trundled forwards with the security man bent over between us. He held the door closed till we got inside. The grief I get, he said, from Jack-the-lads. He stalked us as we moved to and fro. He looked at his watch and sighed. Sordid, he said. A cigarette he rolled burst open in the rain. When we had the last fridge stacked Marty says to me: Hi Ollie, will you get the *dawk-cue-ments?* drawing out the sound like a fucking gobaloon.

I will, I said.

About time, Mr Jenkins said.

I got the receipt book and handed it over.

What does it say? asked Marty.

What do you mean, what does it say? said the security man in consternation. It says ten fucking fridges and six computers.

There, said Marty pointing.

Mr Jenkins scrutinized the docket again.

I see nothing.

He handed it to me.

Can you see anything?

What am I supposed to see? I said.

Mr Jenkins flapped his hands. Ask your boss, why don't you?

Marty said nothing.

Well? Mr Jenkins said, turning to me.

I don't know, I said.

Well, I do, says Marty and he pointed. It says ten, doesn't it? *Deliver at ten* – right?

Is that what it says? the security man asked me.

I read the docket again

That's what it says, Mr Jenkins, I said.

Well, if it does, that's not what they told me. He took a pen from behind his ear and wearily ticked off the items. I just can't believe it. Incompetents, he said. Don't they know it's Sunday?

Marty took his cheque and climbed into the cab and I went ahead to guide him out.

Good luck, Mr Jenkins, I said.

It's just a laugh, ain't it? he said. No harm, right? He pulled the gate to. You tell your boss it's just a laugh. Right?

Did you hear him? said Marty as we drove off.

I did, I said.

You'll get that.

You will.

It's lucky, he said, that you and me are programmed to be random.

That's right, I said.

He gave me twenty.

That was my first wages in England.

Watch your back!

We went to an Irish pub to meet a ganger who promised me the start Monday week with this English gang. You'll have to pay tax on that job, he said. Okey-dokey? I didn't like the sound of that, but it stood to me in the long run. I told him I was a chippie, but in the event he must have thought I was in demolition. Maybe he didn't hear me right.

There was a morning session of music in progress at the time.

The walls had old boots, bodhrans and photos of Ireland in the Twenties. Everyone was stooking wheat. Or sitting by turf fires. In a poster for the Theatre Royal in Dublin, Paddy Crosbie was holding The Pick of the Schools. He was to be accompanied by Freddie Marshall and The Royalettes. Over the bar scenes from *The Quiet Man* were being re-enacted. Then along the walls were portraits of Cyril Cusack, Noel Purcell, Milo O'Shea, Darby O'Gill and The Little People. I went to the bar to get a drink.

Will you go back? said this man at the bar.

Never, I said.

He turned to the Chinese fellow beside him.

As we revolutionize the technology and I get to know more about our product, it gets exciting.

His companion nodded. I sailed back with two pints of Carling. In the centre of the lounge was a long table at which there were maybe fifteen Connemaras, men and women, speaking Irish. I was intrigued by them, and whenever I got the chance I nodded across but got little response. They must have thought I was a jack-in-the-box. When the boys on the bandstand took a break, this middle-aged woman, dressed in a beret and black raincoat, sat down at the top of the table, and sang *as Gaeilge Ochon is Ochon*. Sorrow and more sorrow. I thought it was beautiful. So I approached her table to thank her for the song. Just as I got near I could hear one man say: *Feach Le do Chul. Feach le do Chul.* Watch your back! Watch your back! I didn't know what he was on about. I said to her: *Bhi sin go halainn.* That was lovely. She didn't move her head to look at me or nod. It was as if she were under orders. You have a great voice, I said. She smiled nervously. I think if the others had not been there she would have spoken.

177

I continued on to the toilet. This gent followed me in.

Everywhere I went in London I met folk in toilets.

An bfhuil Gaeilge agat? he asked me.

Beaganin, I said, knowing he must have been one of the Connies at the table. I have only a bit of the language.

You should be ashamed of yourself to have no Irish, he said.

I am, I answered.

What do you want with us?

Nothing, I said. I just thought that lady had a nice voice.

You don't talk to any of our women. You don't approach any of our women, all right?

But I'm from Ireland like yourself, I said.

I don't give two fucks where you're from, he said. Do you hear me?

I do, I said, ashamed of myself.

I walked by the table back to Marty. The gent came in and sat and threw a glance back at me like a curse.

Satan

All right, said Marty and we went for a ramble in the park. He said he was thinking of becoming a Muslim. He'd been working on fixings in a hotel and the Arab clerk of works had stopped the elevator all of a sudden. He asked Marty whether he believed in Satan.

What did you say?

I didn't know what to say, said Marty. I said I didn't know. Then he said: *I thought all you Irish believe in Satan.* But when I left that job, said Marty, I was convinced. But first I have to make the shekels.

We drove round the city to Brixton and went to the pictures. It was a horror double bill. When we stepped onto the street at five the sun was shining.

Not so bad, says Marty. We went down to the public toilets to have a piss and while we were standing there at the long line of urinals this female voice reached us from above.

David?

We said nothing. She came down a few steps.

David, you down there?

We looked at each other. There was a clack of high heels. Hesitantly she came another few steps. Then we saw her legs. She stopped halfway.

David, you there.

There's no David, I said.

Are you sure? she asked in an American accent.

Well, I said, there's only two of us here I think.

Do you mind if I check?

Just a moment, I said.

We put the lads away.

C'mon, I said.

She came down the steps walking very unsteadily. She had a small fur over her shoulders and wore a tiny pleated skirt above the knees. The nylons were thick and black. She had a necklace of shells and a small polite pink handbag.

Sorry, she said.

She walked along opening the doors of the various toilets. You in there, David? she said. C'mon David, she said, don't do this to me. When she reached the end she did the same all over again. Then she looked at us.

Was there anyone here when you came in?

No, said Marty.

This is terrible, she said. He said he would be here.

We walked back up the steps into the sunlight. She looked all around. She lit a fag and her hands shook.

Is there something wrong?

I was supposed to get married, she said.

179

Oh.

We agreed to meet here at the toilet. We agreed yesterday.

I see, I said.

He said right here on this spot at five. I'm six minutes late.

Well, don't worry, I said, he might turn up.

And he has my stash.

Oh.

Do you mind looking down in the washrooms again?

I walked the toilets again.

No, I said, there's no one.

We have to go, said Marty.

Do you have to?

We have to get back, he said.

He gave her a fiver. She looked at the money and nodded.

I'll wait a while longer, she said but still and all she followed us to the lorry like she wanted to come along with us.

Trigger

We landed back to the site. Marty cooked a meal of bacon and cabbage and we finished off a few cans of cider. We sat on the blocks and listened to the music.

Didn't you have a dog who ate apples? I said.

Trigger.

That was him, I said. That was him.

A wino came roaring and began shaking the fence.

Stop the music! he shouted. Stop the fucking music!

He began a long harangue. We slept content. Next morning I took my bag of tools and headed off on the underground and ended up off Liverpool Street in a nice hard hat knocking down fucking walls.

19

the drive

This Friday night Marty picked me up in a pub in Kilburn. Not so bad, he said. He couldn't talk, he said, until we got outside.

He got into the lorry and had a smoke.

Fuck it, he said. You want to go for a spin?

Work away, I said.

I think we'll go and see an auld friend of yours.

Who?

Wait and see, he says.

So we took off for a drive. He said he was thinking of hiring himself out to a bloke called Silver John. He was going to make a few bob and bring the wagon home. Things were too tight in England. Everyone was going home. Fly-tipping was not his idea of a job. There were these cunts after him.

The Irish, said Marty, are worse than the fucking English.

We stopped on the motorway and had another smoke. He asked me if I would join him if he went back to Sligo. He'd need a chippie. Marty was the only man I knew who relished me as a chippie. Still and all I'd look an idiot if I went home so soon. But I said I would. We drove all the way to Luton airport and knocked on the back door. Out came La Loo in his security uniform. He pinned two name badges to our collars and we walked the airport with him. At various watches he turned the key. We walked down long corridors and into the empty departure lounge. Then on to arrivals. We stepped into the ghostly bar. An air-traffic controller made us tea. Lights blinked for miles around. Then we went off on another watch. All was well that night in Luton. At four he knocked off and we drove him back to his lodgings.

Keep in touch, says Marty.

I will, says La Loo.

We turned to London. I fell asleep and woke to find morning was breaking as we came thundering down Western Avenue.

He dropped me at Liverpool Street.

See you later, says Marty.

Sound, I said.

do you think it's all in my head?

That Saturday night when I arrived back off the job Marty was afflicted. He sat frowning at the little table, then was out the door or to the window.

What's wrong? I asked him.

Do you have the feeling that this place is being – watched?

I couldn't tell you, I said.

He tipped the curtain open slightly and stared outside. He sat again.

I feel there's some fucker out there.

Like who?

I don't know. Some fucker.

Watching us?

That's right.

Jazus.

This is a serious joint, you know.

You want to take a look?

I don't know. He laughed. I don't know whether I really want to. Maybe it's best to leave the fucker out there. Hah?

Whatever you want.

All right then.

Sound.

He grabbed me by the shoulder.

Do you believe me?

O' course I do.

I don't know.

Let's take a look, I said.

With lights blazing we walked the site together but found no one.

Now I suppose you think that I was imagining things, he said.

If you think there was someone out there, Marty, then that's good enough for me.

Do you know something, Ollie? he said, I'm glad you're here.

I'm glad to be here, too, I said.

But there's someone out there, he said, somewhere.

We checked the padlock on the gate and jammed a log against the inside of the door in the mobile. We waited there in the dark, frightening each other with our thoughts. He took his binoculars, lifted the plastic curtain and scanned the site. He handed them to me and I did the same.

Anyone?

No.

Do you think it's all in my head?

No, Marty.

Believe me, he said, there's cunts after me.

We lay there listening. Near three, a taxi, its radio blaring, stopped on the street outside the church. We watched her through the curtains. These dudes got out, the doors slammed. Then they stood looking towards us. Marty's hand came down hard on my shoulder.

Whist, he says.

The three blokes stood in a line and pissed through the fence into the site. They went off. Marty got into my bed. We talked of home. We played a few games of cards and listened to this late night station where they were playing record after record by Roy Orbison. Finally, just to help us out, they played The Monster Mash. Then on came Harry Belafonte, whose voice, in the long ago, Mohammad Ali said sounded like straw.

cartoon sounds

I woke to find the mobile basking in wet heat. The windows had steamed up. Marty was gone.

Then I heard these fucking cartoon sounds. Like as if someone was listening to a TV in another room. Little jibbity noises and the click of tiny heels. Beep, beeps, boom! Buff! Ba-da! Tockety-tockety tock! I shook the head. I was afraid to open the fucking door for what I might find outside. Maybe the fairies had followed me over from Sligo. Marty had me spaced out. This is it, you see. This is it. I tried to start with what I'd forgotten. What was it? What is it? It's that thing again nagging at me.

I have to watch that.

I heard the welcome sound of Marty leaning on the horn at the gate.

Things were getting out of order.

I was out of line completely.

Yes.

not far from the trains

We went to the park. It was grand. These South Americans playing netball and the sound of birds and a crowd of lads playing G.A.A. We watched the match and had an orange. I remember I was very happy. Then we took off for a walk across London and found our way to another small park not far from the trains.

There was no more talk of the place being watched.

We went to the pictures and I slept that night the sleep of the dead.

Chef sauce

We had a lovely system going. We'd meet in the York around seven, and have a pint or two, then head back to his site. Meticulously Marty did his *dawk-cue-ments* and his sums and I wrote up my diary. He'd light incense, we'd roll a joint and sit on the blocks with a few cans or lie in bed talking in the dark with the music going. Often I fell asleep into dreams where this singing voice was leading me through another language.

Up in the morning to sausages and Chef sauce I'd brought from home. On Tuesdays and Thursdays we went to the pictures. Other nights we might stroll along the King's Road. Or saunter through cardboard city and back again by underground from Waterloo. And we did a lot of walking. We inspected sites where theatres and aquariums were to be built. We did a couple of jobs for a chain of Indian restaurants working well into the night. Put a roof on a cricket club. Then added a kitchen on to a house in Hampstead.

There I was put to knocking down walls again. The story was the old kitchen had to go and a new extended one had to be built. Marty dropped me off. My orders were to quietly tap the gable wall down from outside without making too much of a scene. Then with a bar work holes into the cement filling. I threw a sheet inside over the shelves and sink. Then I stopped outside tapping plaster off the outer wall, chiselling in between the blocks and trying to wrench them free. I was getting nowhere. Marty came and went. After two hours I had realized only a few blocks. The Jewish woman of the house looked at me every so often, then she invited me in for a cup of tea.

I dare say you have your reasons for knocking the wall in rather than out?

Not really, I said.

So why, says she, don't you just knock it out onto the lawn from here?

Ah.

Wouldn't that be quicker?

Oh, I said, we were about to do that.

You were?

Yes.

When, pray?

After I've cleaned the outside of plaster.

Seems a waste of time to me, she said curtly.

The minute she was gone I knocked the old wall down from within in half-an-hour. When Marty got back from the builder's yard it was finished.

Jazus, he says. Why didn't I think of that?

Well, I said. Neither did I. Your woman it was that copped it. Ah!

You sham ya, I said.

the Reverend

Marty cooked curries and lasagnes and I did stews and fish soups. He was a demon for spice. Saturday afternoons I drove with him delivering stuff. Then we hit the bookies or maybe went round the Natural History or the War museums. Sundays we took her handy. He might tinker with the lorry or just sit there.

You could sit with Marty for hours without him saying anything. Maybe he'd draw, or maybe he'd read. Once we even went to the church to hear the choir. There were few people there. The Reverend Dawson was very interested to find that his nearest worshippers were living across the road in a mobile.

When they build over there, he said, we will have disappeared entirely. I often hear your music.

That's right, said Marty.

He asked could he visit sometime.

You'd be very welcome, I said.

So some Sundays we found ourselves going to the church, to stamp sales and flower shows. The Reverend Dawson led his Irish friends from stall to stall and introduced us to the ladies. We drank clear soup with him in plastic cups and bought a wicker chair, a lamp stand, a couple of Ruth Rendell mysteries and a set of assorted stamps illustrating the fish of the world. The Reverend helped us carry the items across the road.

Do you mind if I take a peep?

Not at all.

He stepped in for tea.

It's very pleasant, he said.

Over the following Sundays we discussed sailing and megalithic tombs. He became our guide to graveyards where victims of the plague were buried.

Were you ever in prison? he asked me.

No, I said.

I'm sorry, he said. I once saw someone very like you in Wandsworth jail.

What was he in for? asked Marty.

I don't know. But if my memory serves me right it was a long sentence.

That wasn't me, I said.

You have a *dopplegänger* then, he said.

Was he Irish?

I couldn't say. He cleared his lap of spilt ash. All I can say is that he looked like you, he said cheerfully.

Lovely, I said. I'm glad to hear it, Father.

fuckers

One night Marty told me he'd been summoned up north to Manchester on business.

Do you think should I go?

Why not.

I could be walking into trouble. I've a bad feeling about this one. These cunts have me plagued.

Who are they, Marty?

Just fuckers.

What fuckers?

I can't say. It's best not to involve yourself.

We made tea and sat out on the blocks.

Fuck it anyway, he said.

Take her handy, I said.

They'll get me, you know. One way or another.

Looka Marty, you go. I'll be all right here by myself.

I don't want to go. I'm in trouble. I wish to fuck you would believe me.

I do.

No, Ollie, you don't. If you believed me you would not let me go.

Well, don't go.

I don't blame you for not believing me. Fuck it. I'll go in the morning. I'll be gone a few days. And Ollie?

Yeh?

Let no fucker in, no matter who they say they are. Right?

Right.

No one.

No one.

He slapped me on the back. We sat there for a couple of hours. I heard him the next morning rummaging around the mobile. I got up to let him out the gate.

See ya, Ollie, he said.

gone north

He gave me the key so I had the site to myself. I cleaned out the mobile and built the blocks into two concrete seats so that we could sit back in comfort outside. I mended one of the gas rings. I was proud to be left in control. I walked the site with his torch, checked the perimeter fence, fed the wildlife and studied the atlas. One evening I heard a crash at the gates. When I went out there was this big middle-aged bloke with a moustache standing there. He had a bad eye in his head.

Hallo, I said.

You security?

Yes. Mr Kilgallon is gone north for a few days, so I'm looking after the place.

Really? he said. Well now, I'd be obliged if you'd let me in.

I can't do that.

But I'm foreman of the site, he said.

Oh.

So come ahead, son.

But, you see, he told me not to let anyone in.

Well, I'll be blowed.

That was my orders.

OK, mate. Look, I understand security but this is taking it a mite far. He laughed. Just open the fucking gates, mate.

No.

Well, fuck me. He put his head in his hands and kneaded his

scalp, then he put his face up against the wire mesh, caught a hold of the steel bars, shook the gate, widened his eyes and said: Open the fucking gate!

No.

Fuck!

What do you want?

I wanna get in.

For what!

Fuck you!

Have you any identity?

I'm going crazy here, you hear me?

I do. Have you anything that tells me who you are?

I don't fucking believe this.

You see, I said, you could be anyone.

Open the gates! he roared.

If you're going to talk to me like that, I said, I'm going.

You what?

I'm going, I said. Come back when Marty is here.

I walked off.

Oi, mate! Come back here!

I rounded the corner behind the foundations.

You're dead! he shouted after me again, you thick Irish fucking cunt!

I peered through the girders. He drew a kick at the gate. Then another.

Fuck him.

me auld mate

I spent a few anxious nights after that wondering would the same bollacks come back. I could have sworn I saw him alight from a bus at Liverpool Street but it was someone else. Then there he

190

was standing outside a fish shop at Hammersmith underground. I nearly cracked up.

But it wasn't him.

I tried to reason with myself. It was a one-off. *Take her handy, Ollie.* Easy does it. Remember the cartoons. And the worst thing was I began to imagine that one evening I'd come home and find the lock was changed because your man really was the foreman. So each day I took all my belongings with me into Liverpool Street. Then when I came home from work I checked the site from all asides, went up all the side streets in case the cunt at the gate who called me names was around. Then came the moment to try the lock. I'd put in the key and when I felt her turn my relief was enormous.

Walking through the shadows, I did my tour of duty jumping at every sound.

I heard things.

I saw things.

I did.

The head was not right.

No.

I was afraid to play the music in case I'd miss someone crossing the site or at the gate. But the silence was more threatening. So what I did most nights was batten down the hatches, play the music loud and read about trips to Brazil or go through the planets. Venus, the rogue. As the moon moves away from us, our day will grow longer. The African and American plates drawing apart from each other in the centre of the South Atlantic Ocean. *What was that?* India careered into Asia fifty million years ago. Rain pounded on the roof.

Come home, Marty, I said.

Me auld mate.

Once I got back from work I couldn't really go far from the site because I had the key and I wanted to be there when Marty came home. Every evening I waited for the blast of his horn, but it never came.

A week passed.

Then a week and a half. I had read all the atlases from cover to cover. I had the planets off pat. I'd read the poetry. No one came.

20

I'll be blowed

I was looking for my best friend in Hammersmith. I had been searching for days for him. I'd get word here, and move on. That's when I began losing the thing that tells me who I am. I told the Reverend Dawson that Marty should have been back days ago. I hadn't a clue how to find him. I thought I'd go see my friends the divers in the London Fire Brigade to see if they could help me. I set out after work and found the station down at the docks and asked for Al.

Well, I'll be blowed, it's Oliver, said Al.

That's me.

What you doing here?

I'm searching for my friend, I said. Marty Kilgallon.

Is he in the drink?

No, I said, I don't know where he is.

Hi, Ollie, you all right?

No.

He took me into their canteen and I told him the story.

Your mate will be back in no time, don't you worry, he said.

I don't know.

Look mate, you're just lonely and you're worried. Just put it out of your head, OK?

OK.

So he took me for a ride up the Thames in their boat and dropped me at a pier near Hammersmith.

You keep in touch now, he said. Give me a ring if you think you're having any trouble.

I will, I said.

And don't drive yourself bonkers.

No.

I felt stupid. All that worrying. I was an idiot. I'll have to stop that, I thought. I was reading the whole thing wrong.

the jeep

And then, yes, a fucking cunt with a diesel Datsun Patrol, with big wide wheels on it, tried to do me in.

They were building a new roundabout at the place and I had taken it as a shortcut. I was in the middle of it on my way home to Marty's site. I had my sleeping bag and bag of tools. I thought the driver was going one way, then he went another. He flew across sign posts and blocked the road just to have a friendly chat.

That's what he said, anyway.

I had to jump back from the car. He was speaking. I put a hand to my chest. He leapt out of the jeep.

That's right, Irish, knife me! he shouted.

the windows begin to steam up

This maybe was not long after Marty left. I was having problems with perspective. Plus I was stinking. I was just in to the launderette with a pair of trousers and probably a jumper to go out dancing in. I was there a while. I had her going nice and handy. I took my clothes out of the washing machine but the woman there was not cooperating with me to get the stuff dried, whatever sort of an outfit it was. I noticed the windows begin to steam up. You could see nothing. I just grabbed the trousers and left. Whatever the crack was there I don't know.

blue guys

A lot of these cunts seemed to be wearing blue on the building site.

The paddy was wary of them.

Marty had warned me. *Ollie, take care!* When I got the bucket of water on my head they were working next door. Two guys with blue jumpers. They were sent from next door to do the job on me.

I don't know what was the reason for throwing water on a man who was trying to do a bit of work.

I must have annoyed them somehow.

my father

I thought of going up to see my father in Coventry, but I didn't. I could have. But I had responsibilities where I was.

speed-drug

The day the laundry windows steamed up, speed was put into my sandwiches in this fancy restaurant I went to. A real posh place. I went in for a toasted cheese and lost the run of things. I was brought into hospital and that was what was found in my urine. It would have been a fucking Thursday. Always a fucking Thursday. Maybe I forgot to leave the woman a tip in the restaurant.

not well

I got very afraid on that site. But then I knew I had to stay there till Marty came home. I began having these sleepless nights. I was not well.

Not well at all.

On Sunday morning I saw the Reverend cross the road from the church, then I heard him rattle the gates. I kept my head low. He rattled them again. I felt bad about not answering him. The place went quiet. I peered through the curtains. He was standing in the doorway of the church, watching the mobile. When I looked out a few moments he was still there but this time he had moved over to the fence and was standing with both hands holding the wire apart. I ducked out of sight. Then I heard him calling my name.

Oliver! he shouted.

Oliver!

But I stopped where I was. Why I did not answer him I could not say. I just lay there on the bed. The whole Sunday I never moved. A few times I thought I recognized the sound of the lorry approaching but it just went on by, or maybe I only heard it in my imagination.

rifles from high buildings

This is difficult. I was just walking down the street minding my own business. That evening I had gone to a flat with these guys from work. Then I'd fallen out with them.

The argument started over protection rackets. I said that Marty had gone missing. That it must have been these protection rackets he told me about. They said he was out of his head. I wasn't having that. It was a Thursday mind, a fucking Thursday. I had to get onto the street. I went walking at eleven o'clock at night. I closed the door and found myself in alien territory. I was off my rocker at this stage. I headed downtown with my bag of tools and my sleeping bag.

I could have gone anywhere – just once I got away from there.

It had become too much for me. You can't turn to the fellow beside you and tell what you'd been really thinking. So I'd become angry with the lads – fuck you, I said – and left. I was finished with them. But which direction did I take? I walked about twenty minutes thinking about getting a nice woman, or a place to lie down, or breaking in somewhere. I don't know what I was doing rightly.

Or maybe just head home. That would have meant walking halfway across London. I just strolled along. And stopped every so often to see would a night bus come. I wasn't bothered, till I spotted this buck on the top of a high building with a gun. So I sprinted across the road, shouting, and shouting.

I got a hop. I ran up the road a bit, and then I leapt a hedge or wall. Anyway I lay there as long as I could and thought my moment had come. But there was no sound. Only my ears popping. The river one way, cars the other. Me, listening, but no shot, not that you'd notice anyway. I looked back over the wall. It was a really tall building and when I looked up out of this small garden – one of those allotments you see when the tube comes overground – I could still see him weaving. Spinning around like, looking to see where I went. So I decided the best thing to do was to get in through the window of the house behind me. But first I knocked on the door. Then I landed in on a carpet at the bottom of the stairs. There was another fellow there with a gun to my head.

I said there'a fucker out there with a rifle!

Calm down, he said.

He was all right. He was a decent fellow.

He rang the guards.

I didn't budge till they came. I was terrified when we stepped onto the street. I was put in a cell for the night for breaking and

197

entering. At three o'clock the next day they decided I should be in hospital. They brought me to a hospital. When I got there they discovered the speed drying out in my urine.

I told them I never take drugs. I'm hypersensitive as it is. I can go like a rocket. Who did it? Someone in the restaurant, someone at work, someone in that fucking flat, I don't know. I reported Marty missing. They told me the man was not pressing charges. I was in the hospital for a week. At night only. They used let me out during the day for a pint and all. And each day I went to the site to check whether Marty had come home. He hadn't. When I got out of hospital, the boss at Liverpool Street had kept my job, fair fucks, so I worked like a dog and went to find him, my mate.

the glass-sprinklers

This is a short confession. I have just seen the one in action and that was round that time. They are like a tank. They can spit glass round in a ring. One night I saw one when I was out walking, it never touched me. It was on a flyover at the motorway. You could hear the glass going whoosh, definitely glass. Some sort of yoke for breaking glass.

It was serious. I walked away from that.

frequency modulators

What Marty said is that when the solidomite is in your head they can send a current through you. They have some way of controlling you. They say you will tell the truth for ever after. But I don't know what to believe anymore.

No.

Since the day they poured the stuff on Ollie's hair – I don't know how – I don't know what to think.

my watch

This protection crowd. I can't figure it out. Confused I am. The protection crowd in blue broke a piece out of my watch so that it wouldn't go anymore. But later I took the glass out and started mending it and got it going. I'm able to look after myself or I would not be alive today.

When they fucked the water on me I was drenched. But nevertheless I saved my watch, I put a tape on it to stop the water getting in. It got broke when they attacked me, but afterwards I was able to mend it. It's going still, look!

National Front

I don't know much about them. I'd say they were the dangerous bastards in the blue jumpers.

bookies

I have that in the nature. This day I lost a lot of money. I left the bookies down-hearted of a Saturday and just set off looking for Marty.

I must have walked Hammersmith over and back, up side streets, under the flyover, past skyscrapers, landscape painters, off-licences, road works. *Come back, you fucker you, Marty!* I saw a falcon above the Thames. I counted the cranes in the sky and walked to each but couldn't find him. All that gambling had my brain unhinged. Still and all I went on searching.

I sat in a Greek caff where I once had coffee with Marty. After midnight, I walked to his site. It was dark and silent. I shook the padlocked gate. Marty! I shouted. I went round the fence and saw in the distance the blocks we used to sit on at night, smoking and watching the sky. But there was no sign of anyone. I shook the gate again. Marty! The echo came back to me.

Then I let myself in. A night bus rumbled by. Sunday morning, I trek off again.

best friend

Missing. My best friend. Missing for two to three weeks. Were there fuckers after him? I didn't know. But I went through the whole of London looking for him. Because there were a lot of things I wanted to tell him. Like *I believe you Marty. I believe you.* But I was leaving those things till I was better. Except we never got better. Not the way we think anyway. So I went looking from one shop to another, one site to another.

And then at last I saw the lorry.

H122 ZFY.

It was up a side street, the front inside wheels jerked up on the footpath and the nose turned slightly in. I looked in the cab. No one. She wasn't locked. I went down the road to the caff, and searched the pubs but he was in none of them. Then I looked in the back to size up the job. There was definitely a man in the lorry but you can't identify a man by his bones.

21

self-destruction

I don't know where or how to explain that. A mate of mine was done in with that. A mate of mine was found dead in the back of his truck with that. There was just the same bones. I had spent weeks looking for him. I asked around the shops and pubs.

Marty Kilgallon, I said.

I asked the woman in the caff he used go to. But there was no sign of him. I walked the streets there at night. Then I saw the truck. He must have pulled in on his way home to get some groceries. There was half-a-pound of ham and four tomatoes in two little bags on the driver's seat. A few cans on the floor. I found him in the tipper part of it, in the body of the truck, covered in 5 or 6 litres of what I took to be paint. It burned my feet as I walked round the truck. My feet were destroyed in London. It would take the toenails off you.

It's serious.

But I saved my watch.

There was a lady in a caff nearby – a good friend of mine. She rang the guards. I didn't want anything more to do with him then. He was gone beyond me. He was my friend, I'd looked for him and found him. Ollie's feet were burning him. The police arrived in style.

Then ambulances. I had to get new socks and shoes.

They had to lift me. Then two women police questioned me. I

was drinking cans – drowning my sorrow – on the scene. The police disclosed nothing. All they knew was what I found out. I told them he was afraid of some protection racket. Then he went north and disappeared. So then I went looking for him and saw the scenes. He was making too much money and the other boys were making nothing. Whether they were English or Irish I don't know.

I think they were English.

fuck all

I told the police all I knew. You can tell fuck all really. I gave them his address at home and they rang the Sligo barracks in Ireland. They brought me to the morgue. I was not able to identify him but I said that they were his shoes. And that might be his ring. It looked like the cut of him, I said. They took me to the site.

I showed them the mobile and the garage.

Who owns this place, Oliver? the cop asked me.

I don't know.

You squatting here?

No, guard, I said.

If you're living here, how come you don't know who owns the place?

Marty, I said, was in charge. A Japanese crowd I think. But the builders are known as McKenna's.

I see, he said.

He just looked around but touched nothing. Then they brought me back to the station to make a statement.

I told them I had been looking for him for days.

Why? they said.

He was a mate of mine, I said. And then he went north and disappeared.

They asked me was he into politics.

I said he was thinking of becoming a Muslim. He was a spiritual man. He was always given to such things.

And you, Oliver?

Me, guard? I have no politics, I said. I take no interest.

None of you do, huh?

Some do. Not me.

Right. And you work where?

Liverpool Street. I have my tax cards here in me pocket.

Right. He looked at them, sent them to be copied, then said: Tell me, Oliver, who was Marty?

He was a neighbour of mine from home. We sang in the choir together. He was always my friend. He looked after me when I came over.

Why did you come to London?

I came, I said, to broaden my horizons.

And what education have you?

Four honours in the Leaving.

What does that mean?

Four A-levels, I said.

You have four A-levels?

Yes.

He has four A-levels, he said to his mate. He shook his head. Do you go home to Ireland often, Oliver?

Sure, I've only just come over.

Quite. Now why did you not report Marty missing?

I did.

To the police?

Yes, I said. I was in this hospital and I told the police he was missing.

The police made me tea and sympathized with my loss. They took my fingerprints, then the key to the site and left me there in the station a long time.

Then the detective came and said, I see from the report that

203

you've been in hospital.

Yes, guard, I said.

You were sick?

I was, I said. Someone put speed in my sandwiches.

And then what happened?

A fellow on a roof took a rifle to me.

Oh, he said.

Mr Kilgallon

In stepped Mr Kilgallon.

Ollie, he said.

We shook hands.

Can I bring you somewhere? asked the detective.

No, said Marty's father. We'll make our own way.

The two of us walked to the site.

I opened the gate.

Is this where he lived? he asked.

Yes, I said.

I often wondered.

He walked around the interior of the mobile looking at the books, the bearded fishermen, he opened the cooker and looked in.

This all his stuff?

Yes.

God of almighty.

We sat on the sofa together. He lifted up an atlas and leafed through the pages, over and back, seemed to study an item, for a second he was elsewhere, then he slapped the book closed and put it away, carefully.

Will you look after his things?

I will.

These are sudden times, he said.

He got up and went outside. I followed him. We walked round the site, stopping to look at the foundations, the flag on the crane waving overhead, the heaps of bricks in polythene.

I can't think, he said.

Do you want to see where the truck is?

I suppose so.

I closed the gate and felt this great pressure on the back of my neck. We walked the side streets. He said nothing. He retched a little and spat. When we reached the place where Marty had been killed the truck was gone. He stood looking a while.

And you say he was thinking of coming home?

Yes.

Now this.

We were to go back together, I said.

Aye. He turned away. I don't know what to think.

We left that street and went into another then he stopped again.

I'm not blaming anyone, he said. Neither him nor you.

I nodded.

There's nothing I can do here, he said. They won't be releasing the body for months. I'll go home tomorrow.

Yes, Mr Kilgallon.

And what about you, Ollie?

I'll be all right.

I don't know, he said. I don't know.

Honestly, I'll be all right.

He offered his hand.

There's things to be done, he said. Take care.

I will.

He headed down into the underground.

I bought some jelly and light soya sauce and chicken and port and stir fry. I went back to the mobile to cook a meal.

But didn't.

I drank a few glasses of port.

These sightseers came. There were a lot of people going to and fro. I began to feel lightheaded and all. I turned on all the overhead lamps and trained them on the site till near midnight. Not long after I had switched them off a handful of stones rained on the roof. The heart went crossways on me. Then I went apeshit. I flew screaming through the site, brandishing my hammer, but there was no one to be seen.

Come out, you fuckers! I shouted.

Yelling, I dragged the hammer along the fence and beat the gate. I hammered till I was sick of it. I went back to the mobile and began to pack away Marty's books and his porcelain heads. I'm getting out of here! Right now! I crawled though the site in the dark and listened. Nothing. I lay on the unopened sofa with a blanket over me and my woollen hat on my head and these hallucinations blinked on and off. Sometimes I'd get a clear run of sanity and know that what I was going through was not grief but some fucking madness. I kept seeing Marty in the back of the lorry. He was a bright-blue corpse with charred clothing sticking to him. One knee drawn up. The skull sideways. The burnt hand splayed.

This was no good.

If I closed my eyes I saw him emerge out of the dark. If I opened them he was there burning bright in my brain. Back and forth the image went. His bones ballooned. His breath rose like froth. I put on the light and saw that the windows had steamed up again. So I opened the door and let the night air glide though the mobile. I heard the first planes. The cartoon sounds of the city. Barrels. The roar of exhausts. Buses. Then came the early-morning cheers of the bin men as they came up the side street heaving garbage into the truck that screeched and strained as it bit into the waste.

I dressed for work.

I couldn't tell you what day it was, but I was glad to have someplace to go.

Ollah

That evening after work I went back to the caff. Just. I was high, with the lips going, after all the interrogation the police had put me through. My mate was dead. I was looking for someone to explain this. I didn't give a fuck at the time. I would now. So I travelled back to Hammersmith and headed to the caff just across the street from where the truck was found.

I asked the Greek.

Who else was out there at the lorry?

And he said, Ollah, Ollah, the police have asked me all this. Now you. What can I say?

I said, You know.

No, no, he said, not me. Your friends, he says, they know. I do not want to get mixed up in this.

I'm not a coward, I said. I might pretend to be but I'm not.

I understand.

Who were they?

Men, men, men! he said.

He went off down the far side of the counter to serve people. I followed him. No, please, Ollah, no! he said. Then he got on the telephone. So the police came. They brought me back to the site. It was then they asked me did I ever consider going back to Ireland. That night I thought about clearing out of there but I couldn't go. The site was my responsibility now that Marty was dead.

That night I saw the squad car cruise by a couple of times but I was too tired to care.

Then, near dawn, someone knocked on the door of the mobile and tried the handle.

Hallo? a voice called.

I jumped up in panic.

Hallo in there! Open up, please.

I looked out of the window and saw this cheeky bloke in a suit.

Excuse me, I said, till I get dressed.

You Mr Ewing?

Yes.

Right. I'll be outside.

He was standing by a white van talking to the driver. He stood like a mongoose, hands held out like flippers at his chest as he watched to see where the danger might come from. Behind the van was a white Jag with three men stting in it. He smiled at me.

Good morning, he said.

Good morning, I said

I'm McKenna.

We shook hands.

I believe, ah, Mr Kilgallon has met with an accident.

He was killed.

A terrible thing, he said.

It is.

I'm dreadfully sorry. Quite honestly, I was devastated. We owe him a great deal for looking after things here. Ah. Very, very trustworthy.

He folded his hands behind his back, nodded and strolled away with me in tow.

I'm afraid, he said, I have rather more bad news for you.

Like what?

He stopped, spun round and faced me.

Well, you see, actually, he said, construction is about to begin here soon.

Oh, I said.

So I'm afraid I'll have to ask you to evacuate the site.

You mean today?

Yes.

Now?

Yes, unfortunately.

At six in the morning?

He nodded at the driver.

Dick here will drop you wherever you want to go. And you might leave the key with him. You will have no need of it now.

He offered his hand. And I took it.

where to?

Where to? asked Dick.

Lovely Luton, I said.

You must be joking.

Sure. I'm only joking.

So where to, mate?

I don't know. Liverpool Street?

Liverpool Street it is.

I should have said the wonders of Sligo for the crack. He hit the ignition. We shot through the gates. I copped the police in a car up an alley. They were there I suppose in case I was reluctant to go. But Ollie went. Sometimes you are a beat ahead of the possibilities, things go wrong, and serendipity does not show its face. No.

And I never saw that site no more.

22

a house off the road, with flowers

It was seven in the morning. Islington. A house off the road, with flowers.

So I knocked.

The ganger came out in his boots and shirt.

He looked at me.

Come in, he said.

I have a van waiting, I said.

Let him wait. Those chaps know how to wait.

He was at his breakfast alone.

I know what happened, he said.

He buttered a piece of toast and poured me tea. I could feel the tiredness coming over me what with the heat.

You look fucked, he said.

This is it, I said. But I feel mighty.

So what can I do for you?

Can I stop with my gear on the site?

You can, he said, for a while. You see there could be repercussions. Have you no friends?

Not at the moment.

He nodded. Someone upstairs turned a radio on. Children ran across the floorboards.

You ready for work? he asked, reaching for his helmet.

I bedded down in what would be some sort of government building, maybe a Treasury office, maybe the World Bank, in Liverpool
Street all the next few weeks and disappeared from the scene.
I made a bed for myself on the tenth storey and bought a lamp
that I left on all night in case I woke and had to take a piss in
the dark. That would be dangerous. There was a only few planks
running across a steep fall once you went beyond a certain point
and I didn't trust myself to wake and know where I was. Up there
I walked all points of the compass in my dreams.

I might have thought I was back in the mobile.

Which wouldn't do.

Things were different in Liverpool Street. Once the door to the
site closed I was in there for the night. There were no keys to the
joint. No way out for Ollie. So I sat with Marty's things in what
would one day be a director's office. It was strange being there
at night listening to the city, but I was safe and I wasn't lonely.

I was looking down on London town.

Wind blasted through plastic. A bucket flew. All this crowd. Taxis
honked. The sound of lorries at night. Steel-cutters in the morning.
Shoppers in the evening on their way to the shopping malls. In a
multi-storey car park across the way I watched cars come and go.
Pigeons land. Far below, police sirens screamed and motorcyclists
walked with their helmets under their arms. As darkness fell, lights
flooded the office blocks. I could see into flights of stairs climbing
behind glass like snakes-and-ladders. A plasterer working a night
shift skimmed the sill of a window with a trowel. A solitary man on
his rounds headed down a long corridor with a huge roll of paper
towels. Another man, who worked late most evenings, swung his
jacket over his shoulders, took one last look at his computer screen,
paused, shook the jacket on, and left.

Yellow street light climbed to my right. Signs zipped on and off. For hours I stood watching the world round me bed down.

The blue hands of the clock in the tower in the distance moved a fraction. An ambulance turned down a side street. A TV came on in the dark corner of a dark room in a block of flats. A shadow passed by in Gotham City. On the roof of the multi-storey car park, the black security man and his girlfriend talked in his wooden cabin. Cleaners moved from floor to floor of the offices. One lady arrived with her young daughter into an office where a man was still at his desk. She started to dust. The girl sat into a chair. He worked on without considering them. Below him, men in their shirts laboured over texts. Screens were wheeled to and fro. A large fan that stood with its back to the window was moving so fast, it was at a standstill.

In other empty rooms, computers, with their eyes closed, watched all that went on.

Another night companion of mine in Liverpool Street, two floors down, flicked through files, stapled pages together, put them away and turned to others, his body becoming smaller as he concentrated. Grey filing cabinets stood like sentries guarding the door. I could see across into a round pot of pens, a box of paperclips, I could even see figures on a large sheet of paper pinned to a wall like a map. The office worker hunched, grew in intensity, then relaxed. He stood back.

Some conundrum had been mastered.

I was glad for him. Soon he left, and the others followed, the men labouring on texts, the cleaning lady and her daughter; the plasterer, with one backward glance on to the street below, was gone. All that worked on through the night was a drink-dispensing machine, jumping from Coke to Fanta and back again; and then some security video monitors that remained focused on long corridors, doors and offices, and across their screens I imagined I could see ghosts flit by every so often.

Then in the pink darkness the rain-stick and the didgeridoo began to play. A top-of-the-head wind, that you find at the foot of office blocks and skyscrapers, flew through the half-finished storeys. The polythene cracked. A dust sheet danced across the floors. The pipes whistled. The scaffolding played aboriginal airs. It was a céilidh. Then back to me came the names of reels and jigs I had long forgotten. Like "The Tent in the Attic", where I was now. Then there was "Don't They Know It's Sunday?". Followed by "Rifles from High Buildings", "Glass-Sprinklers", "Protection Rackets", "Mr McKenna", "Come Back me Auld Mate", "Is the Place Being Watched?"

It all fitted. I was making up my own tunes.

Stroll on.

Amo, amare, amen.

I had my own pigeons, thank you, and my own music, and I was alive, which was not a bad thing, but I was still plagued. *Like what was the story?* As if I didn't know. I could have done with a lady. It was hard to make sense of it – this band playing Greek tunes a few storeys up, above a city going about its night life. I had dreams of sitting in the front row of a cinema and the seat I was in was bucketing in water. I tried to right myself but it got worse. I bobbed to and fro, blocking the view of those behind. My feet could get no purchase.

You might well ask.

I'm not saying I felt like topping myself, but I had too many chemicals – and I don't mean drugs – in me, I think.

Maybe I'm a bit of a joker but this was serious. Plus you have to remember the dead.

He was the only friend I knew at that time. So on the Friday I phoned La loo in Luton airport and he gave me the address of some lads from Sligo who were hanging out in Clapham. Saturday afternoon at quitting time the ganger paid me off. My time was up.

Take care, he said.

I will.

Try me again in a few weeks.

I thanked him and took a taxi to their door and loaded the gear onto the step. There was nobody home, but these two gay bucks in the basement said they were quite happy if I left my stuff with them till the Irish lads came home. It was a relief. I set off round the pubs and bookies and in the third pub met McGlouglin from Streedagh. He was done up like a cowboy in a wide-brimmed hat and white mackintosh.

Hallo there, I said.

He looked at me askance.

I like the hat, I said.

Don't tell me, he said. He shook a finger in my face and made bird noises. Is it, Ollie?

That's me.

Ollie Ewing?

Right.

Well, fuck me.

There you go.

Jazus.

I've had a few experiences, I said, and I need a place to kip down in for a while.

No problem, he said. What are you having?

A port.

Very good.

What are you at these days? I asked him.

Insurance, he said.

He handed me the port.

Welcome, he said, to South Sligo. Did you know that London is just a series of villages?

I did, I said.

above the trains

I was landed in a back room above the trains.

My new home was perched next to a railway line. I spread Marty's things around the room. I hung the fishermen on hooks, set up the transistor, and made a book shelf for the atlases, the books on the planets, the poetry. His ledger I lay on the dressing table. It was a long time since I had a room to myself. For three days I stopped in bed listening to the trains as they thundered past heading north, heading south. It was like listening to demented armies on the move. I fried spam and eggs and lay down. I had nearly forgotten all about it – sleeping in a bed in a house. Got up to go to the toilet – that has to happen – and lay down again. Daydreamed and nightmared.

A rush of air boomed by. Titan, Jupiter's Great Red Spot, Cassini's Division. With each train the the friction in the railtracks grew. At rush hour in the morning a heavy pall hung over the lines. It felt that if you struck a match the whole place would go up. Entire tribes were on the move. Hurtling. Jaunting. Copulation. Population. That was the sounds of the trains.

Copulation. Population.

Copulation. Population.

Japan – 124 million. China – 1.17 billion. Brunei – 267,000. Turkey – 59.5 million. Germany – 80 million. Monaco – 30,000.

No you don't. Yes I will.

No, you don't. Yes I will.

Once twelve at night came the trains passed less frequently, the distance between them grew, the last passengers were heading for foreign parts. I used watch them sometimes, sitting in their lit carriages, looking out at nothing, reading, as they careered through the night. Commuters framed in windows, like sorrowful portraits.

Longing came over me. I cherish longing.

For a while I began to relish the memory of the site – the long nights, the silence, everything at a distance, the frogs in the foundation pools, the robin washing herself, the cat tucking her paws neatly together like a lady. Eventually I got out of that bed and nipped out the glass and put in double-glazing, but still the room and the walls shook every two minutes. I hung a large Persian rug across it at night, which deadened the roar. I stopped there and was happy enough. The lads didn't know what had been happening. When I told them they backed off. I didn't blame them. I lay staring at the ceiling and was full of regret but for what I could not say. It was enough to know I was sorry. But sorrow helped me sleep. Sorrow can be like joy.

On the third morning I tidied up the flat after the night before and brought my bag of tools and took the tube to go day-labouring with another ganger that they told me of.

underground

I turned up at the Crown and stood around waiting to be hired. Eventually I was taken by this subcontractor from Kilburn. That was the day we went underground, and when we were coming back in the lorry one of the men said *I heard about your friend. A bad business.*

He rolled a fag.

Who was he working for? he asked.

You ever hear about Silver John? There's a tosser called Silver

John that he mentioned. Have you heard of him?

I have, he says. He hangs out in the Lag in Wood Green.

Thanks, I said, I won't forget you.

Was your Marty with him?

I think so.

Marty, he said, was not wise.

The ganger paid me off. I asked him for another day's work but he said there was nothing doing. *But,* he says, *Look there's a few contractors taking on casuals and foreigners.* He wrote down the address. Then I set off for the Lag.

Silver John

I took a bus across the city. I was feeling light-headed again, a bad sign. There was a fierce buck at the door in a dress suit with one red rose in his buttonhole.

Evenin', he says.

Evenin', I said. Can I go in?

He laughed.

Go ahead, son, it's a free country.

Inside at a table a group of foreign-looking men, Romanians, Serbs, Croatians, were hanging around in working gear. Chippies, plumbers, doctors, lawyers, drivers, civil servants, all reduced by war to labouring. A lot of London Underground folk at the bar in their peaked caps. The place was done in pine with various hunt jockeys in pastel colours and comic faces hanging off the wall. Lester Piggot, looking a little daft on a pony that was all out of proportion, was there too. Another bouncer in a dress suit came out from behind the bar and relieved the first fellow, who took a tall blue ledger from behind the bar and sat down at a table. A wad of notes crossed the counter. He flicked through them and handed them back to the barman. It must have been a fucking

Friday, pay-day. I bought a pint of Heineken and sat near the door, watching. The thing was going and coming. These men beside me were from Wexford. I went to the toilet but couldn't piss, though I wanted to, and it was while I was standing there that this buck in a grey linen suit came in and stood by the wash basin. He flicked his moustache with his thumb and forefinger, then leaning heavily on the wash basin he looked into his eyes, dashed water on his face, then resting his palms together, he slid his hands up and down, dabbed his hair lightly, wrung his hands, then shook them, and looked at me.

Anything wrong with you? he asked.

Nothing, I said.

So I just left, though I hadn't even started. The man I had asked to mind my bag of tools had bought me a pint and we started talking. He had wild hair stiffened with grit. And after a while I asked after Silver John.

You don't want to know him, he said.

It's business, I said.

He shook his head.

You've just been to the toilet with him, he said.

The buck with all the rings?

That's him.

help

After a while I found myself talking about boats with Arklow men. The place was flying. The East Europeans and the Irish and the English men lined up to be paid and the bouncer entered the figure into the ledger, then Silver John handed over a cheque. The cheques were cashed behind the bar and it was explained to me that three per cent was going to the landlord. *They have it well worked out* I was told. The ledger went back behind the bar and Silver John ordered a round, then sat at a long table with some other men and women. So I approached him.

Are you Silver John?

Who's asking?

Ollie Ewing.

You want something? he said.

My friend was killed a little while back, I said.

So?

And I heard you might be able to help me.

You hear this, Bob?

I hear him, said his mate.

So how can I help you?

I don't know.

He must think, said Bob laughing, that you might be able to bring him back from the grave?

It's not right to speak like that, I said.

Do you hear this? said Bob to the others, but they weren't smiling.

Silver John turned back to me. How was he killed?

He was burnt by acid in the back of his lorry.

He stalled a second.

What has this to do with me?

Someone told me he worked for you.

Someone told someone something they know nothing about, said Silver John.

I was only asking.

Look, he said, I might have heard something about a young fellow being killed, but that's all I know. OK?

All right, I said.

So fucking leave it, said Bob.

If that's what you want.

That's what I want, he said. He stood. Are you from the news-papers or what?

No I'm not.

I don't want to hear from any cunt that's prying around. I don't want any cunt here looking for trouble. OK?

OK.

I went back to the bar and was standing there with the others when a hand came down on my shoulder.

Are you still here? said Silver John's mate.

I'm having a drink, I said.

Are you talking about me? Is he talking about me?

No, said one of the men.

He tapped me furiously on the shoulder.

Are you with a newspaper or wha'?

No, I said, I'm a chippie.

You better not be with some newspaper, he said. You hear me?

I do, I said.

He went on by.

Who was that? I asked

That was Scots Bob, one said.

He doesn't sound Scottish to me.

That's because he's not. Not by a long shot. He worked up there a while and he'd sicken you with Celtic.

Nothing is what it seems.

Now you have it. Watch him!

blows

The Arklow men were all high. I told them about what happened and they cherished me. They were standing with me on the street having the crack when Silver John arrived with Scots Bob. Silver John came up to me,

Come here, you, he said.

I followed him and we stood on a traffic island in the middle of the street.

Look, he said, tapping me, I know nothing about some fellow that was killed.

That's not what you said inside.

A lorry roared past.

What are you talking about? he asked.

That's not what you said a moment ago. You said you heard of a young fellow being killed.

The best thing for you to do is disappear, boss, he shouted. Now I'll only tell you once – I know fuck all about a fellow killed in a lorry.

That's not what you said a moment ago.

Are you fucking deaf?

He walked off the traffic island towards his crowd and I followed him.

Look, he said to one of the Arklow men, you better take that fucker there home.

He's all right, John, said one.

He's not all right. And he won't be all right.

He lost a friend.

Jesus Christ! said Silver John. Look I know nothing of a fellow killed in a lorry.

I approached him.

The others went quiet. I knew I was overdoing it, but I couldn't stop myself.

That's not what you said a moment ago, I said.

Is he a fucking echo chamber or what? said Scots Bob.

If you don't take him away, said Silver John, I won't be responsible for what will happen.

His crowd gathered. At any moment I knew he would turn on me.

Why can't you tell me? I say.

You fuck off! shouted Scots Bob.

No, I say.

You want me to sort him out John?

You're out of your depth, says one of his friends.

Never mind that, I say.

Silver John goes to walk away and I lay a hand on his shoulder. He freezes and turns round slowly. In the street light it looks like he is wearing a wig. His black mane of hair makes his eyebrows huge. He grabs my hand in his and begins to squeeze it. The huge rings gouge in. He looks into my eyes for the first spurt of pain. This woman who is there shouts, Stop, John!

Go away, Meg, he says.

Stop, she says. He's only –

I want to know what happened my friend, I say.

He smiles at me.

Someone take this fucker away, he says, releasing my hand, before I kill him.

He stands there smiling with his hands in his coat pockets but I go closer to him. He looks one way then the other. Scots Bob brings his knee fast up into my stomach. I go down.

I told you, said Silver John. The other fellow is on top of me. And that's how I know what blows feel like.

23

the door please

I woke in a small flat in Wood Green on a settee in a plumber's kitchen. He was shaving in the mirror and his wife was blow-drying her hair. One of his eyes was closed.

I sat up.

Stay there, he said, go back to sleep.

Thank you for looking after me, I said.

It was nothing.

You took a bad hiding, said his wife.

Jesus, I said.

He's dangerous, said the plumber. That man is a dangerous fucker.

The woman was hanging wet clothes on a wooden clothes hanger in front of a gas Superser. She hung shirts, knickers, socks.

Will you have a cup of tea? she asked me.

I will, I said.

Stay there and I'll bring it to you.

I drank the tea and lay down.

Do us a favour, she said, and turn off the fire before you go.

Then I heard a door close, other bodies start moving overhead, a woman's voice, then nothing. When I woke again it was late afternoon. I was terrified that some of the clothes might have burnt. I turned off the fire. On the table was a loaf of bread, teabags and an egg. I sat in the strange flat for an hour, maybe longer, feeling like staying there but knowing I had to go sometime. I didn't want them to come back and find me there. So I stepped outside, but didn't want to close the door. If I closed the door I might never get back in. So I went into the kitchen for maybe another hour then I wrote a note and left. This time I pulled the door to before I changed my mind.

I got directions for the tube and found myself again standing at the entrance to the underground outside the Lag. I looked in.

You still alive? asked the barman.

"Mrs McCloud's Reel"

Next Monday morning I turned up at this yard I'd been told about. They were hiring all manner of people for casual work. A bus had broke down on me so I was late. I arrived at seven-thirty after leaving the house an hour before to find that nearly all the lorries and vans were full of men chatting quietly in different languages.

I walked over to one of the subcontractors sitting in the cab to explain my situation.

What happened you? he asked.

I got held up, I said.

I mean, what happened to your face?

Nothing, I said.

You're some tulip.

Is there a chance of a start?

Sorry, boss, he said.

Please, I said.

No way. He shook his head. He mustn't have liked you, whoever he was.

I went on to another lorry that was pulling out, held up my hand and stepped up on the running board.

Any chance, I asked, of a day's work?

We have our quota.

I'm after coming all the way from Clapham.

And I've come from fucking Slough! shouted a fellow behind.

Tell us this, said the driver. Who did that to you?

A fucker called Silver John.

You what?

The driver looked at the subee and the subee kept his head facing forwards as if I wasn't there and just lifted his finger and pointed ahead. The driver hit the ignition and the subcontractor wound the window up. Just before they accelerated off he stared at me through the glass and moved his lips saying something I couldn't make out. The lorry began moving. I let go of the handle and dropped down. The men in the back of the lorry averted their eyes. They moved off onto the streets like survivors from some catastrophe. It was then that I heard in the back of my head "Mrs McCloud's Reel".

looking for the start

They put out a number on me. When I turned up in the yard for the start next morning and the morning after none of the gangers took me on. It was *You! You!* and *You!* but not me. No eye would light on mine. I was bad news. I'm maybe five foot nine, tall enough to be seen, but still I was left with the winos and the hardmen as the lorries drove off towards the airports and the diggings.

Every morning it was the same story. I was a man looking for work. I just came to the yard every day with my bag of tools. I had to leave the house at half-past six and take the tube to Kilburn, the *Mirrors* and the *Suns* out, the lamp-lit city, then get down, walk a little, take a bus, two stops, walk up Meadow Street and into the yard where crowds of men from Romania and Russia, Serbia and Ireland stood chatting in a cloud of smoke.

The lorries pulled in and the gangers stood out the back and said *You! You!* and *You!* like they were picking a football team.

Then they were gone and we that were left behind went and sat in a small park and ate our sandwiches and waited.

So they won't take you on? this drinking man called Jack Mannion of Manchester asked me.

No.

So what did you do on them?

Nothing.

Are you a druggie or what?

It's not like that, I said.

It never is, he said.

the chessplayers

I went morning after morning but got nowhere. At least my face healed. Then this client from Serbia suggested to Jack Mannion that a few of us might do a bit of washing up and general kitchen work at some hotels in the city.

He knew a chef on the job. So for a few days I found myself off Regent's Park in a dungeon with white plaster walls and oak doors, dropping spuds into a peeler while people walked overhead on the pavement above. The chef introduced us to a seasonal job in Regent's Park proper, in a type of cafeteria, outside which the chessplayers, mostly East European, sat on an open veranda playing chess throughout the day, sometimes into the early evenings. Beyond the wide windows they set clocks, studied their opponents, wandered off to watch games at other tables or else lined up on deck chairs and white iron seats to meet the champion, a small nimble-fingered Estonian in a blue-and-red woollen beret. If it rained they came indoors, but mostly they sat out under the trees, not speaking till a game would suddenly stop with a flurry, then each move was argued backwards, the new man sat in and the quiet began again.

I served them lemonade, sometimes hot, sometimes cold, and all manner of coffees.

It was a bright breezy place with kites rising into the air and in the distance people on horseback. Lads played soccer. Girls drank white wine with pink marshmallows. Bearded Jewish men sipped lemon tea. Wolves howled in the zoo. I was happy enough. I might even have forgotten my situation. They gave me a nice waiter's uniform and Mannion walked round behind me with a sweeping brush. The job ended when the waiters who had been on holiday returned. Mannion and me found ourselves back in the yard at seven the following morning.

On the first truck that backed into the yard stood Silver John and Scots Bob.

Them's the fuckers, I said to Jack.

Silver John got up to pick his gang. The Serbs went up onto their toes. He picked men to the right of me and men to the left till I was on my own. He even picked Jack Mannion. Then he jumped down off the lorry and came over and tapped me on the shoulder.

You! he said.

What?

You.

the chat

I was not sure I was doing the right thing as I climbed onto the lorry with the other men. Silver John got into the cab with the driver and took one long look around at me and smiled. We stopped off at a caff at eight for breakfast. Some men had steaks, some had beans. Silver John had chips and sausages and pulled up a chair opposite me.

I want to have a chat with this man, he said to Mannion. Mannion moved to another table.

So how are things? asked Silver John.

Things are fine.

I heard the gangers wouldn't touch you.

That's true.

So, you see what happens in this town when you start wrongly accusing a man. He forked a sausage. Did you find what happened to your mate?

No.

Well, I had nothing to do with it, he said.

I didn't say you had. I was only asking what you knew.

How would I know anything?

Someone told me.

Someone? he said. he lowered his fork and studied his rings. Who?

A friend of mine.

Well, he should have keep his trap shut. He put more red sauce on the edge of his plate and wiped it with a slice of bread. He laid a hand flat on the table. Now listen.

I'm listening.

You annoyed me once, don't annoy me again. He lit a cigarette. You're putting out a story about me.

I'm not.

I heard, he whispered. The men told me. You don't know what you're dealing with here. He stirred his tea and drummed a tune with his fingers on the table top. Do you want to keep this job?

I don't mind.

Well, let's forget about the other night. Right? I don't want anyone thinking the wrong thing about me. Right?

Right, I said.

And your friend never worked for me. I had no job going in Hammersmith. OK?

OK, I said.

He got up.

Everyone got up and followed him to the till.

Heave!

We pulled in beside a drain along Ealing Broadway. Ahead, a JCB tore a path for us. The winch whined and Scots Bob strolled the pavement shouting *Heave! Heave!* I can still hear him. Behind me a man puked and said, *Dear God. Heave! Dear God. Heave! Shut him up, someone. Heave! Dear God. Heave!* A lane of angry traffic moved beside us. *Heave!* People watched from the tops of buses.

In front of me Mannion was hauling the cable when his trousers gave. He stood up and gingerly fingered the split on his backside. Jesus, he said. *Heave!* He bent down to pull and his balls appeared through the hole. *Heave!* As we came back on our heels his balls disappeared again. In and out, up and down they went all day like a yo-yo. By the time we had finished that evening I knew John Mannion's balls very well.

Silver John handed me a fifty as I stepped down off the lorry.

There's more where that came from, he said. He tapped his nose and winked. Mr Ewing, isn't it?

That's right, I said. Ollie.

Well, Ollie, and he shook my hand, I'll see you in the morning.

Myself and Mannion strolled through Finsbury Park.

You'll have to watch yourself from this out, partner, he said. Keep a cool head and a dry butt. He's a wrong'un.

I know.

24

let the hare sit

The following Friday was pay-day. The lorry stopped outside The Lag. I was dreading this – that I'd be seen in the company of the men that clocked me. This was bad news. Silver John came round from the cab. Bob was on duty. We followed the subee through the swing doors.

Evenin', says Bob to me. No hard feelings, huh?

He offered his hand.

And I took it.

I did.

I took it.

The place was full of labouring men and the same underground workers. Lester Piggot looked worse than ever and now there were bad versions of Irish songs coming over the jukebox.

I hung back and let Mannion go to the bar. Silver John sat down at the table I'd seen him at before. The wad of money came over the bar, was counted, went back again. Silver John took out a cheque book, looked up at the first man and wrote out a figure. The man handed the cheque to Scots Bob. Scots Bob entered the amount in a ledger. Then the landlord paid the cash over the bar. I presented myself because I wanted to get out of there fast.

Hi you, the barman shouted.

Yeh? I said.

I don't want any trouble, he said.

Leave him be, said Silver John. He's a friend of mine.

You're joking.

He's one of us now.

The barman looked at me very uncertainly.

If you say so, John, he said.

He's my mate now, too, said Scots Bob.

Oh?

What are you having, Ollie? Silver John asked as he wrote out my name.

I'm all right. I'm leaving.

What's your hurry? he said grinning. Go on, have something.

A pint. I'll have a pint.

A pint for the lad and one for Mr Mannion. He handed me the cheque.

I was turning away when I saw the plumber who had befriended me in the fight. He must have come in the door just in time to hear all that had been said. He looked at me in consternation.

What sort of a bollacks are you? he said quietly.

He glanced at Silver John.

What the fuck is going on?

I'll explain, I mumbled.

Then Silver John rose from his table.

And give my friend a pint too, he called.

I'll buy my own, thank you, said the plumber.

Makes no odds to me, said the subcontractor and he went back to his cheques. Makes no odds to me, son.

Mannion put a hand on my knee.

Let the hare sit, he said.

hold it there

I waited till I saw the plumber going to the toilet and followed him down the steps into the basement.

He stopped and turned outside the ladies.

Keep well away from me, he said.

Just give me a minute.

What the fuck do you want?

I want to talk to you.

I think, he said very slowly, that you mean trouble.

He stepped into the gents and I went with him.

Look, I said, I know what you're thinking.

He stepped straight into a cubicle and pulled to the door.

I know what I'm doing, I called.

Are you still here? he said.

I took the job because I had to.

Do you know what you can do?

What?

Keep it for a year and a day.

I'm serious.

You want to watch it, big fella.

I will.

Look, he said, can a man not have a shit in privacy?

All right.

Do you hear me?

I do.

Then hold it there, just hold it there.

In came Scots Bob.

Anything wrong here?

No.

Good, he said.

Some other men came in, so I went back to the bar. For the rest of the night the plumber kept his back to me and we didn't speak no more. I had lost a decent man.

a clout

On the Monday I was dropped off near the airport with another bloke. Planes flew low over our heads and the traffic poured alongside us. We were heeling kerb stones all morning together.

You with John long? I asked him.

A while.

So you know him well?

What are you getting at?

Nothing.

The best thing you could do, he said, is mind your business. John is John.

All right.

All right, fuck. He has a lot of things going, has John. I wouldn't like to cross him.

No.

He straightened up.

I was there the night he did ya, you know.

I don't remember.

If I was to hit you a clout you'd remember, he said, and laughed.

is this a Free House?

One evening the gang came back to the yard and we climbed down from the lorry. Silver John, as he did each evening, sat in a Ford Sierra with his two minders. He beckoned me over.

Ollie, he said, you're south London?

That's right.

Well, we're going that way.

OK, I said.

I got into the back beside him. He clapped a hand on my knee.

So where are we for?

233

Clapham North.

Good enough.

I saw Mannion eyeing me as the car turned into the traffic.

This is Ollie, said Silver John. And this is Phil.

How are ya doing?

Fine, said the driver.

And that fellow there is Bert.

All right? said Bert, without turning.

We came by Finsbury, Islington and Victoria. The car smelled of sweat, *eau de Cologne* and a strong whiff of aftershave from Bert whose chin was smooth, almost silky. Every so often Phil shrugged his shoulders and sighed. It was a long journey. I was in the back all right with Silver John. I seemed to be all alone in the world with him and I smelt something else – fear. He asked for Willie Nelson. The tape played as we swung through the traffic like there was no such thing as gravity or home or rings around Saturn. I had jumped ahead in time to where we might land up. A fellow at a set of traffic lights washed our windscreen. I could see his smiling face swirl round in the suds. For a few seconds the city disappeared and we were in this car with the windscreen blinded. Then Phil hit the wipers and the lad stepped back.

Silver John opened his window and tossed him a pound.

Thank you, said the skinhead cheerfully.

His voice sounded otherworldly, like he was living in a different dimension. The lights changed. We went on over the rail tracks, past takeaways, clinics, car showrooms, charity shops, Indian clothes shops, trees, workers, buses, underground stations, under bridges. The streets hummed.

Not so far now, I said.

No, said Silver John.

No one else said anything. As we got nearer home I gave an address round the corner from me.

So what are you having for the dinner? asked Silver John.

Oh fish and chips, maybe.

Very nice.

Just take a left here, I said, into Manor Street.

Manor Street, Phil.

Number 34.

Right, said the driver.

He stopped the car.

Thanks a lot, I said, and reached for my gear.

It was nothing.

See ya.

Are you going at that?

What do you mean?

Are you not asking me in? said Silver John.

Well, you see, I'm only dossing here.

Fair enough.

Good luck so.

I stood on the footpath waiting for them to take off but they didn't. The driver lit a fag and changed the tape. The front-seat passenger, Bert, lifted out a road map. Silver John just sat there looking straight ahead. So I had to climb those steps and knock on the door of a strange house in which I knew no one. I pretended to lean on the bell, looked back and they were still there. Fuck. So I rang again. I stood back and surveyed the house. I knocked on the passenger window and Silver John opened the door.

Having trouble?

They're not back yet, I said. Do you want a pint?

Why not. I'd be delighted with a pint.

When he stepped out of the car, so did Bert. We walked to the nearest bar. Silver John stood aside to let me go first and seemed strangely shy. The usual crowd from Kildare were there talking bowling. The elderly Jamaican was sitting alone by the table inside the door humming to himself. The printer from the *Mirror* newspaper with his baby son in a pushchair called out a greeting.

The couple from Dorset in their finery smiled. The Connemaras speaking Irish nodded knowingly.

Dia dhuit, I said.

I saw them take stock of Silver John's rings. The jeans cut off above the high boots. The jet black hair that looked like a wig. They fell to whispering. Silver John seemed to levitate, he went off, then returned a few seconds later to find himself back in his human frame. Flustered, he threw a twenty onto the bar.

Is this a Free House?

No, said the barman, it's a Young's.

I'll have a pint of Special, then, old son, he said loudly to show he knew where he was. That he knew his way around. He looked at Bert.

A scotch, said Bert. No ice.

Ollie?

A pint of Winter Warmer.

So this is your local?

That'd be her.

He nodded to himself, taking it all in, then he lowered his head, dropped a spit and stirred it with his toes.

You nervous or something? he asked.

No.

I don't know, he said slowly.

You don't know what?

Ah Ollie, he smiled. He took a sip of his pint. Is there a phone in this joint?

In the corner he made a call to someone. It seemed to take a long time. He hung up and came back. I have to go, he said. He took another sip of his pint. I'll be seeing you, Ollie. See you in the morning.

Good luck, John, I said.

See ya, mate, said Bert.

the leg of the chair

That night there was this wild banging on the door. I could hear someone shouting on the street. I didn't know what the fuck was going on. So I took the leg of a kitchen chair down three flights, but when I swung open the front door it was my brother I found standing on the step.

Redmond, I said.

Good man, Ollie!

Keep it down!

What are you doing with the leg of the chair?

Never mind.

You're tough, he said.

Come on, come on.

He plonked his case in the kitchen and told his story. He'd arrived from Sligo and gone to Coventry to stop with the father, but there had been nothing doing so he had come on to me.

He was stoned.

I put him into my bed.

Me big brother, says he.

Keep it down.

I will.

He started laughing and so did I.

I made it, he said. I made it.

I lit a fag and listened to him breathe. He laughed again and again to himself, then fell asleep. When I woke in the middle of the night I thought he was a lady. Next thing I heard him opening the wardrobe and feeling his way inside.

Where's the light? he asked. I can't find the light.

I led him to the toilet.

Where am I? he said.

London town.

Now, he said, laughing. What would Ry Cooder do now?

In the kitchen at six next morning I was tapping open an egg when the brother came in.

I heard about Marty, he said, the whole crowd at home are talking about it.

What are they saying?

That he got killed.

He did.

Murdered?

Yes.

Jesus. That's serious shit. He sat on the edge of the bad chair. They say you were there.

Is that what they're saying?

Yes.

Well, I wasn't.

Well, that's what they're saying.

Who was it said that?

I can't remember.

Well, when you meet them again tell them they're wrong. I came along after. I found him. And then I got arrested.

For killing him.

No, for fuck sake. I went off the head.

I heard that too.

Then they let me go.

You were lucky.

I got up and poured himself and myself a cup of tea.

I was in the hospital a while, I said.

He stirred in two spoons of sugar.

Are you better now, Ollie?

I don't know, I said.

I made a breast of chicken sandwich for myself and he ate a leg.

Could I get a few days with you? he asked.

Take her handy. Have a rest. I'll see.

Can't I go along with you?

No, I said.

Why.

I have a problem.

With who?

The ganger.

What's wrong with him?

I'll tell you again. He's lamping me. It's tricky. The less you know the better.

Couldn't I get the start with someone else?

Maybe.

C'mon, Ollie. Bring me.

And it was travelling on the bus with him down Wandsworth Road that I heard my name called out of the void. It was a warning that I did not heed. A sorry rain was falling in the yard on the Russians and the Serbs when we got there. Mannion shook the brother's hand. We got soaked waiting for the lorries. When mine arrives, Silver John is not on it. You! shouts Scots Bob. I get on. You! he shouts. Mannion gets on.

He with you? asks Scots Bob.

I hesitated.

Yes, I said.

You, he shouted.

Redmond got on.

25

the story

All that week we worked the road at the airport by ourselves.
We brewed up tea and ate ham boiled in scrumpy in the cabin.
Everything was ticking along nicely. They were pet days. Silver
John arrived out in his car a couple of times with his minders and
had a smoke, talked to the brother as if they were old friends, other-
wise we saw nothing but endless cars till evening when we took
the traffic cones in and the lorry came to ferry us back to town.
We toured Leicester Square and Soho at night, ate in China Town,
went to the pictures and the clubs where Redmond found a lady
from home. I slept on a sofa in the kitchen and he slept in the bed.

It was like old times.

Whenever Redmond asked me what the story was I could not tell
him. It came out in dribs and drabs and sounded like something
made up. I could not get the order right as regards events.

Protection rackets, he said, what sort of protection rackets?

I don't know, I said. But Marty got done.

Those nights walking London town came back to me. The hospital. The ganger's house with the flowers in the garden. The Greek
caff. What the story was I couldn't say. The brother grew protective
of me. He began planning a party. I started to think nothing bad
had happened at all. I didn't know how I took a job with the man
I thought might have killed my mate. I still don't know now. And
worse, I had brought my brother onto the job.

Then on the Friday morning Silver John drew up alongside us in his car.

Good men, he said.

How are ya? said Redmond.

A word, he said to me.

Fire away.

By yourself, said Silver John.

There's nothing you can say to my brother, said Redmond, that you can't say to me.

This is private son, OK?

It's all right, Redmond, I said.

Are you sure?

This is between him and me, said Silver John.

I nodded and followed him along the footpath. It was like the night I had followed him out on to the traffic island at the Lag. The traffic roared past. He lay up against the wall and considered me.

34 Manor Street

I was in your part of town the other night, said Silver John.

Oh yeh?

I was up there on a bit of business and I thought I might have a pint. So I thought, *I'll call on my old friend Ollie.*

Ah.

So you know what, I went round to 34, number 34 Manor Street. Isn't that right?

That's right.

That the correct address?

Yes.

I thought so. He nodded. And I knocked and you know what?

Yeh?

They never heard of you.

241

I felt sick.

I've just moved, I said.

Strange.

You see myself and the brother found a new pad.

Is that so? But they've been living there for years and they never heard of you.

I was only dossing on the floor there for a few nights.

Ollie Ewing, I said. *Ollie Ewing.* No, they said, no one of that name ever lived here.

But they wouldn't have noticed me.

Yeh, but you see Ollie, there's only the one family in the house. Do you get me now? It's a family house.

I do.

You picked the wrong door, boss.

I said nothing.

Why, I said to myself, *did Ollie give me a wrong address?* he says, pretending concern. *Why?* I asked myself. He strode away, turned, came back. *Now*, I said, *that's a quandary. That's a quare one.* Isn't it, Ollie? He tipped me on the shoulder. And then do you know what I did? I did the obvious thing. I went to the pub, the Young's house, to see if my old friend was in his local. Like, maybe I've made a mistake or something. And he's not there. *No sign of Ollie anywhere.* So I fell into conversation with this bloke. I bought him a pint. You know how it goes. One thing led to another and then I said *I'm looking for my mate, Ollie – Ollie Ewing*, I said – and he led me outside and said, *There, man, that's where he lives, just over there. A nice man, Ollie,* he said. So I'm looking at number 9 Olive Street. Am I right? Do you follow me?

I do.

What are you saying? Hah? What are you saying?

I'm saying I understand.

We'll have to have a little chat, Ollie, I'm afraid.

242

It's like this, I said, John.

I'm listening.

The lads I'm with are into the bit of dope and I thought you mightn't like it. You know what I mean. They could be up there off their heads and then next thing I'd arrive in with you.

He started laughing.

Is that the story?

That's the story, I said. You see, they're paranoid.

So am I, he said. Who do you think you're fooling?

I'm not trying to fool anyone.

You're trying too hard, Ollie. Far too hard.

I mean it, John.

Do you think I believe this shit?

I don't care whether you do.

Whoa! he shouted. The boy is cross. I like you, Ollie. Ollie Ewing. The wee carpenter. I like it. The wee carpenter and his bag.

Fuck off.

He walked away and came back again.

So, you've nothing against me?

No.

You trust me?

I do, I said.

Ha-ha, he said. Me not know. Me not know.

Me neither.

And you boys like a bit a' smoke?

Yes, I said. And we're having a party tomorrow night, Saturday, if you want to come along.

You're moving too fast for me. A party is it?

For the brother.

He lit a fag.

You're asking me to a party?

243

Yes.

Wonders will never cease.

So?

I like a draw myself, he said. And I like a snort. You like a snort?

I do, I lied.

C'mon, he said. And bring your brother.

He went back to the car.

C'mon, I said to Redmond.

Where are we going? he asked.

In the car, I said.

With that mad bastard?

Yes, I said.

We got in. Redmond sat rigid in the front passenger seat. I moved a pile of site maps and a pair of wellingtons and got in the back. Silver John lifted a silver wrapping from his pocket. Nice, he said, opening it. Redmond caught my eye in the mirror. John inched out three lines of coke with a penknife onto a shaving mirror.

So you like a snort?

I do, said Redmond, surely.

He handed an empty biro tube to the brother.

There you are son, he said, get that down ya.

The brother aimed the biro and snorted one of the lines. He smiled back at me. I looked at the cocaine and thought of the speed some fucker had put in my tea. I saw my face in the mirror. Flip me. I shot a line and handed the coke back.

So we're for a party? smiled Silver John.

That's right, I said. And by the way it's fancy dress.

That's right, said Redmond and he went into a fit of laughter.

You don't mind if I bring a couple of the lads?

No problem.

Is that good stuff?

Fuck me, said the brother.

Silver John snorted the last line. Whoa! he shouted. He whacked the steering column then closed his eyes.

The wee carpenter, he said.

That's me, I said.

I like it, he said.

So do I, I said.

Ollie Ewing, he said, and I heard it, I suppose the way we all do, our names on another's lips, in a newspaper, at the end of an exam, on a TV, on a lover's lips, in secrecy, loudly, quietly, in the mind, all the days of my life the whisper of the name someone gave you, like tadpoles. Whatever that means. We sat in the car watching the world whoosh past. Suddenly a white Jaguar shot by on the inside lane where we had been working a few minutes before. It scattered the traffic cones into the air then swerved out into the centre.

What the fuck?! said Silver John.

Then a cop car that was chasing the Jaguar came screaming by, throwing the cones further across the road.

Let's go for it, said Silver John.

The three of us got out and ran through the traffic, collecting the cones. I walked back up the road and fetched the sign that said STAY IN MIDDLE LANE – MEN AT WORK. It had been thrown in the air and landed on the hard shoulder. Myself and the brother walked the loose kerb stones along the path while Silver John stacked them one on top of the other. We covered the sand with plastic and clamped her down with stones. We washed out the cement mixer and cleaned down the shovels. We put the cement bags in the cabin. We locked the cabin. I got my bag of tools.

I think we can call it a day, boys, said Silver John.

We turned for London.

That Saturday was a long day. The lads worked hard for the party. We had a whip-round and went down to the off-licence and bought, oh, maybe six dozen cans of cider and beer, a few bottles of vodka and bags of nuts. Redmond went up to Notting Hill and came back in a black cloak with silver tassels round his neck. Joe from Carney threw four chickens in the oven. Brendan McGlouglin from Easkey made potato salad.

I made a pile of burgers with plenty of chilli and garlic. Then Joe's woman, Sally, came round with a few bowls of salads. She was in khaki. We bought candles and incense. I stepped into a sari. Two girls from Sligo dressed as angels arrived with lentil curry. A crowd from home came up from Slough, and La Loo even made it from Luton, dressed as Boy George. A pair of farm labourers tipped in from Oxford. Redmond ran a broom around the flat singing *Galileo! Galileo! Galileo!*

We told the gay bucks below us about the party and they arrived with meringues for dessert and extra chairs. The old man above gave us his blessing and said he might drop by. Jim the Jamaican came as a clergyman and brought over his stereo and reggae collection and hung around cutting sandwiches. And Mannion came in a blue suit with a bottle of poitín wrapped in Christmas paper.

We were motoring.

Then we all went down to the pub.

Word had spread.

What's the party for? asked the woman from Dorset.

No good reason, I said.

What will we come as? she asked.

Come as yourselves, I said.

We were fairly flying when Silver John and Scots Bob arrived to the door of the house wearing togas. Meg was hanging off Bob's arm.

So this is your pad? said Scots Bob.

Very nice, said Silver John.

Delighted, said Meg.

Then Flo from Tubber came as a nurse. I only knew her to see at home. She was looking lovely.

Silver John called me into the kitchen.

He had a little phial of acid. He popped a tab into my mouth, took one himself and so did Bob and Meg.

There you go, he said, and handed me the rest.

I know where you live now, said Silver John.

So what?

Nothing.

Well, I gave them round to the gang. The tabs were not too strong, just right. Redmond brought round meringues thinking they were savouries.

Your brother is sweet, Meg said to me.

Soon we were sitting in the candlelight while the gay lads in sombreros and sequin jackets danced. The man from above came down looking neat in a wide black hat and cravat. The reggae went with us. The priest kept her going. I could feel the presence of Silver John somewhere out there in the shadows but I just let it be.

I heard that you're a subee, said La Loo.

You heard right, said Silver John.

I have a nice number in Luton.

Is that so?

But what I'd like to be is a male nurse, explained La Loo. Do you know anyone in nursing?

No.

Neither do I.

La Loo shuffled off to talk to someone else. I began having a little trouble, but I got over that. It was only a small crisis. I went out to the toilet and Scots Bob stepped in behind me.

This mate of yours got burnt.

That's right.

What did he do to deserve that?

I don't know. Forget it.

Have you forgotten about it?

No.

Neither have I. He washed his hands and looked at his face. The Irish, he said, are too fucking Irish, don't you agree? He looked at me. You look pale son. Feeling all right?

I'm fine.

I went back in and sat down. The heart was going.

are they real, Flo?

The trouble started between Bob and Redmond near midnight.

There's something wrong over there, said La Loo.

Leave it, I said, it'll sort itself out.

It was happening at a great distance from me, but I knew it was happening. I heard a voice, but I didn't obey. It was to do with Meg. She'd sat down with Redmond and they were rapping. She'd taken a shine to him. I heard them laughing. Then Bob was saying something to Meg that Redmond didn't like. It was in the words, not what they said, but in their sound. It would stop, then start again with a shiver. You wanted it to stop.

And it did when the food was served. The lights went on. I found a chicken wing. It took me a long time to eat that. Then I moved on to the lentils. I was picking there for hours. Flo put the burgers on. I found a bottle of white wine and drank some with the potato salad that Brendan had made.

Are you happy? asked Flo.

I am, I said.

Joe was looking very carefully at a *Playboy* magazine that Sally, his girlfriend, had found someplace in the flat. He was stunned. He turned the pages very slowly while she watched him. The couple from Dorset politely chewed chicken at a low table by the door. My burgers went round in a bed of lettuce. Joe handed the magazine on to Brendan McGlouglin. He handed it on to La Loo. Bob lit a joint and blew a line of smoke up Meg's nostrils. Then she blew a line up Redmond's. The old man ate with a handkerchief tucked into the wings of his gleaming shirt. Silver John was serving in the kitchen with Flo's apron on. It was decorated with apples and oranges.

He was in his element.

Jim put on Queen and Redmond and Meg danced. The lights went out. *Galileo! Galileo! Galileo!* sang Queen. Redmond called for Queen to be put on again.

Can you not play something fucking else? sneered Bob.

Take her easy, said Silver John.

Mannion lay down full length on the carpet and poured me a thimbleful of poitín. The candles purred. I took a draw of a joint and found I was pinned to the ceiling. After a while I came back down gently and saw Flo's breasts faintly breathing. Then I went back up again. I was a long time on the ceiling. I was in a ball above. I saw Flo away down there. Her eyes came up to the ceiling. I plummeted back in the armchair and leant forwards to touch her.

Are they real? I asked Flo.

What do you think?

I launched myself on to her bosom.

I'm sorry, I said to her.

Then I launched myself again.

Jesus, said Redmond, take it handy there, Ollie.

I came to myself with Jim the priest beside me in an empty cold room.

Hey man, you all right?

What happened? Where's Flo? I said.

Here, came her voice from the shadows.

Where?

Over here.

I can't see you.

I'm here, she said.

Will you come back beside me?

I am beside you.

Oh.

You're not going to do that all over again?

No, I said.

Her face came very close to mine.

It was very funny really, she said.

Does anyone remember *Daithi Locha*? asked La Loo.

I certainly do, I said.

So do I, said Redmond. That was in that programme *Murphy Agus A Chairde*.

Who was he when he was at home? asked the old man.

He was a duck who spoke Irish, said La Loo earnestly.

Pavarotti

It was sometime after this that Reverend Jim put on Pavarotti singing *Questa O Quella*. I don't how it happened. He must have found it among the stash of cassettes I'd taken from Marty's mobile. All of a sudden I was sitting on the blocks on the site watching the fox stop in the clearing.

The music was blaring out of the door.

This darkness swooped.

I'll swing for you

I could see these people moving round on a white screen. It was just before something bad is going to happen. Then these things started to hop off the walls like mushrooms. Something soft popped on my face. This goo hit Flo. I thought it was to do with the acid. Then Reverend Jim switched on the lights after something struck the stereo. The place went quiet. That's when we heard Meg screech. I saw her crying. She was covered in mush. Beside her Scots Bob was standing with a tray of leftovers and he lobbing food.

You cunt, said Redmond, what the fuck are you at?

Bob laughing to himself threw the carcass of a chicken at him.

What the fuck? shouted Redmond.

Then everything happened in slow motion – the Dorset couple leaving, Silver John sitting perfectly still, the lads rushing. Then Redmond threw himself at Scots Bob. They fell onto the kitchen floor.

I'll kill ye! he shouted at Redmond.

You'll kill no one, I said.

The lads helped me haul him off.

Redmond came to his feet and stood there shaking.

What the fuck are you at?

Having a wee bit a' fun.

Do you call that fucking fun? shouted Redmond.

Look, I said, he'll have to go.

Do you think so? said Silver John.

I'm certain.

I'd take every one of you! shouted Scots Bob.

All right, said Silver John. They want you to go. We'll go.

Yeh! said Joe, Get him out of here.

They propelled Scots Bob along the corridor.

C'mon you! Bob shouted at Meg.

She said nothing.

C'mon! he screamed.

I'm staying, she said.

You what?

I'm staying.

He lunged at her and we grabbed him.

Fucking cunts, screamed Scots Bob.

Get out of here, I said.

You call us fucking murderers. We'll fucking murder you all right, and he dived at me.

We'll go, said Silver John catching him.

But we'll be back – you hear me? shouted Scots Bob.

They were trying to throw him out onto the landing.

You hear me, Meg? he shouted. He was kicking and lunging. I caught him by the hair. I'll do for you! he screamed at me. I caught him a tap on the ear with my fist. You hear me? he roared. I'll swing for you! As they carried him he held onto the door jambs. Silver John just stood on the landing in his toga eyeing me. Someone kicked Bob's fingers. He let go. They got him out and slammed the door. He began kicking it.

Meg! he roared.

He tore at it with his fingernails.

MEG!

After a while they left.

We sat in the living room. First one window came in, then the other.

A car drew away.

What was all that? asked the old man.

Maybe I should have gone with them, said Meg.

You'll be all right, said Redmond.

I don't know, she said. I'm scared.

There's nothing to be scared of.

Yes, she said, there is.

the knock

I don't know what time it was when the knock on the door came. We had cleaned up the flat and Mannion had nailed cardboard to the windows and lain down chatting about home. Reverend Jim was humming to himself. His mumble grew ecstatic. He stopped abruptly.

You hear something man?

No, I said.

Wow!

The foreman will keep me on, said La Loo, because I don't mind work. I like tidying up round the airport.

Then we were just sitting there drinking a few cans. Maybe it was five in the morning. Flo had made coffee. The dancing had long ago stopped. Redmond was talking of disappearing with Meg.

They were planning to head off to Coventry, one thing was sure, they had to get out of that place.

Right now, said Meg. Let's get out of here.

In a while.

Now, she said. Now!

Settle, he said.

He was on his way to the toilet when the knock came. It was La Loo heard it first. A polite tap. He thought it might have been the gays come back for their gear. Anyway, Redmond it was opened the door. Inside the living room we were just sitting there. Then I heard a scream and a whoosh. The smell of petrol taking. I ran to the corridor. Redmond and Scots Bob were standing in flames.

VI

The Case History of Ollie

26

the head

The father came from Coventry, the mother from Sligo. They were sitting by his bed when I entered the room and none spoke to me, except Redmond.

Is that you, Ollie?

It is.

It's tough, he said.

I could hear the father whispering behind me. I didn't want to turn, for fear of what I might find. He called me outside. I went with him.

Fuck off now! he shouted.

I came to see Redmond.

Go away from here.

What's wrong with you?

Fuck off! he said.

I'm not going.

He hurled himself at me.

The angry tics began. Look, he said shaking me, he was your responsibility. You hear? He was your brother! You hear me? First Marty Kilgallon, now Redmond. What the fuck are you at?

A nurse came down the corridor.

I said what the fuck are you at?

Leave it, Daddy.

Leave it? he sneered.

Yeh, leave it. My head is done in.

What do you mean your head is done in? What does that mean? Your brother is in there dying and you're thinking of your bloody head.

I'm sorry.

The mother opened the door and whispered: He's asking for you, Ollie.

after the party

When I got back from the hospital the house and garden were ringed with blue and white tape. I stood a while outside wondering could I go in. Were the cops about? I went up the stairs. There was a black tape across our door but when I turned the key she opened. I half-expected these policemen to rush me, but there was no one.

The place was a shambles. It smelt of petrol. In the living room the cardboard had fallen in and the wind was racing round. So I went down to the hardware shop and got two window panes to measure, some putty, and tapped them in.

People gathered across the street.

I pulled the curtains

Take her handy.

The carpet in the corridor was burnt black and soaking. His body had made a shape on the wall. I washed it down and took the carpet up the road to a skip.

I swept the old boards and shook water on them to keep down the dust and swept them again. The smell of burning followed me. I got a box of Flash and washed the skirting. I painted the wall another coat of green. Then I got a can of floor polish and did the boards. Outside it got dark. Still the place smelt. So I went down to the late-night supermarket and got air fresheners and more incense. I collected the empty bottles and cans into a box and took them to the bottle bank. People were staring at me on the street. I started on the kitchen and found the tabs that Silver John had brought the night of the party. I broke them down to a fine powder and flushed them down the toilet. I flushed four five six seven times. I collected the broken delph in a rubbish bag and washed the dirty dishes.

I stacked my bag of tools and left it by the front door in case I had to go anywhere in a hurry.

I lit a fag and got my breath back, then I attacked the living room. In there was the food thrown by Scots Bob. Chilli stuck to the armchairs, meringues crushed into the rugs. I shook them out the back then beat them. There was shattered glass under the windows. I was down on my hunkers when someone knocked.

Who is that? I asked, thinking it might be the cops.

It's Tim, said a voice.

And Mark, said another.

It was the gay bucks. I had their chairs stacked in the kitchen. In the fracas they had left behind their jackets but I had them hung up in my bedroom. They thanked me. They said how sorry they were about what had happened. I said I was cleaning up. They brought a hoover down from their room and did the carpet in the living room.

Watch the glass, I said.

It's all right, Oliver, said Tim.

No, I said, watch the shagging glass. It'll cut through the bag.

Right, he said.

And be careful emptying it.

I will.

They did the armchairs. We took a break and I went up to their pad to eat. We had toasted cheese and wine.

I came back down and finished the job. I lit the incense and the candles and sat down to wait. I rang the lads to say we had the flat back. The boys returned after closing time, they packed their bags and split. Everyone disappeared. I was with the ghosts. I listened to the street and heard someone say, *Thank you, blossom.*

Thank you.

the police

At dawn I woke to find a policeman at the end of the bed.

Geezer here in bed, he shouted.

Another policeman came in.

Who the fuck are you?

Ollie Ewing.

What are you doing here?

I live here, I said.

You live here?

Yes.

They looked at each other.

You should not be in this apartment.

What do you mean?

We're not finished here.

Well, how was I to know?

And he's fucking cleaned the whole place out, said the other.

Shit.

Somebody's fucked up. Somebody has fucked up badly.

They made me get dressed and took me down to the station. I was there for hours. Eventually they let me go to see Redmond.

fast countries

The father was asleep with the newspaper in his lap. The mother was having a yogurt. They had both slept in the corridor the last few nights.

Redmond lapsed in and out of consciousness.

He was lying stock still, wrapped in a sheet of white plastic that used to slip up his arms. I fed him water.

Ollie?

Redmond.

I can see, he said, with my eyes closed.

Is that right?

No bother, he said.

Will you stand on the chair? he asked me after a while.

I stood on the chair by his bed, and he swivelled his head very gently and looked a long time at my shoes.

If I come through this, he said, I'm going to buy a pair of shoes like that.

A Thai nurse wearing black slippers shuffled in, pushing a trolley. The wings of her hat made her look both stern and amazed.

What are you doing? she asked.

He wanted to see his brother's shoes, said my father.

Oh.

I climbed down.

Please, you will leave now for a while, yes?

Yes, said my mother.

We walked the corridor.

You read the newspapers today? asked my father.

No.

Well you should. You're in them. You want to hear what they say? He stopped, opened the paper and read: IRISH DRUGS BASH ENDS IN MURDER. You like that?

It's not true.

You're in deep shit boy.

I know that.

The police do you any harm?

No. They were all right.

These, he said, are fast countries.

the lift

Then one day I arrived to the hospital and took the lift to the wrong floor. Every floor looked the same, so I made my way to where I thought Redmond was. Then I saw a solitary policeman standing at the far end on his own by a door.

I passed the nurses' station and turned right and found I was lost. I went back to ask the way and pressed the button at the desk. Just then the policeman stood aside and the door opened. Scots Bob hobbled out in his pyjamas, both arms heavily bandaged. He and the policeman came towards me. I couldn't move. As they wheeled away left to the toilet the policeman said, You all right there, mate?

Yeh, I'm all right, I said.

Scots Bob suddenly saw me and stood transfixed, strangely comic in his pyjamas.

You know each other?

Yes, I said.

Move along then, said the policeman.

So I turned away and started back down the corridor. Every time I turned back there was Bob looking after me. He's looking at me still.

the empty bed

We sat in that canteen most days while they changed Redmond's bandages, that were not bandages at all. One day I came up and there was a cop standing at the door, so I said to myself *I've done it again, I've gone to the wrong floor*, and I was about take off when the policeman called after me.

Oi you!

Yes?

You a relative?

Yes, I said.

He held the door open. I walked in. The bed was empty.

I'm sorry, he said.

27

the trial

Scots Bob was charged with manslaughter. He claimed in court that we were all drugged out of our minds. That I had put drugs into the food. That he had been provoked and beaten.

That he had only meant to frighten us. It was a joke that got out of hand.

He just meant to frighten Redmond, not kill him. If Redmond had not fought with him, neither of them would have got burnt.

His woman was in that flat and he wanted her back.

He said that I had claimed he was a murderer. That I had tried to involve him in another killing. A lad that had been burnt in the back of the lorry. Everyone knew that I was insane. That they had tried to be nice to me. Given me a job though I was useless. Every man in the gang could prove that. That I had provoked him by spreading rumours. That I was under the illusion that I was a carpenter. Everyone knew that I had been locked up before.

He is not right in the head, he said, pointing at me.

Even on the night of the party I had dived on a woman and tried to rape her.

Silver John sat very correct in the chair and faced the judge, without once turning back to the barrister.

The deceased worked for you?

For a number of weeks.

And his brother?

I think for a period of two months.

Was Oliver Ewing a capable worker?

No.

Then why did you continue to employ him?

I was sorry for him.

The deceased's brother – Oliver Ewing – assaulted you, I believe, in Wood Green.

He did.

Why did he assault you?

It was something to do with an accusation he was making, that somehow I was involved in the death of a friend of his.

A Mr Martin Kilgallon?

That might be. I never heard his name, your lordship, he said, addressing the judge. I never met the bloke. The first I heard of him was when this fellow Ollie Ewing starts hurling abuse at me.

Did you know how he died?

No. Not then.

Did you have any association with Mr Kilgallon?

Never.

And out of the blue, the deceased's brother assaults you?

That is correct.

And yet you employed him.

Because I had not the heart, your lordship, to see him standing there in the yard looking for work each morning.

You felt obliged to help him?

Yes.

Because he was helpless?

Because he begged me for a job. He was there every morning. He was a miserable, hopeless wretch.

I see. And I suppose it was for the same reason that you employed his brother?

Correct.

They were down-and-outs?

They were.

And you felt you must help them?

To my shame, said Silver John, and my loss.

Quite. The barrister looked back towards the door where someone had entered the courtroom. The deceased's brother asked you to this party?

He did.

Why did you go?

I suppose to show him that I bore no grudges over the assault.

Surely you had demonstrated this, Mr Reynolds, the judge interrupted, by employing both brothers?

I felt he was still suspicious of me.

He still made accusations?

Not verbally. It was in his eyes. The way he looked at me.

Carry on, the judge said to the barrister.

Thank you, your honour. Again the barrister looked towards the door. So you decided to go to this party?

I did.

And you brought Robert MacVeigh and his companion, Miss Farrell?

They were happy to go.

So what did you find when you arrived?

There were a lot of Irish there, mostly men. The minute I entered the joint I could feel the hostility.

What do you mean, exactly?

266

I felt we'd been set up. That once they had us inside anything might happen. They were talking politics, your honour.

Irish politics?

Yes.

About Northern Ireland?

Things like that. They started speaking in Irish. But I could make out some of it.

I see.

They were stoned, said Silver John, and for the first time he turned towards the barrister. They were trying to terrify us. Then Ewing –

Oliver Ewing?

– Oliver Ewing started on about his friend that had died. How he had been burnt. They started ganging up on us. I said we would go, but before we could leave they set upon us. They called us English bastards and three or four of them starting booting Bob. I asked them to stop, but they wouldn't. I was flung out the door, then Bob was thrown out. He was badly wounded. He began screaming for Meg, but they wouldn't let her go.

Your witness.

the bad things

And so my man stood and began to interrogate Silver John but it was like I never heard him.

All I could hear were the bad things.

Meg

Meg took the stand.

You are Margaret Farrell?

Yes.

The accused – Robert MacVeigh – is your companion?

Yes, said Meg.

And you accompanied him to this party?

Yes, she said, with Silver John.

John Reynolds?

Yes.

Now there was some disagreement, a falling out of sorts with the accused and the deceased?

They had words.

And Mr Reynolds left and Mr MacVeigh left?

Bob and John decided to go.

In fact they were thrown out.

That's right.

They were physically hurled out of the flat isn't that right?

That's true.

Now could you explain since you came with them – with Mr MacVeigh and Mr Reynolds – could you explain to the court why you did not accompany them?

I couldn't.

Speak up, said the judge.

Please, Miss Farrell, said the barrister, will you please address his lordship. Why did you not accompany your friends when they left?

I just couldn't.

Miss Farrell, I put it to you again: why did you not just leave? Your friends were going. You were among strangers. You did not know anyone there.

I knew Ollie, she said.

Mr Ewing, the brother of the deceased?

Yes. I knew him. He worked with Bob.

But did you know anyone else?

No. Not till that night.

So why did you not go.

I –

Yes?

I – she said softly.

Miss Farrell, will you please address his lordship. Let's put it this way – did you want to leave?

I did, but that was after I . . .

Please answer the question. Did you want to leave?

Yes.

And why did you not leave?

I was told not to go.

By whom?

By Redmond.

Redmond Ewing – the deceased – threatened you?

Not in so many words.

Miss Farrell – either the deceased threatened you or didn't threaten you. Well?

He said things to me.

Could you please explain what *things*?

He said I should not go.

And –

That I would be in trouble if I left.

So, in fact what happened was, your friends were ejected from the apartment – with great violence – and you were held there against your will. Is that not so? Come, Miss Farrell, is that not so?

Yes, she said sadly.

And so it would be understandable if your companion – Mr MacVeigh – Robert – should wish to rescue you, isn't that right?

Yes.

In fact you wanted him to. You begged him to save you. Is that correct?

Yes.

269

He would have been terrified of what might happen to you. Isn't that right, Miss Farrell? Miss Farrell?

Yes.

I walked back towards the flat

Scots Bob looked at the floor.

When you were ejected from the apartment what did you do?

I drove away with Silver John, then asked him to stop the car.

And he stopped the car where?

On some street, I couldn't tell you where.

Some distance away from the apartment, I take it?

Quite a distance.

You were not near a petrol station?

No.

Nowhere near?

No.

And then what happened?

I asked Silver John to go on. I told him that I needed some fresh air.

You were upset.

Yes.

Understandably, in the circumstances.

Yes.

And what did – ah, ah – Mr Reynolds – say?

He told me to get back in the car.

But you didn't.

No. I was upset. I told him I would get a taxi later on and eventually he left.

But he did so reluctantly?

Yes.

And then?

I walked back towards the flat.

Alone?

Yes.

You walked back to the flat. Why?

I was worried about Meg.

Miss Farrell. I see. And what did you intend to do?

Nothing. I don't know. I just thought I should go back.

You imagined all kind of things.

I did.

So why, said the judge, did you not phone the police?

I couldn't think straight. My head was going round. I had received a few blows to the head. I'd been kicked, I was sore, I didn't think of the police.

Go on.

Then I saw this all-night garage.

You just happened upon it?

Yes.

I want to be clear about this. Not until you saw the filling station did you ever consider retaliation of any kind?

That's right.

Thank you. Please continue.

I bought a container and got a fill of petrol.

Why did you do that, Mr MacVeigh?

He – and he pointed at me – had put it in my head. With all that talk of burning. If he had never accused me of that killing, nothing would have happened. It was like he had got inside my brain. I didn't know what I was doing. It was like I was being ordered to do what I did.

So you bought the petrol, Mr MacVeigh?

I did.

And you walked back to the flat?

Yes.

271

And how did you get in?

The front door was open. I went up the stairs.

And what did you intend to do with the petrol?

To burn down the door.

You had no intention of harming anyone?

No.

Your chief concern was to get Miss Farrell safely from the apartment?

Yes.

And then what happened?

As I was lighting a rag soaked in petrol, the door opened and there was Redmond Ewing. We started to struggle and the can caught fire.

Did you throw petrol on him?

No.

My friend, here, will say you did.

I did not. It was an accident. If he hadn't struggled with me it wouldn't have happened.

You are quite sure, Mr MacVeigh?

I am.

And what happened?

The can went up. We both got burned.

You, in fact, got badly burned.

Yes.

So, in fact, what you are saying is that if you had intended to throw petrol on the deceased – Mr Redmond Ewing – you yourself would not have suffered?

That's right.

Thank you, Mr MacVeigh. That will be all for now.

Mr Ewing, you have been resident in London for – how long?

A year.

Speak louder, please.

A year.

And when you arrived you were resident – where?

On a site in Hammersmith.

With Mr Martin Kilgallon?

That's right.

You were living there illegally.

I was not.

Mr Ewing, I have papers here to the effect that you were living illegally on the site, without the knowledge of the contractor Mr McKenna.

That's not true.

I'm afraid it is.

No, it's not. I was acting as security while Marty was away.

Indeed. How are we to know that is true?

That's what I was.

I have a sworn statement here from Mr McKenna that to the best of his recollection he had no knowledge nor written permission that you were resident on the site.

He's lying.

Is that so? Had you not to be ejected from that site?

That was after Marty died. McKenna said building work was about to begin. He had no more need of me.

I put it to you, Mr Ewing, that you were not only living illegally on the site but that you in fact refused entry on to the site to a foreman employed by Mr McKenna.

What?

I said you refused entry to a foreman on the site.

I didn't know who he was.

So much for security. You in fact threatened him.

I did not.

He will swear you did.

It was him threatened me.

It seems you labour under an illusion, Mr Ewing, that the world is against you. He paused. Mr Ewing, it appears to me that you are the one who has threatened not only the foreman, but Mr McKenna, you threatened Mr Reynolds, you threatened Margaret Farrell and you threatened the accused, Mr MacVeigh. Is that not so? Speak up, Mr Ewing, I can't hear you.

I didn't threaten anyone.

I put it to you, Mr Ewing, that this whole tragic affair arose because of you. Is that not so?

No.

rifles from high buildings

He lifted a sheet of paper. Do you know what this is?

No.

This is a statement you made to the police. June 18th. He handed it to me. Does it look familiar?

Yes.

Could you, please, read paragraph 10, . . . I said could you read paragraph I0?

When I got –

Speak up, please, Mr Ewing!

When I got the bucket of water on my head, they were working next door. Two guys with blue jumpers. They were sent from next door to do the job on me. I don't know what was the reason for throwing water on a man who was trying to do a bit of work.

So even at work you were threatened?

That's right.

274

Because you were Irish?

Maybe.

I see. Now could you please read paragraph 15?

The day the laundry windows steamed up, speed was put into my sandwiches in this fancy restaurant that I went to. A real posh place. I went in for a toasted cheese and lost the run of things. I was brought into hospital and that was what was found in my urine.

And that was what was found in your urine – speed?

That's right.

Someone put amphetamines into your sandwich?

I don't know.

Why would someone – a complete stranger to you – do that?

I don't know.

You don't know, indeed. Life has been very unkind to you, Mr Ewing, don't you think?

I'm not the defendant here.

You were arrested some time back, were you not? June 5th, to be precise.

What?

Are you saying you were never arrested by the police? Mr Ewing, I am asking you a question.

That was different.

I see. Please turn to page 3. Paragraph 6. You have it?

Yes.

Good. I believe you were walking near Clapham at the time. Is that so?

That's right.

Please read it for his Lordship.

I just strolled along, and stopped every so often to see would a night bus come. I wasn't bothered, till I spotted this buck on the top of a high building with a gun. So I sprinted across the road, shouting, and shouting.

I wasn't bothered till I spotted this buck on the top of a high building with a gun, he repeated. Indeed, Mr Ewing. These are your words?

Yes.

Extraordinary. And after your encounter with this – er – assassin what did you do?

I broke into a house to take shelter.

How convenient. You *broke into a house to take shelter.*

That's right.

As you had formerly broken into the site in Hammersmith. Is that not so?

No.

Speak up, Mr Ewing.

I broke in no place.

In your own words you *broke into a house.*

That was different. I knocked first.

How gracious of you.

I was trying to hide.

And you were arrested.

I was. But then I was released. There were no charges.

Do you really expect the court to believe that you saw an assassin with a rifle?

I saw him.

In their report of the affair the police were inclined to wonder.

I saw no report.

And one wonders did you see any assassin.

I did.

But no one else did. Would you agree that you fabricated this whole encounter with a would-be assassin in your imagination in order to justify breaking and entering?

I saw him, I swear!

Did the police find any evidence of a gunman?

Not that I know of.

So?

They might not have, but then they didn't find my friend Marty when he went missing, did they? And then they found him dead, didn't they?

I'm coming to that, Mr Ewing, I'm coming to that. But first I think – and he shuffled the papers in front of him – I think we should discuss, let me see – and he chuckled – *glass-sprinklers.*

28

paragraph 5

Could you read paragraph 5, page 3.

    Why do you want me to read it out?

    The court would like to hear your observations on this phenomenon.

    Why?

    Leave the questions to me, Mr Ewing. Please read.

    I don't want to.

    Mr Ewing, if you don't read from the document somebody else will. Do you understand?

    I understand.

    Lift the document and read. Paragraph 5, page 3. Right?

    Glass-sprinklers. I have just seen the one in action.

    Please, go on.

    They are like a tank.

    Indeed. He smiled broadly. Continue, Mr Ewing.

    They can spit glass in a ring. One night I saw one when I was out walking, it never touched me. It was on a motorway flyover.

    Yes?

    You could hear the glass going whoosh, definitely glass.

    And the next line reads, your honour: *Some sort of yoke for breaking glass.* Is that correct, Mr Ewing?

    Yes.

You may put the document down. He smiled at me. Now would you not say that some of your observations are a trifle bizarre.

Maybe.

Glass-sprinklers?

That's right.

Glass-sprinklers, Mr Ewing?

What else could you call it?

Indeed. He laughed. What else indeed? He laughed again and then spun on his toes. Mr Ewing, are you telling us that you encountered a machine for breaking glass on a motorway flyover?

I did that night.

But not since?

No.

Nor ever before?

No.

And why do you think that is?

Maybe they've gone out of production.

I would not try to be funny if I was you. I'd like to remind you that two people who were associates of yours are dead. I don't think that is a laughing matter, do you?

No.

Explain to the court what *glass-sprinklers* are?

I don't know.

Do they come under the same heading as assassins with rifles? Do they, Mr Ewing?

I can't explain it.

I can appreciate that.

It's difficult.

The court – he swung away from me – can appreciate, Mr Ewing, that you have a capacity to observe phenomena some of us lesser creatures will never see. But what we are doing is trying to separate fact from fiction. Do you understand?

279

Yes.

So let me put it to you that what you are saying is unbelievable.

It's what happened.

Come, come. Men with rifles, *glass-sprinklers*? What next? What next indeed.

protection rackets

Let us go back to June 18th.

All right.

You had been searching for your friend, Mr Kilgallon.

Yes.

Your statement to the police says he was worried about protection rackets.

That's right.

What manner of protection racket?

I don't know. Something to do with the building trade. Something to do with haulage. I don't know.

And who ran these protection rackets?

I don't know.

Do you know of any specific reason why anyone would want to murder your friend?

No.

Your statement reads: *He was making too much money and the other boys were making nothing. Whether they were English or Irish I don't know. I think they were English.* Is that correct? Is that what you said to the police?

If you say I said it, I must have.

You don't remember saying it? Please turn to page 4 of the document in front of you.

No, it's all right. I accept I said it.

You accept you said it. Thank you, Mr Ewing, he said, then bowed to me and turned away. *I think they were English.* What do you mean by that?

I mean what it says.

That he was killed by some English gang?

It means maybe he was killed by some English lads.

Do you have any evidence for that assertion?

No.

Why not an Irish gang for instance?

I don't know.

What have you got against the English, Mr Ewing?

politics

Would you say you are a political person, Mr Ewing?

No. Definitely not.

And Mr Kilgallon, was he a political person?

No.

In fact, you said he was a Muslim.

I said he was thinking of becoming a Muslim.

Would you not consider that a political act?

No.

To my mind that would be a very political act.

It was the religious aspect that attracted him.

Is that so? And you, who claim you are also not political, can make an assertion that – I quote – *some English lads* – unquote – killed your friend.

That's not political.

Is it not? Why – since you had no evidence to back up this assertion, did you say it?

I said *maybe*.

Why *English lads*, Mr Ewing?

It must have been something Marty said.

Ah, but unfortunately Mr Kilgallon is dead.

Yes. They killed him.

Who killed him, Mr Ewing? You just said *they killed him*. Who? I repeat, who killed your friend Mr Kilgallon?

I don't know. I thought this court case was about who killed my brother.

Yes it is. But, you see, Mr Ewing, you yourself implicated Mr Reynolds and the accused, Mr MacVeigh, in the death of Martin Kilgallon. Didn't you?

hiding out

You say your friend, Mr Kilgallon, prior to his death, went north.

On business.

What type of business?

I don't know.

You don't know. How many times have we heard you say those words – *I don't know* – over the last few days?

I haven't counted them.

Quite. Neither have I. But would you say that you have continued to mislead this court by claiming you don't remember, or you don't know, or in some cases using a combination of the two, in order to safeguard yourself?

I'm trying to tell the truth.

Good, the court is pleased to hear that, Mr Ewing. And he smiled. Now on what business did Mr Kilgallon go north?

I don't know, I say.

Have you any evidence that he went north?

That's where he said he was going.

But that is the problem, Mr Ewing. We have only your word that he intended going north, haven't we?

What difference does it matter where he went?

Well, if he remained in London, while you say he went north – it makes a big difference, doesn't it.

I can't see why.

Because it means you're lying.

I'm not lying. I believe he went north because that's where he said he was going.

And where was he found dead?

In Hammersmith.

A few streets away, in fact, from where you were illegally living on a building site.

I was not there illegally.

Why did you implicate Mr Reynolds and Mr MacVeigh in the death of your friend Mr Kilgallon?

Because Marty told me he was thinking of going to work for Silver John.

Again the court has only your word as to what Mr Kilgallon might or might not have said.

I can't help that. He told me he was thinking of going to work for Silver John. Then he disappeared. Then I found him dead. That's the story.

Tell me this, Mr Ewing. After you left the site at Hammersmith where did you go?

To Clapham.

Not so fast, Mr Ewing. Where did you spend the next few weeks living?

The next weeks?

Yes.

In Liverpool Street.

Where, exactly?

On the site I was working on.

So you moved from one site to another?

That's right.

Why did you not get an apartment? You were working. Why

did you not get a flat or lodgings like any other person in your position?

It fell out like that. I hadn't time.

I see. I put it to you that you were trying to avoid having proper accommodation.

I was not. It just happened that way.

You arrive in London and you live illegally on a site. Your friend is killed and what do you do? You move on to another site where you cannot be detected or found. Why was that ?

It just happened.

Why were you trying to avoid normal accommodation?

I wasn't.

I put it to you that you were in fact hiding out.

No.

Did you leave your new address with the police?

No.

Your friend Martin Kilgallon has just been killed and what do you do? – You disappear.

I didn't disappear.

You did not tell the police where you were moving because you wanted to disappear.

I told them that I was working on the buildings.

But did you tell them where?

I showed them my tax forms.

Did you?

I did.

Well, Mr Ewing, we have only your word for that. What's recorded here is your address at the site. *Occupation*: *labourer*. *Education*: *4 A-levels*. *Nationality*: *Irish*. All the police knew at that juncture was that you were living on that site. After you left Hammersmith they had no record of you. By the time they discovered you were working in Liverpool Street you had disappeared again. Do you make a habit of disguising where you live?

No.

So why did you give a false address to your employer?

What?

Olive Street

Mr Ewing – do you recall Mr John Reynolds and two of his employees driving you home on a certain date towards the end of July?

Yes.

So, please explain to the court what happened.

They left me to Clapham.

Yes. What else?

There's nothing else.

Oh but there is, Mr Ewing. You in fact gave them a bogus address. Mr Reynolds will give evidence, as will his two employees, Mr Raynard and Mr Magus, that you in fact brought them to an address – in Manor Street I believe – where you did not live. Why did you do that, Mr Ewing?

I wanted to keep my address to myself.

Why?

Just.

I see. And then a few days later Mr Reynolds called at that address only to discover that you had lied to him. Is that right?

Yes.

You had never lived there?

No.

You in fact lived in Olive Street. Correct?

Yes.

So again we have this wish to deceive.

No.

You are, in fact, a compulsive liar.

I am not! Didn't I invite them to the party?

Ah but, Mr Ewing, look what happened to those gentlemen there. Look what happened to your brother, Redmond Ewing. You deliberately set up this party so that a gang of youths could launch an assault on Mr Reynolds and Mr MacVeigh. Isn't that right? Isn't that right, Mr Ewing?

fucking Irish cunt

On the night you found your friend Martin Kilgallon dead you claimed that you had been searching for him for days.

And nights.

How many days and nights?

About two weeks, maybe more.

And you stopped in the Portakabin each night while he was away?

Yes. Except for the time I was at work.

Did you have any callers over the period that you were staying in the Portakabin?

Except for that madman claiming to be the foreman of the site there was nobody.

He was the foreman.

I didn't know that.

Why did you not let him in?

I'd never met him. He had no identification on him. Marty told me not to allow anyone onto the site.

Indeed. Did you have any other callers?

No.

Are you sure?

Certain.

Are you familiar with the Pastor of St James's Church, Reverend Dawson?

Yes, I knew him. We both did.

And did he call to see you?

He might have.

I'll ask you again. Did Reverend Dawson call to see you during this period?

He shook the gate one night.

In fact, he saw you in the Portakabin and called out your name. Is that right?

Yes.

And what did you do?

Nothing. I didn't answer him.

In fact, you cowered down out of sight.

Maybe.

Why?

I don't know.

Reverend Dawson, who had befriended you both, visits you, and not only do you not let him in, you refuse to answer his call and then hide from view. Why, Mr Ewing?

I wasn't in the mood for company.

Oh. What were you hiding?

I wasn't hiding anything.

Then explain to the court why you not only refused entry to the foreman of the site, but then refused the visit of Reverend Dawson.

I was panicking.

Panicking?

Yes. Because Marty was gone and I thought this crowd might be after me.

If he was missing, surely the most obvious thing to do was to speak to someone. To tell the foreman. To explain to Reverend Dawson. To contact the police. Why did you do none of these things, Mr Ewing?

I couldn't think.

But you were able to deny the rightful owner entrance on to his own site.

I tell you I did not know who he was. He started calling me names.

Oh, did he?

He called me a *thick fucking Irish cunt.*

I suppose he was English too.

Yes.

Are you sure about that?

No.

He leant down and spoke to someone at his elbow then turned back to me. I gather Mr Gaynor, the foreman who works for Mr McKenna, is in fact Irish.

Is he?

Now, if he was Irish why would he call you *a fucking Irish cunt,* Mr Ewing?

Maybe he's been living over here too long.

Ah, I see – they are all against you, aren't they, Mr Ewing?

Including you.

Indeed. He turned to the court and nodded appreciatively.

self-destruction

Mr Kilgallon died of severe burns from acid. Is that right?

Yes.

Are you all right, Mr Ewing?

Yes.

Shall I continue?

Go on.

I believe, in fact, he spoke of this acid to you, referring to its properties of self-destruction?

I suppose you could put it like that.

When did he mention this to you?

Not long after I arrived.

And what did he say?

He said I had to be careful. There was this protection crowd that would throw it over you.

Why would they throw it over you?

I suppose if they had something against you.

Like what?

If you didn't pay up.

And?

I don't know. It could be for anything.

Have you heard of it happening?

Yes.

You have? Please tell the court.

Didn't Marty die of it?

Mr Ewing, the court is aware of the manner of Mr Kilgallon's death. What the court wishes to know is whether you know of any other instances of these so-called protection gangs throwing acid on persons in the building trade?

No. But I'm sure it has happened.

But not to your knowledge?

Is it not enough that Marty died of it?

Mr Ewing, do you know of someone other than Mr Kilgallon who died in the building trade by having acid poured over them?

You don't have to use acid.

No?

No. You can use petrol, can't you?

back in the Lag

After the death of your friend Martin Kilgallon you went to the Lagoon Bar in Wood Green.

Not immediately.

But soon after.

That's right.

Why?

Marty had mentioned that he had intended to work for a man called Silver John.

I see. At this juncture did he say anything at all derogatory about Mr Reynolds?

No.

Did he impute to you that Mr Reynolds had anything to do with these so-called protection rackets?

No.

So, in fact, as far as Mr Kilgallon was concerned, Mr Reynolds was a worthy, honest employer. Would he have suggested going to work for him if he did not trust him?

I suppose not.

Good, thank you, Mr Ewing. So you went to the Lagoon Bar to see him?

Yes.

Why?

I wanted to ask Silver John did he know anything about what happened to Marty.

I see. Why should he know anything of what had happened to your friend Mr Kilgallon?

Because Marty might have gone to work for him.

But he hadn't had he?

Not that I know.

You were told that, were you not?

Yes.

Not once, or twice, but many times.

I was told he had not worked for Silver John.

But you persisted in insulting Mr Reynolds.

I did not.

Then you attacked him.

I did not.

We have witnesses to say you attacked him on the street and that Mr MacVeigh had to come to his rescue.

That's not true. And I have a witness who will say different.

And who is this, pray?

There was a plumber who came to my aid.

Mr McDonagh?

I don't know his name. He was from Wexford.

Yes, we have spoken to Mr McDonagh, who is from Wexford in the Irish Free State. He says that you attacked Mr Reynolds.

He would not say that. I'm afraid you have the wrong man.

Did you stay in his house – the house of this plumber?

Yes.

Well, that is Mr McDonagh.

He wouldn't say I attacked Silver John.

I'm afraid he does.

I don't believe it.

He says that you grabbed Mr Reynolds by the shoulders and began to scream abuse. Do you remember that?

No. I might have tapped him on the shoulder.

I see. Tapped him on the shoulder.

That's right.

How much did you have to drink that night?

A few pints.

The landlord, Mr Robert Vaynes, says you had in the region of eight or nine pints of Heineken. Is that not correct?

I can't remember.

And that you continued throughout the evening to interrupt the company of Mr Reynolds and Mr MacVeigh. Is that not correct?

No.

And then, outside the pub, you lay in wait and attacked Mr Reynolds.

No.

That's what Mr McDonagh says.

I don't believe he would say that.

As does Mr MacVeigh, as does Miss Farrell. You waited outside the pub and you attacked him.

It's not true.

Mr Ewing, why did you attack Mr Reynolds?

I didn't attack him.

Mr Ewing, the court will understand that after the death of your friend you would be upset. Is that not right?

I was upset.

So you attacked him.

I didn't attack him. I didn't attack him! You hear me?

I hear you, but I don't believe you. You arrive at a pub and make wild accusations to a complete stranger. You wait outside the pub and, though asked to desist, you keep shouting at Mr Reynolds when he emerges with his friends. This is a man you have never met prior to that night! This is a man who has never met or heard of your friend Martin Kilgallon! He is totally innocent of any crime against you or your friend, and yet you grab him by the shoulders and start shouting obscenities. He tells you over and over that he knows nothing about the death of your friend. Then suddenly you launch into a wild attack on him. Is that not so?

No.

Did you have any evidence that he was involved in the death of your friend Martin Kilgallon?

No.

Do you have any now?

No.

Had you ever?

No.

Thank you, Mr Ewing. Thank you.

30

accepting the job with regret

Despite having no evidence to back up your assertions, did you continue to believe, after the fracas that night at the Lagoon Bar, July 10th, that Mr Reynolds was involved in the death of Mr Martin Kilgallon?

I wasn't sure.

And yet, when Mr Reynolds offered you employment with his building firm you took it.

I was in need of a job.

You took it gladly, didn't you?

I took it.

How could you take a job with this man if you still harboured suspicions about his involvement in the death of Martin Kilgallon?

I don't know. I don't know.

I think we have two options here, Mr Ewing. I put it to you that either you took that job believing Mr Reynolds to be totally innocent of any connection with the death of Mr Kilgallon, or – and I would listen carefully if I were you – you accepted employment with him in order to exact revenge. Which is it to be?

He offered me a job. I took it.

Do you really want me to believe it was as simple as that? Let's go back a bit shall we? Did you go to that yard knowing Mr Reynolds would be there?

I suppose I knew he would be there.

Are there not other places in London where day-labouring can be obtained?

There are.

Why did you not go to them?

It just happened like that.

Mr Ewing, are you telling the court that all that happened to you is the result of chance?

Most things in life happen like that.

Like what?

Suddenly.

Do they indeed?

That's what I think anyway.

So you only happened to go to the Lagoon Bar?

No. I intended to go there.

I see. But you didn't intend to go to the yard at Rose Avenue?

I did, I suppose.

I thought *you just happened to go there*?

That too.

So you didn't go there knowing that this was the place where Mr Reynolds hired men for day labouring?

I found out that.

Thank you. So you went deliberately seeking work from Mr Reynolds?

No. Not only from him. From anyone.

But they didn't hire you, did they?

No.

Only Mr Reynolds offered you employment, isn't that right?

Yes.

So why did you accept employment from Mr Reynolds?

Why did he offer it to me?

You have heard, Mr Ewing, what Mr Reynolds said. You were out of work. Your friend had just died. He felt sorry for you. Why did you accept that job? By taking that job you set in motion a series of events which eventually led to the unfortunate night of the party on October 2nd. I ask you again: why did you accept the job?

I should never have taken it.

No. You should not have. Your plan went wrong, didn't it, Mr Ewing? It backfired, didn't it?

I had no plan.

So why did you accept the job?

I should never have taken it. And . . .

And what?

. . . he should never have offered it.

So he's to blame now, is he?

No.

So you agree you should not have taken it?

I should not have taken it, no.

Just as you should never have gone to the Lagoon Bar to persecute Mr Reynolds! Just as you should never have held a party to deliberately set up an assault on Mr MacVeigh and Mr Reynolds! There are a lot of things, that with hindsight, you now regret, are there not, Mr Ewing?

Yes.

When you accepted that job you deliberately set out on a course of action which led to the death of your brother, is that not right? Would you like to take a break, Mr Ewing?

No.

the plan

So you accept you had a plan?

No.

A moment ago you admitted that you had.

No. I had no plan.

In other words you had complete faith in Mr Reynolds. Yes?

296

I suppose so.

Well then, will you please explain to the court why you began questioning men in his employment about Mr Reynolds's personal history.

I only asked a few questions.

Did you ask someone – *Are there any protection rackets on this job?*

Maybe.

Did you, Mr Ewing?

Yes.

And what were you told?

That there were none.

Does that sound like you trusted Mr Reynolds?

No.

Did you state to numerous people that you believed Mr Reynolds was involved in the death of your friend Mr Martin Kilgallon. Did you, Mr Ewing?

I don't remember saying that.

So what did you say?

I can't remember.

And did Mr Reynolds not challenge you as regards these stories?

He did.

And yet you persisted.

No.

So I put it to you that when you accepted this job, which Mr Reynolds so generously offered you, you had already thought out a plan of action to wreak havoc with his life.

No.

And the worst thing is – you have succeeded.

I don't know what you mean.

Are you aware that Mr Reynolds's business has folded?

No. I was not aware.

Are you aware of what this court case and the newspaper reports and your accusations have done to his life?

No.

And all because of you, Mr Ewing. From the day you met him, you have stalked Mr Reynolds. You assault him, you spread rumours about him, you invite him to a party and then a crowd of your friends, including yourself, set upon him. You hold a friend of his against her will in your apartment. You insinuate again, in this court, that Mr Reynolds is behind the death of your friend Mr Kilgallon. Witnesses in this trial have stated that you implied that Mr Reynolds incited Mr MacVeigh to do what he did. Isn't this what you've done, Mr Ewing? Hm?

Redmond

Your brother also received employment through the good offices of Mr Reynolds. Is that not so?

Yes.

If you believed that Mr Reynolds was involved in so-called protection rackets why would you expose your brother to such an enterprise?

It was a mistake.

It certainly was. Another of your regrets?

I regret it.

And why, Mr Ewing, did you encourage your brother to seek work with Mr Reynolds?

I didn't encourage him.

But you brought your brother to the yard at Rose Avenue?

Yes. I should never have done it.

And you introduced him to Mr MacVeigh?

In a way.

And he hired the deceased because he was your brother?

Yes.

He was glad of the job?

Yes.

And so were you?

Yes.

And all the time you and your brother were conniving and plotting to bring about the downfall of John Reynolds.

No. We never spoke of it.

Never, Mr Ewing? Did you say *never*?

I did.

Tell me this. Would your brother have known Martin Kilgallon?

He would have a' course.

Because Mr Kilgallon was a neighbour of yours back in Eire.

Yes.

In fact, he would have known him very well.

He would have.

And he had heard of his death?

Yes.

He was upset by the death, I'm sure.

He was.

And then you introduce your brother Redmond Ewing into the employment of a man you suspected of being involved in the death of your friend Mr Kilgallon and never mentioned your reservations.

I suppose I did. In a way.

Thank you. And what do you think your brother Redmond Ewing would have made of such insinuations?

I don't know.

I think you do, Mr Ewing. Sadly, I think you know only too well.

Why did you invite Mr Reynolds to your home?

To go to a party.

I know that. But why?

It just happened.

Did you and Mr Reynolds have a discussion in which he asked you whether you – I quote – *held anything against him*?

We might have.

And did you say – I quote – you *held nothing against him*?

I think so.

Did you say you trusted him?

I don't know.

Did you or didn't you?

I did.

And all the time you didn't?

Yes.

So you lied?

I did.

You invited him to the party?

Yes.

And he accepted?

Yes.

Would he have gone, do you think, if you had not told him you trusted him?

I suppose he wouldn't.

So you lied to get him to go?

No. I invited him because I was afraid of him.

Are you telling the court that you invited a man who you were afraid of to a party in your house?

Yes.

But why invite him?

I don't know.

Was there any reason to invite him?

No.

Did Mr Reynolds threaten you in any way? Did he say for instance *I want to go to this party*?

No.

In fact, you brought it up?

Yes. I was on the spot. I was trying to make up to him for giving the wrong address.

So you invited him because you had lied to him?

I suppose so.

And then, when he asked you did you trust him, you lied to him again?

Yes.

Have I got that right?

Yes.

Very good, Mr Ewing. We are getting somewhere at last.

31

the Irish

How many people attended this party, Mr Ewing?

About sixteen.

Mostly Irish friends of yours?

There were about seven, maybe eight people, who weren't Irish.

But the majority were Irish?

No. It was about even.

But counting yourself and your brother, the deceased, Redmond Ewing?

We were in the majority until Silver John and Scots Bob arrived.

I see. So what was the purpose of the party?

There was none really. Maybe to celebrate Redmond coming to England.

I see. There was plenty of alcohol I take it?

Yes. And plenty to eat.

Indeed. Did you mention to your friends that Mr Reynolds, your employer, and Mr MacVeigh were coming to the party?

I might have mentioned that Silver John was –

Mr Reynolds?

I might have mentioned that Mr Reynolds was coming. I wouldn't have known who he was bringing with him.

Your friends who you invited would have known Martin Kilgallon?

Yes.

They would have known him very well?

Yes.

And did you tell them that you suspected Mr Reynolds was involved in his death? I ask you again, Mr Ewing, did you tell them that you believed Mr Reynolds was involved in Martin Kilgallon's death?

No.

La Loo

Your name is Larry Loonan?

Yes, said La Loo

And you attended the party on the night in question?

I did.

You reside in Luton.

I'm studying there.

Who contacted you?

Ollie Ewing.

And did he say what the party was for?

No. He just said there was a party.

He didn't say he needed your help with something?

No, he didn't.

And you came all that way for a small party?

I came for the crack.

What do you mean by *crack*?

The fun.

I see. It was some fun wasn't it, Mr Loonan?

It was not funny, sir.

And what time did you arrive in Olive Street?

Some time in the late afternoon. I had a pint at the station and looked into the bookies.

And when you arrived at the flat in Olive Street what happened?

Well, the boys were knocking together a bit of grub with the help of the ladies.

Then what happened?

We went across to the pub.

So you sat around drinking?

And talking.

And what were you discussing?

Jobs, work, study, Sligo, all kinds of things.

Nothing else?

No.

Did Mr Ewing discuss the possibility that there might be trouble later on and that he wanted you to be ready for it?

No.

Did he mention that he had asked his employer, Mr Reynolds, to the party?

He did.

And what did he say about him?

He said he didn't think he'd turn up.

And were you surprised at that?

No. He didn't know him that well, I took it.

Did he at any stage allege that Mr Reynolds might have been involved in the death of your friend Mr Kilgallon?

No.

Let's put it another way. Why do you think Oliver Ewing said he didn't expect Mr Reynolds to attend?

I don't know.

Did he ask you to be wary of Mr Reynolds?

No.

Are you telling the court that Mr Ewing never alluded to his suspicions?

No. He never did.

Did you have any knowledge prior to the party that Mr Ewing

suspected Mr Reynolds was involved in the death of Martin Kilgallon?

No.

You're certain?

Yes.

Thank you. Just one final question. When you physically ejected Mr Reynolds and Mr MacVeigh, did you not verbally abuse them about their involvement in the death of your friend Mr Kilgallon?

There were things said.

Things?

Yes.

By you?

Yes.

So by then you knew of Mr Ewing's suspicions, didn't you? That he believed that Mr Reynolds had somehow being connected to the death –

He didn't believe that, he only suspected that. He didn't really believe it.

He suspected?

Yes.

But he didn't believe it?

No, he didn't.

I see. Again the barrister looked towards the door where someone had entered the courtroom. Slowly he turned to La Loo. How did you know that?

Know what?

That he didn't believe but only suspected? How did you know?

I heard it.

But you've just said you were not told in the pub.

I learnt it later.

So you later learnt that Mr Ewing suspected Mr Reynolds of being involved in the death of Martin Kilgallon?

Yes.

When?

I learnt it at the party.

Ah, so Mr Ewing, the brother of the deceased, told you at the party?

No. Ollie never mentioned it.

I repeat – Mr Oliver Ewing told you, isn't that right?

No.

Remember you are on oath, Mr Loonan. I put it to you that Mr Ewing told you of his suspicions.

No.

That he warned you and the others to be ready to attack Mr Reynolds.

No he didn't, he never did.

You have already agreed that you knew of his suspicions as regards his employer.

That's right.

So, Mr Loonan, it's obvious to the court that Mr Oliver Ewing told you.

No, he didn't.

Mr Loonan. Who else but Mr Ewing could tell you of the suspicions he had?

He didn't tell me.

Your honour, it's obvious to me that Mr Oliver Ewing told the witness of his suspicions.

Mr Loonan?

Yes, your honour.

You say Mr Oliver Ewing did not impart to you his suspicions of Mr Reynolds.

No, he did not.

But you have already agreed that you later knew of his suspicions at the party.

That's right.

But he didn't tell you?

No.

Then how did you come by this knowledge?

I was told.

Who told you?

Redmond. Redmond told me.

Redmond Ewing?

Yes.

The deceased told you?

Yes.

Thank you, Mr Loonan.

Thank you, your honour.

Mr Loonan?

Yes.

We have heard from two witnesses that politics was discussed at this party.

No. Never.

Both witnesses stated that you and Mr Ewing started to speak in Irish. Is that correct?

I can't recall, sir.

Well, the court will be patient. Now, do you remember speaking in Irish?

I don't think we did.

Please, Mr Loonan. If you spoke in Irish would this not be an attempt to communicate with each other without Mr Reynolds or Mr MacVeigh knowing what was being said.

Yes, I suppose so.

So what did you speak about?

Suddenly La Loo broke out into a fit of laughter.

You find it funny, Mr Loonan? Indeed. So what did you speak of?

The only Irish we spoke was of *Murphy Agus A Chairde*.

And what does that mean?

Murphy and His Friends. It was a programme for children that used to be on Irish television when we were young.

A children's programme?

Yes.

drugs

There was plenty of alcohol available at this party?

Yes.

And drugs? I repeat, Mr Ewing, were there drugs available?

Ham.

I'm sorry?

Nothing.

We already know there were drugs available through an autopsy carried out on your brother, the deceased. You have heard evidence to that effect, have you not?

Yes.

So you admit there were drugs available at this party?

Yes.

Thank you.

And did you partake of LSD?

No.

You are certain of that?

Yes.

But your brother did?

Yes.

And your friends?

I can't say.

But you didn't?

No.

I see. I have a police report here before me, Mr Ewing. It states that your eyes were dilated and you were suffering from hallucinations when the police arrived. Is that correct?

I was all over the place after what had happened.

Indeed. *All over the place.*

That's right.

Why are you lying?

I am not lying.

I put it to you that you were doped out of your head!

No.

Do you think a man in your condition would in fact be able to recall in a lucid manner the actual run of events at the party?

I can remember.

Can you?

I'm not likely to forget.

Well let's see, shall we, Mr Ewing?

things started flying

When things started flying that's when it started.

What things?

Food.

And who was throwing this food?

Scots Bob.

Mr MacVeigh?

That's him.

And because of some light-hearted fun on the part of Mr MacVeigh you decided to eject him from the party?

It was not light-hearted fun.

Throwing food? Come, come, Mr Ewing. Isn't it true to say that you were only waiting for your chance?

He was out of order.

Then what happened?

I asked him to go.

And when he refused?

I asked him again.

And then you struck him, yes?

No.

And forcibly restrained his companion Miss Farrell from leaving?

That's not true.

You heard her evidence.

She's lying.

Why would a young woman, who came to the party with Mr MacVeigh, decide not to go with him when he was leaving?

It happens.

And why would she lie to the court?

That happens too.

So, lying to the court is something that *happens*?

If you feel threatened.

Is that why you are lying about drugs, Mr Ewing? Do you feel threatened?

No.

What? Is that not your *modus operandi*? Is that not why we are standing in court today? What of all the imaginary threats we've heard over the last few days? In fact, because you felt threatened one man – if not two – are dead.

What the fuck are you saying?

Please control your language, Mr Ewing.

I'm sorry, your honour.

So *things started flying* did they, Mr Ewing?

Yes.

And so you decided to eject Mr MacVeigh?

Yes.

And what of Mr Reynolds?

He said he would go too.

Did Mr Reynolds in any way start to protest?

No.

In fact, he behaved like a gentleman, did he not?

Yes.

But Mr MacVeigh did protest?

Yes.

Understandably, given the circumstances, wouldn't you agree? Oh you don't agree. If by chance you were being thrown out of a party and your hosts refused to let your female companion accompany you, I'm sure you would protest. Wouldn't you?

She said she didn't want to go.

Did she indeed? I am afraid the court has heard a quite different version of events from Miss Farrell. So let's recap. You attacked Mr MacVeigh and hurled him out the doorway of the apartment?

I didn't attack him. No one attacked him.

So you gently hurled him out the doorway?

He didn't go handy.

Handy? Meaning *easily* I take it?

Yes.

I see. And then what happened?

The windows came in.

Just like that?

No, sir, suddenly.

the crux

And now we come to the crux of the whole evening. You say your brother went to the toilet. Yes?

Yes. He headed on out.

This meant he had to leave the living room and walk along a short corridor that passed by the front door of the apartment.

Yes. The front door would have been on his left.

As he was going out?

And on his right side coming in.

Thank you, Mr Ewing. Did anyone accompany him?

No.

311

So there is no witness to what happened out in that corridor?

Yes, there is.

And who is that?

Scots Bob.

Thank you, Mr Ewing. The court is aware of Mr MacVeigh's position at the time. I meant there was no witness among your party who could testify to what took place at that front door?

No.

But you were first out?

I heard a knock. Then a whoosh.

And?

And I found my brother in flames. I found Scots Bob with his arms on fire. The fire was running along the carpet.

And what did you do?

I remember the screaming.

Yes.

And that I had to stop the burning.

Yes.

I tried to throw a blanket over Redmond.

Understandably. Did you do that immediately?

I don't know.

There was a lot of confusion.

Yes.

Did you try to throw something over Mr MacVeigh?

No.

In fact, you struck him.

What?

You struck him repeatedly. Isn't that right?

No.

In fact, before going to the aid of your brother you struck Mr MacVeigh.

No, no, I did not.

Mr Robinson?

That's me.

You live above the apartment where this tragic affair occurred.

I do, for ten years. People come and go. I stayed on.

And you attended the party on the night in question.

I did. It was fancy dress. Everyone came as someone else. Not me, though.

And a certain fracas arose.

It did.

And then Mr MacVeigh and Mr Reynolds –

I don't know their names.

– left the party in violent circumstances. Right?

There was a ta-do.

After they left, you were seated directly inside the living-room door, the door that lead on to the corridor. Yes?

I was seated at the entrance.

And then, after a certain length of time, Mr Oliver Ewing rushed by you when more commotion arose in the corridor.

There was screaming.

And what did you do?

I looked out.

And what did you see?

Nothing at first. There was a great deal of smoke. The stench was terrible. It was very frightening.

And then what did you see?

Oliver.

And what was he doing?

He was stamping on the carpet.

And then – ?

He started screaming at the other man, the intruder.

You mean Mr MacVeigh, the accused?

313

Yes.

Go on.

Then he threw some garment – a blanket – over his brother.

But first, Mr Robinson, before he got the blanket to throw over his brother, did he strike Mr MacVeigh?

It might have been after he covered his brother.

You think it was after he covered his brother?

Yes, now I think, it was after he covered his brother.

I see. Well now, whether it was before or after he got the blanket for his brother, you admit that he struck Mr MacVeigh?

It's all so difficult.

Please, Mr Robinson, I have your statement here before me. You state he struck Mr MacVeigh, yes?

Yes. But you see . . .

Thank you, Mr Robinson.

But you see, now I think, he was trying to put out the flames.

By striking a man?

Yes.

I doubt it, Mr Robinson. I think what you witnessed was Mr Ewing physically assaulting a severely burnt man who could not defend himself. Is that not so?

Yes. That is true.

Thank you.

But begging your pardon, sir, why did he then strike his brother in the same manner?

Are you telling us he struck his brother also?

Yes, sir, he did.

He struck his brother?

Yes.

314

Just a few more questions, Mr Ewing. All right?

Yes.

Is it true that you surreptitiously made your way to the room in St Thomas's where Mr MacVeigh, severely ill after the fire, was hospitalized?

What?

Were you not found by the police lurking on that floor of the hospital?

But my brother Redmond was being treated in the same hospital. I didn't even know Scots Bob was a patient there.

You didn't know?

No.

And yet you were found facing the exact room in which he was a patient.

It happened by pure chance.

Chance again? *Pure chance?* Of all the rooms in the hospital, you ended up outside his very door?

I took the lift to the wrong floor.

Did you indeed?

I did.

One wonders what would have happened had the police not been on permanent duty there.

I tell you I didn't even know he was in the hospital!

And yet you were found outside the door of the chief witness in this trial, the only person who could tell us what exactly took place on the tragic night of this party.

I took the lift to the wrong floor.

Indeed? Let's return to your apartment in Olive Street. Before the police had conducted a proper search of the house what did you do?

What do you mean what did I do?

Did you not, in fact, clean the entire flat from top to bottom?

I did.

Why?

Because the place was a mess.

Were you not trying to hide any evidence?

The police had already been through the flat. I was not trying to hide anything.

Your brother is lying in hospital severely ill, and instead of staying with him, you find yourself outside Mr MacVeigh's door, and then you return to the apartment and give it a thorough going over. Would you not consider your actions suspicious?

I'm tidy.

I see.

I always was. It's in my nature.

Is that so. And is selfishness in your nature? Why did you not stay in the hospital with your brother?

I can't say.

And is deception in your nature, would you say? Is deception equally abundant in your nature?

No.

So what did you throw out?

Rubbish.

Is that all?

Yes.

Well, we shall never know, shall we?

Ollie Ewing

I went to stand with the prosecutor outside the courtroom. He was congratulating me on staying the course. La Loo was lighting a fag. I looked over his shoulder and saw Silver John standing with his barristers. They were going great guns. He turned away from them in disgust and his eyes alighted on mine.

He smiled over at me. Then I saw it – his mouth went into an *O*, he wagged a finger at me, slowly shaking his head, as if to say *You shouldn't have!* Someone spoke to him and he replied without looking at them. Then he raised his hand and flicked two fingers fast across his neck as though he were brushing away a fly. He mouthed something.

He started walking towards me. I backed away but he kept coming.

Someone must have understood then what was happening, for his crowd surrounded him, but he still kept at it, wagging his finger and then he whispered to me again. Even though I was standing some distance from him, I could read my name on his lips. *Ollie Ewing,* he was saying, *Ollie Ewing.*

VII

An Afterlife

32

the drums

The morning after the trial I closed the door to the Clapham flat and lit out for Luton with La Loo.

I was glad to be away from there. The mother and La Loo had stayed a few days, but mostly I was there on my own since the night of the party. Traipsing. Sometimes I imagined there were folk under the arches of the railway watching the house. Once night fell I didn't stir. I waited for the windows to come in. The doorbell would ring at all hours and there'd be nobody there. Soon, none of the tenants would answer the door. Instead they'd call out *Hallo* from their window.

Hallo, anybody there? I'd hear the gay bucks call.

No answer.

It was silence all round. I never spoke. I never answered the door. I never called out. One night this fucking car parked directly outside and whoever it was had this drumbeat playing. They threw the door ajar. It must have lasted maybe only a minute but it seemed to go on for ever. The same pounding rhythm over and over. I could do without that.

the point

So, La Loo says, come on down to Luton.

We shared the one room. He headed off in the morning to his

toxicology and I hung a few laps around the town looking for work. I stopped off at Vauxhall Motors but had no luck. Then I saw a sign in a window. They wanted pickers. *£4.25 in the hand, plus bonus. Training and uniform provided. Own safety shoes an advantage.* So I said, right. I know potatoes, but what did I want a uniform for? So I stepped in. I'm sorry, sir, the secretary says, but this is actual factory work. I didn't understand, but Thank you, I said. In the event, I went into the Arndale Centre.

How are you today, sir? Morella in the arcade asked as he served me cappuccino.

I could be better, I said.

Oh, he said with dismay. You not find a job?

What is the point? I asked him.

Hah?

I'm saying, what is the point of it all?

The point? Ha-ha, he said, avoiding me.

With great bluster he poured frothing milk into my cup from a jug held on high and moved on quickly to the next customer.

How are you today, madam? All right?

I got myself a seat on a long bench. The floor rocked under my feet as if it was suspended. Then, at the other end of the bench someone farted. It reached me after passing along the buttocks of the other sitters.

Lovely, ain't it? said the bloke beside me.

Then a woman carrying coffee fell across him as she made her way past us. He watched the coffee run across his trousers.

Hallo, he says, wha' we got here?

Sorry, she said.

Put more water in it, love, he said.

He looked at me and lifted his hands.

What can you do?

Nothing, I said.

Right. Right. So what you been at?

322

Been through a court trial.

Nothing political, I 'ope.

No.

You win?

I couldn't win.

Yeh, but did the other bloke go down?

Yeh. Seven years.

That's all right then. Fuck 'im, right?

fuck him

Fuck him.

Luton ladies

I was there maybe a week when one day I found myself reading a monument to the men and women of Luton who died in the war. Three Indian girls in flowing white saris emerged from the town hall. One of them was pregnant. It was the lovely pitch of the raised sari over the swell that attracted me.

He's not mad, one said.

No, said the other, but she's going mental.

And then you get, like, dance stuff.

See you later, she said to the others.

See you later, they said.

I followed the pregnant lady through the shopping arcade.

This fascination with pregnant women took me on various jaunts round the city. I might be minding my own business then this woman would stroll by, just taking a walk. Maybe she wanted to get out of the house. Sometimes we walked for hours and hours. Sometimes she'd stop and straighten up as if some distant command had reached her. She'd push out her breasts and tap the small of her back. Then on. Or maybe rest a hand on her hip as if she'd run out of breath.

Then on we'd go to travel agents' windows, hairdressers and especially vegetable stalls, for lettuce maybe, radishes, sometimes mushrooms. We'd drop into a seat in Queen's Park and watch children playing. She might eat Pot Noodles or a baguette or a doughnut. We watched the people.

For hours I sat to the left of a certain Nigerian woman in the Arndale Centre. She wore a puffed-out silver jacket, her hair in clasps, huge bangle earrings and a satchel on her back. She was huge round the stomach. Old men sat in front of us under indoor trees. And beyond them: florists, Superdrug, Woolworth's, W. H. Smith, H. Samuel for rings. It was H. Samuel's she was looking into. Every so often she went across to look at the rings, came back and sat.

She held her pregnancy closer to her. We strolled to Burger King and back. As darkness fell, we went up streets I shouldn't go. We headed past Balti cafés, she went into the Kashmir take-away, then on to R. Johal's & Co. store and off-licence. She looked into Lodge's exclusive lingerie, then stopped somewhere in Moore Park and went in.

A gang of youths came towards me.

I was frightened they might throw acid in my face, so I crossed the street and so did they. I passed a man sitting on the front doorstep of his house. He was bouncing a shuttle on a badminton bat. From inside came rap music.

I asked directions for town.

He pointed.

I sat down beside him and we had a little chat. I explained some of what had happened me. He nodded and listened and asked me to go away.

revenge

At night I dreamed of revenge. I saw myself entering the Lag to confront him. I stood on the threshold. Silver John rose from his chair and turned to me. He was wearing football socks.

You survivin'? he says.

I am.

Redmond was behind the bar, shining glasses. It seemed to me that he had just come in by bike from evening mass on a Saturday and was doing a late shift in Gerties. We moved from the Lag back to Sligo and Silver John came with us, except now he was only a blur over there, somewhere to the left, where dreaming people sit.

But Redmond was very real, in a striped shirt, the hair slicked back.

I didn't know he was dead, not at all, he was mad alive. He held a glass up to the light. Very high. Then he walked towards me. I was delighted to see him and started to explain in a hurry all that had happened.

Never mind that, he says.

I just came up to see you for a minute, I said.

Work away, he says.

I'm sorry, I said. I couldn't get here earlier.

Never mind.

I've been trying to, but I got held up, you know.

Sure.

Then our mother breezed past, her head down. Something snapped in my skull and I awoke, soaked. I lay there convinced Redmond was alive. Or else I was dead. Then the knowledge of recent times intervened. I wanted to stay where I'd been. But I knew it was impossible. So I tried to convince myself that he was dead, but I couldn't, because there he was, inches away from the bed, still burning in the halo of the living. Then I saw the daylight come coldly into the room. He was dead.

I recalled the hospital with his scarred body. I heard it again –
the crackle of the plastic. A body moving.

Ta-ta, says the man in the next bed.

A male nurse in a short white coat appears with a love-bite on
the throat.

All right? he says.

And it was not something terrible, but comforting, in a terrible
way.

walking

I went on what I thought might be my last walk. The final lap. Barges
drifting along quietly. The suburbs growing darker as I headed in.
A red and white pavilion by a go-cart track in Milton Keynes.

The russet-tiled roofs of middle England.

I walked the streets, jealous of all the book-lined rooms and fires
burning and places to go. I sensed the devilment and impishness
of the English girls; their comic style and the anger in their
boots. A Coca-Cola sign bucketed. A smell of hops. Dinosaurs in
the subways. A poster said Neil Young was playing somewhere.
The Swan. The George. The Portakabin raised on scaffolding and
reached by stairs.

The Mayo flag.

That will do.

I turned back.

Yes pet?

Then another day I found myself in the centre of Luton at the
junction between Silver Street and John Street.

I was terrified.

I had been visited.

I could not take another step. I sat down at a wooden table in Debenham's and shook. I should get up and go. An old man approached me, a small frail Indian with a goatee. He wore a tweed coat and cap, and was carrying a child. The weight of the child made his mouth sag on either side.

I went, Sir?

He went, Yes, pet?

I need to get away from here. I'm trapped.

I see.

Can you bring me?

Now?

Yes.

OK.

We stood. We stepped through Debenham's doors. Yes, we go through Debenham's doors. Slowly. We walked like old people. And still we walked on along the town centre.

33

child's eye

I dreamt that night that I had a third eye pinned to my forehead. It was a child's eye. I wondered in the dream why people were looking at me oddly. I was round the back of the house in a shed making spokes for some sort of red tourist cart. The men and women were about other business.

We stopped up to talk. Then I found their eyes lift beyond mine to a point on my forehead. They seemed aghast and turned away in embarrassment, but no one wanted to tell me what was wrong.

I worked on anyway till the forenoon. Then as I began to sweat I passed a hand across my face and found this thing pinned to my forehead. I thought, *What's that blooming thing?* It was not a rose or a blister but a round plaster. I didn't know what it was.

So I went indoors but there was no mirror anywhere in the house. Where there used to be mirrors, now there were only blank walls. Though I knew my way around and it was all familiar, it was hardly my home at all. So I stepped in the kitchen door and called to my mother who was entertaining some labouring men.

Mother! I called.

Be with ye in a minute, she said to the others.

She followed me out to the porch.

Yes? she said. What now?

I said nothing but waited for her to see what was on my forehead. She did not seem at first to notice it, then a few seconds later she withdrew suddenly and rose a hand to her mouth.

Oliver! she said.

What is it? I said. I can't see it.

She led me to her room and took out her handbag and handed me a small mirror. Then I saw the child's eye. It was stuck on to my forehead by the sucker behind the pupil. I could put my finger in behind the socket and it moved freely. I wanted to tear it off immediately but instead I found I was looking through it at myself in the mirror.

The other eyes were seeing normal things but this eye was seeing something else, something I myself didn't want to see.

the thing with the words

When I got up to walk around Luton the eye came with me, even though there was no eye there. I had this straight perspective. I could only go by certain signals. My body was being commanded from elsewhere.

I decided to follow a street sweeper pushing his barrow. When I had exhausted his itinerary, I followed another fellow who stepped out of the Firkin Brewery but only for a few paces, then he turned into The Dog and Donut. Others I went after kept disappearing like that. They would never stay the course. Then the thing with the words happened. The words for the things escaped me.

Escaped me.

I thought I should have a word with the authorities but something told me to leave it.

As I stood there I knew there was a certain loss, of that I was certain. And yet somehow this was to my benefit. But still and all it was sad to know the loss. This was when a shadow intervened.

the shadow

It came down a side street and close to me.

That you, Ollie?

A man from the Point arrived who was apparently a jockey in Chester.

I was filled with joy. I could do anything. I shook his hand fervently.

What are you doing there? he asked me.

I'm seeing the new pollution through, I said. You see we haven't learnt our lesson since the last industrial revolution.

I see, he said, wincing.

Come on, I said, and we'll have a chat.

No, he says, I'm tied up.

Ah, go on.

No, Oliver, I have to hit the high road.

Be seeing you then.

Good luck.

So I went on to where I could see a crane in the sky. It meant going through the Arndale Centre again, a place I liked, I liked the bustle, then on by the railway station where they were shouting out the names of destinations. Bedford calling at Flitwick. Sheffield calling at Kettering. Then I marched through the galvanized door by the signs for helmets. Up high was a single crane-driver in his little cabin, controlling everything. The arm and chain swung by like a fishing rod, to and fro, the line taut, the catch nearly landed.

Another shadow approached me.

What you want, boss?

I'm just looking.

Best now if you get off the site.

But I'm a chippie. I'm looking for work.

There's no work.

I have some friends, I said.

Easy now lad, best leave now.

But I just smiled.

Seriously, I said, but he was incensed.

You're a big lad.

He was talking, he was talking about controlling the situation. He marched me across the site.

Do you realize, I said, that –

We'll talk about that outside.

Then there's the corporation and there's reverberations there, you know.

I'm sure.

I worry about that. Do you?

I don't, actually.

Well, I certainly worry about that.

Good.

We reached the street.

If you have a problem, he says, take it elsewhere, and he lifts his hand and shakes it at me as if to say *Keep your distance*. He divides his face in two with the side of his hand.

Keep going, he says.

I will. Thank you.

So I went over to watch workers on their dinner break kicking a ball about in a children's playground.

this has got to stop

It has.

So I went for it. I went to do what I had been putting off. This Friday I travelled down to London town on the afternoon train. I took my bag of tools: my hammer, the Stanley, tape-measure, wood chisel, saw.

The city did not seem to be the city I'd been in.

All the way out on the Piccadilly line people were chatting normally. I had my demons, they had theirs. I felt sick. But anyway. I stepped out at Wood Green, took a deep breath and climbed the last stairs. Turned to the pub. There it was. A lot of things went through my head. I went into this small park, sat down on a bench and watched the doors of the pub swing.

Darkness soon began to fall.

I sat waiting for the lorry to appear. And Silver John to alight from the BMW with his heavies, but they never came.

I did not know rightly what I would do.

I must have been there maybe two hours and there was no sign. Then I saw the plumber that had helped me come sauntering up the side street. I ran round the railings to the gate.

Hi! I shouted.

What? he said stopping and threw his arms wide.

I didn't mean to shout, I said.

Who the fuck are you?

Ollie Ewing, I said.

Who?

You put me up once.

Ollie Ewing, he says. I don't believe this.

There you go.

Well, fuck me. He laughed. I see you in the newspapers. Jesus, you're still here? I thought by now you'd have cleared out of the country.

Not yet.

Well, if I was you I'd be fucking miles from here.

You turned against me, I said.

He moved back from me.

You still looking for trouble? he says.

I don't mean you any trouble.

You steer clear of me, all right?

He turned to go.

I'm looking for Silver John, I said.

He kicked the railings.

Jesus Christ, he said. Are you fucking right in the head?

I know what I'm at.

He tapped his left temple.

See you son, he said and walked off.

So I worked up the courage to go to the pub. No sign of a bouncer. I pushed the door open and went in. I looked at John's table, but it was empty. The barman recognized me immediately. He looked at me in bewilderment. There were a few labouring men there, not many, and the underground folk, but no sign of Silver John and his cronies. I dropped my bag and went to the bar.

A pint of Carlsberg, I said.

The place went quiet.

I'm not serving you, he said.

OK, I said.

So I went out, stood a moment on the footpath, pulled a comb through my hair, turned and came back into the bar again.

A pint of Carlsberg, I said.

Fuck me, said the barman.

A pint of Carlsberg.

Are you joking or what?

I'm serious.

Look, get out of here.

I'm sober.

Makes no difference to me, lad.

A pint, I said.

No can do, he said. Sorry.

What do you mean *Sorry*?

Will you leave now, mate?

I lost people, I said.

So do we all. He came out from behind the bar. OK mate? You know the score.

All right, I said.

All right, he said. He saw me onto the street. John don't come here any more, OK?

OK.

And neither do you, right?

the warm side

I got the last train home and arrived to find La Loo getting up to do his night shift, so I undressed and got into the warm side of the bed.

Where were you? he asked me.

London, I said.

It's over Ollie, he said.

Is it?

It is, he said. It's over.

He flicked off the light. The voices started.

that sadness

Not so long after that, Redmond's body arrived out in a coffin to Luton. In a few weeks Marty's would follow. La Loo had worked out everything, the flight to Dublin, the tickets, the hearse to Sligo.

I packed my bag for home. I was leaving England. The father came down from Coventry the evening before. We found him

334

knocking on the wrong door. All he had with him was a plastic bag and in it a change of shirt and underwear. La Loo made up a bed on the sofa but the father sat up the entire night in the room making endless cups of tea. Next morning he was still sitting there by the window with this pale haunted look on his face, his hands hanging slack over his knees.

La Loo headed off. I got dressed and sat opposite the father.

How are you? I asked him.

You and me are going to have get on for the next few days, right? he says.

All right, I said.

For the mother's sake. For hers.

OK.

But I don't forgive you.

I know that.

He was your responsibility.

Let's not argue.

I'm not arguing.

All right.

Tell me this, do you ever take anything seriously?

I do, I said.

I doubt it, he said.

I packed away Marty's and Redmond's few things. I took with me all the newspapers that had reported the story. Carrying our cases, we went to the Foresters pub around two in the day. Behind the bar two hurleys were crossed. The men at the bar were all wearing cheap colourful ganseys. The place smelt of wet jumpers and whiskey.

We ordered two pints of Guinness.

I tapped out a Carrolls cigarette.

Answer that question now, said a gypsy man to my left. He was seated with his young son in front of a tired pint. Some labouring men smiled at him indulgently, finished their drinks and left. My father lifted out his airline ticket and studied it. A solitary women threw darts. Sadness hung in the air. The gypsy took stock of our cases then he shouted, Hi Jimmy, are you men just over? but I pretended not to hear. Then his son came over to us.

Me father said could he have one of your cigarettes? he says.

Sure.

My father put the ticket away.

The son returned: Would you like to buy a TV?

No, I said.

A right big one.

No.

What's the time? my father says.

Half-two.

A few hours to go yet.

Aye.

34

some time later

Some time later we alighted in Dublin and I saw the coffin wrapped in grey sheeting come across the tarmac like it was a chest arrived from abroad. The whole gang were there waiting. I kept my head down.

The first man to take my hand was Mr Kilgallon, Marty's father, but I couldn't speak all that well.

You should have come home with me, he says, that time.

I wasn't there. And I was sorry that I felt no grief. No grief but shame. The grief will come some time later I told myself. Some where in the future I'll make that journey I told myself.

I'll go back through the whole thing one day.

just like that

After Marty's funeral a few of us took a taxi to Sligo town for the tear. I don't know. It was another world. It was strange. I used to be here. I . . . We started off in McCrystal's, then to the Rap because it was there. I got the wrong taste of the beer. We made our way to the Yeats's Cellar, made our way by Doyle's for Bargains!, Penny's, Tights from Penny's says Flo, Harmony Hill, High Street and they all seemed like places in the past. But not working, working. I wont make out here, I said to myself. Not me. I was out of order. We drank till we were sick and I found myself on a kind-of-a-long-couch in wherever. There was a woman, fair enough, and this bloke going on and on about what happened to me. Like this. Like the north. Like you know. I went home in the morning and took to the bed. Just like that.

I had enough.

The mother left me alone at the beginning. I still had ambition, you know. I'd go down into the kitchen in the middle of the night and eat something out of the fridge, take a bottle of 7-Up to the room and stroll on. After a while she used to come pounding at the door but I didn't budge. I was off thrashing – paddling though sweat and hallucinations.

Come out of there, she called.

No.

Get out of that bed.

No.

Blast you!

She'd disappear for a while then shout from the bottom of the stairs, Oliver!

No.

There's people here to see you!

Who?

People.

Mummies is it?

What are you saying?

I don't want to see them.

She came flying up the stairs. Threw open the door.

Get out of the bed, Oliver!

No.

After a while she relented. One morning she brought me a tray and I supped anxiously. The nerves were shattered. After that she never gave off to me. Sometimes she'd sit a while going through small talk, talking of anything that came into her head, neighbours,

338

chickens, politicians. How the days were lengthening. Blue lightning. Minks.The Rory Borry Yellows.

We'd go through silences together while our minds raced.

Eventually one afternoon I went downstairs. She was sitting by the fire, alone.

Are you back?

I am, I said.

Well, you're welcome.

a sad case

A few weeks after they threw a party in memory of Marty and Redmond down in Gerties. The Not-So-Bads played. My father came over on the Holyhead boat for the occasion. Himself and my mother at a table to the side of the bandstand. He accepted everyone's hand, stood and listened to their words of consolation, as he'd heard them weeks before at the funeral, then he handed the mourner on to my mother, who sat there, smiling oddly.

Marty's parents went from table to table, then eventually sat alongside my folks.

The band thrashed out medley after medley like demons. Then Mr Gilmartin arrived with his wife and he joined the band to play Dixieland and Jewish rhapsodies. Gilmartin was in his element on the trombone. And often I saw his wife as she moved around stop every so often and look over at him as if she were trying to piece together the face of someone she'd once known.

Who's that over there?

Who were we at all?

We were members of the Where-The-Fuck-Are-We Tribe listening to the Not-So-Bads.

Gilmartin liked old-fashioned jazz. He liked to sing "Because That's My Home", "It's Raining in Georgia" and sometimes he'd slip into country with "Water, Cool Clear Water". Behind him sat Freddy on drums who turned white when he was twenty. *Mammy!* He was doing lovely accurate slaps and strokes away by himself, finishing one rhythm and beginning another, just a hint of another, without telling, heading off into a tune that was not the right one at all, then shouting *Mammy!* into the mike. As he hit the base chords the banjo player jutted his lower teeth. The man on lead was smiling. Mister Gilmartin would turn round to him in mid-tune, then stage left, where tall Gerry the butcher was on base, a trifle pale in the face, his head down, thick fingers curling going round the fretboard.

I forgot where I was and found myself going to the music.

Then the father gives me a nod. I went over to his table.

What do you want? I asked.

He mumbled something but I couldn't hear what he was saying.

What did you say? I said.

He stood.

He shook his head.

Here, get a drink for the band, he says and he handed me some sterling.

this long empty floor

The boys thought it up. La Loo was there and some of the lads who were at the Clapham party. No speeches, just music, drink and food prepared by both families.

After the handshaking, the locals stood sheltering each other at the bar, watching everything. The widows arranged against the walls did not move. It was supposed to be a celebration, but no one asked anyone out. At one stage, in a break between tunes, Johnny came across to the range, tipped a tincture from his glass of whiskey onto the tiles and said, A drop for the dead. He glanced at me, then made his way back out to the shop again.

The music continued. It was strange to listen to a band with no one dancing. In front of us was this long empty floor, this long empty wooden floor and windows that gave on to the Atlantic. The General made an appearance for a few minutes to dance with himself, he worked his fingers and dug his toes into the boards, but then he realized he was out there alone. He was at the wrong do. Shamefaced he made his way to the toilet.

Few people were talking. And soon no one talked at all. All stood or sat without moving while the band played on in another dimension. At last came "The Soldier's Song". We all stood to attention for the anthem. Come the drum roll. Then the place emptied. Some of us stayed on for a while in the dimly lit shop, then we made our way down the blue alt. La Loo and myself said our goodbyes and I wandered the road. I stood in the immense darkness and heard the sea rock in the distance. A lighthouse was pulsing towards Donegal. It was a noble night.

When I got to the house the father was asleep on the sofa with his case beside him packed for going on the morrow. On the ground was a small saucer with a single butt squashed out. For a while I had forgotten about his existence. Now here he was. I looked at him a while and went on to my room where he should have been sleeping.

I don't forgive you, I heard him saying again.

I don't forgive you.

I pulled the hood of my sweater over my head and sat on the bed waiting till the listening stopped